ONE TRUE MATE · 2

Dragon's Heat

LISA LADEW

Book cover by The Final Wrap *smooches* Hi Rebecca!!

Cover model: Scott King

Photographer: Eric Battershell

Special editorial assistance by The Blurb Diva and Savan Robbins. As always, mayo-ing up my world. ;)

Thank you to **Kristine Piiparinen** for your incredible coolness and assistance. <3

Thank you, beta readers, arc readers, babes, and all of my readers. Goodness, you make writing worth doing and so much easier and fun.

I also want to thank Fay Reid for answering *so many questions* from me about Scottish culture, and to Alexis Riddle for her help with the Gaelic language.

You all really need to know that Amanda Quiles, my shifter guru, has ideas for days, and answers for years. Amanda, I hope you like the dragon). Sorry he's not a gingy.

GLOSSARY

Bearen – bear shifters. Almost always work as firefighters.

Citlali – Spiritual leaders of all *Shiften*. They are able to communicate with the deities telepathically, and sometimes bring back prophecies from these communications.

Deae – goddess.

Dragen – dragon shifter. Rare.

Echo – an animal with the same markings of a *shiften*. Usually seen as a harbinger of bad things, but could also be a messenger from the Light.

Felen – big cat shifters. Almost always work as mercenaries. They are also the protectors of Rhen's physical body and a specially-trained group of them can track Khain when he comes into the *Ula*.

Foxen – the *Foxen* were created when Khain forcibly mated with female *wolfen*.

Haven, The – final resting place of all *shiften*. Where The Light resides.

Impot – a *shiften* that cannot shift because of a genetic defect caused by mating too close to their own bloodline. Trent and Troy are not thought to be *impots* because they were born during a *klukwana*.

Khain – also known as the Divided Demon, the Great Destroyer, and the Matchitehew. The hunter of humans and the main nemesis of all *shiften*.

Klukwana – a ceremony where a full-blooded *shiften* who mates another *shiften* does so with both in animal form, then the mother stays in animal form during the entire pregnancy. The young in the litter are always born as their animal. *Wolven* from a *klukwana* always come in at least 4 to 7 young. *Bearen* are always two cubs, and *felen* are unpredictable, sometimes only one. *Shiften* born from a *klukwana* are almost always more powerful, bigger, and stronger than regular *shiften*, but many parents don't try it because of the inherent risks to the mother during the (shorter) pregnancy and the risk that the *shiften* young may choose not to shift into human form. A lesser known possibility is that the *shiften* young will have a harder time learning to shift into human form, especially if no one shifts near them in the first few days after birth.

KSRT – Kilo Special Response Team, or Khain Special Response team. A group of *wolven* police whose primary goal is to hunt down and kill Khain, if that can be done.

Light, The – The creator of the *Ula*, humans, Rhen, Khain, and the angels.

Moonstruck – Insane. *Shiften* who spend too long indoors or too long in human form can become *moonstruck* slowly and not even realize it.

Pravus – Khain's home. A fiery, desolate dimension that sits alongside ours.

Pumaii – a small group of specialized *felen* tasked with tracking Khain when he crosses over into our dimension.

Renqua – a discoloration in a *shiften's* fur which is also seen as a birthmark in human form. Every *renqua* is different. The original *renquas* were pieces of Rhen she put inside the wolves, bears, and big cats to create the *shiften*. Every pure-blooded shifter born since has also had a *renqua*. Half-breeds may or may not have one. Some *foxen* acquired weak *renquas* when they mated with *shiften*. Also called the mark of life.

Rhen – the creator of all *shiften*. A female deity.

Ruhi – the art of speaking telepathically. No humans are known to possess the power to do this. Not all *shiften* are able to do it. It is the preferred form of speaking for the *dragen*.

Shiften – Shifter-kind.

Ula – earth, in the current dimension and time. The home of the *shiften*.

Vahiy – end of the world.

Wolfen – a wolf shifter. Almost always works as a police officer.

Wolven – wolf shifters, plural.

Zyanya – When a *wolfen* dies, the funeral is for the benefit of humans, but the important ceremony is the *zyanya*. The pack mates of the fallen *wolfen* run in wolf form through the forest, heading north to show the spirit the way to the Haven. When they reach a body of water, they all jump in and swim to the other side, then emerge in human form.

CHAPTER 1

*W*ade peered out the windshield at Remington's house as he drove up, dread eating at him. Gah, all those *cats*. They did something to him, got in his mind somehow. No wonder Trevor was the only one who still came out here to check in on Graeme, a full week after his mating and almost two weeks after their successful but costly rescue mission into the *Pravus*.

Wade doubted Trevor wanted to deal with the cats, but Ella wouldn't take no for an answer. Graeme had saved them both, plus Ella's sister, and Ella wouldn't let Trevor forget that, horde of fur balls or not.

Besides, Trevor had two cats *living* in his house now. Wade pulled into the driveway of the large two-story house that looked more like a museum than a doctor's office or home, and shuddered at the thought. Living with cats. How… unnatural.

Wade shut off his engine and hopped out of the Jeep, his work boots crunching on the asphalt of the driveway as he landed. He had dressed down, knowing he'd be heading out to Remington's place and not wanting to draw attention to himself in his official capacity.

Cats appeared as if from nowhere, heading straight for him. A minute before, the place had seemed empty, no people or cars or cats in sight, but now he counted seven, no, twelve cats coming from under the wide porch and appearing as if by magic from under the hedges. He grimaced and began walking for the front door, ignoring them.

A yellow and orange cat yowled and tried to rub up against his boot even while it was in motion. *Show no fear. They are tiny, you could rip them apart if you wanted to.*

One of the cats, a large black and white one, with fur so long it dragged on the ground as it walked—no, slunk—alongside Wade, made a snuffling, snorting sound through its nose.

Is he laughing at me? Little beast. Wade bared his teeth at the cat and started up the steps to the front door. A pied-piper-like clowder of cats followed him, winding between his feet, threatening to trip him. And when they did, they'd be on him, no doubt, little fangs ripping into his skin like needles...

Wade turned and growled at the cats, moving his foot in a wide arc, pushing the ones in his reach back away from him. A few cats hissed at him, but most wound their way in between his feet again, one standing on its hind legs and pawing up at his knee. Weren't there more now? Twenty, at least? Wade turned toward the door and pounded on it, his skin crawling, his fangs growing of their own accord. His animal wanted out, badly, and it wanted to crunch on cat spines like chicken bones. He held his wolf back with everything he had.

Felen-wolfen relations were at an all-time high, and there was no way he would be the cause of any sort of erosion there. War was coming, pups were coming, and they would need the *felen* more than ever.

The screen door bounced in its frame, the heavy door inside open to let in the light, proving Remington had to be around somewhere. If only he would hurry up.

"Remington!" Wade shouted, his voice strangling on the last syllable. Soft cat feet plucked their way up the back of his pant leg. A claw snicked out and brushed his skin.

"Remington, where are you?" he almost screamed, kicking backwards, somehow connecting with nothing.

A male appeared in the yard from around the corner of the house. "Ah, Wade," Remington said, looking up at him as he strolled to the steps that led up onto the porch. "I was taking one of my daily walks. I didn't think you would be here so early."

The sea of what had to be at least thirty cats parted, letting Remington through effortlessly. Wade eyed Remington's college-boy looks, styled hair, and earring in his right ear with distaste. Remington didn't look old enough or distinguished enough to be a doctor at all, but he was the only *shiften* doctor living in the area. Wade made a mental note that they needed to recruit or something. If the fight with Khain was only about to intensify, like he was sure it was, they would need more.

Shiften couldn't shift to heal if they had bullets in them or were unconscious, and no one could forget that there were actually going to be babies born in a few months. Well, nobody knew how long Ella's gestation would be… nine months like a human, or closer to five months, like a *wolfen*?

Claws breached his pant leg again, pulling him out of his

thoughts. He kicked out with his foot, dislodging the little beast. "Call your cats off me, Remington."

"They aren't my cats," Remington said lightly, his smile and tone amused.

"Whatever, just tell them to go away."

Remington took a step backwards and folded his hands, his face smug. "Nobody owns a cat."

"Thanks for the zoology lesson," Wade grunted, backing up into the screen door. "Why do they follow me like this?" he asked, motioning his hands towards the moving mass of cats at his feet.

"Because they know you don't like them."

Wade looked at Remington and cocked his head. That was ridiculous. "So, what do they do with someone who likes them?"

"Depends on their mood. Probably mostly ignore them."

Wade grumbled under his breath, looking down at the backwards felines, most of whom were now staring at him, a few meowing lightly and trying to brush up against him. He could see cat hairs on his boots and his pants. He would throw the uniform away. Maybe burn it, if he ever got out of there. "Ridiculous beasts. No sense."

"What was that?"

Wade looked up sharply. "Can we go inside?"

"Ah, yes." Remington pushed past him and opened the door for Wade, hissing something out of the corner of his mouth.

Wade was relieved to see none of the cats followed him inside. When Remington shut the screen door behind them, Wade was able to breathe a bit easier.

"So, I called you for a reason," Wade said.

"I wanted you to come here for a very important reason," Remington said at the same time.

Wade frowned. "What? Is he worse?"

Remington raised his eyebrows and put out his hand, pointing Wade into the patient care room immediately to the right of the front door. "See for yourself."

Wade walked into the room he'd been inside several times already, distressed to realize that he could tell at a glance what Remington was probably referring to.

Graeme lay on his side in the hospital bed, wires running to his bare arms and chest, a white sheet covering most of him. Behind him, a wooden contraption held eight vials of blood, and Wade noted with alarm that the ones farthest to the right looked almost green, instead of red.

The heart monitor next to Graeme was off. His cheeks were sunken, his dark hair completely lifeless, his skin sallow and diseased-looking. He looked like he'd lost twenty pounds in just the few days since Wade had last been there. "He is worse."

"Touch him," Remington said.

Wade looked up, a sneer on his face. That didn't make any sense.

"Just do it. Anywhere. On his hand."

Wade approached the bed and held out his hand. When his fingers were still a good three inches away from Graeme, a spark leaped out of Graeme's flesh and shocked him.

"Ouch! Motherfucker!" Wade cried, pulling away from the bedside and shaking his hand.

Graeme moaned, and his arm flopped backwards, but something stopped his body from following. Remington stepped forward and pulled a wedge out from the hollow of Graeme's back so he could move.

"That started yesterday. I think it's a bad sign," Remington said, not looking at Wade. "It's why the heart monitor isn't on. He shorted it out."

"Why didn't you get shocked just now?"

"Because you did. You released the buildup of energy. It will take another hour or so before a tiny spark builds up again. The longer I wait to release it, the bigger it gets."

Remington stared Wade in the eye. "That's why I called you. You have to move him. I'm afraid he's going to burn my house down."

Wade shook his head. "Absolutely not. And that's why *I* called *you*. This is taking too long. You need to find an expert on *dragen*. Get him better. You said he needed a rest, but this is looking like a coma, *Doctor*."

Remington's right eyebrow raised, but nothing else did. In the same sickeningly smooth voice he said, "There *are* no experts. I've called every doctor I know, even a few in Scotland who I didn't know. They all thought *dragens* had been gone for centuries. No one knows anything about them."

Wade's fist twisted around the side of the hospital bed, and his voice rose for the second time that visit. "Then find a different expert. Branch out. Start calling veterinarians, if you have to. I don't care how you help him, but you can't just sit here and do nothing!"

Remington curled his lip as if he were going to say something smart—or stupid. Wade heard himself growl deep in his throat and he cut it off mercilessly. He had to keep control.

Wade motioned to the form on the bed. "He saved our asses, he's irreplaceable, and he's an awfully nice male. I'd hate to think that this is how we repay him."

Remington frowned. "Did you ever think maybe he doesn't want to be repaid, or saved?"

Before Wade could answer, Graeme moaned again, his big body twisting under the flimsy sheet that covered him. His mouth opened, and Wade could see his lips were dry and cracked. Wade leaned forward, trying to catch the soft words coming from his lips.

"So cold. So wet. So awful. I'm ready to go. Take me. It's been so long. Too long. I don't want to…" His words trailed off.

When Wade looked up at Remington, fear in his eyes and his heart, Remington only nodded. "He talks like that a lot, especially at night when the moon is high in the sky." He took a deep breath. "I don't think he wants to live anymore."

CHAPTER 2

*E*lla sprinted through the woods in her bare feet, feeling the springy dirt and leaves under her toes. Her breath caught in her throat as her heart trip-hammered inside her chest.

She whipped her head around to look behind her. Was he still there? Was he gaining? She saw nothing but trees and heard nothing but her own blood pounding in her ears and the rasp of her breathing, but she could feel him. He was close, closer than she could even imagine—

Growling sounded far in front of her, and she tried to stop, her heels skidding as she threw her momentum backwards, not wanting to run right into him, not wanting to be caught so easily.

Her eyes wide, trying to take in everything at once, she managed to keep on her feet, but barely. She thrust her hands out and held on to the small saplings on either side of the trail, hearing the rustle of the tiny trees as she moved them, and the minute crackle of the dry leaves beneath her.

When she had come out to these woods, she had been able to see her breath, but now it was invisible in the relative mid-day warmth. Her feet were cold because she had kicked her shoes off at the start of the chase, knowing it was the only chance she had for any sort of evasion, if she even had such a chance.

She heard the growling again, ahead of her and off to her right. Was he toying with her? Enjoying this?

She tiptoed off the trail, knowing it wasn't safe, hoping the noise wouldn't give her away. Maybe she could find a place to go to ground? Or would climbing a tree be smarter? Give her more of a chance?

Ahead of her, the leaf-covered land gave way, sliding down into a dip, then lifting up into a hill on the other side. Between the massive oak trees, she saw a clearing on the top of the hill. She tiptoed closer, wanting to get a better look at what she thought she was seeing. A cabin that looked partially finished. Only holes instead of windows, and a huge stack of logs next to it.

Did Trevor know someone was building a house in his forest?

The thought of her mate's name seemed to conjure more growling, from directly to her left this time.

Ella screamed and spun in that direction, staring down the massive black wolf with the beautiful silver fringes around its head and chest. It was only fifteen feet from her, its head down, its eyes locked on hers. She could clearly see the boomerang-shaped white mark on its left shoulder. It advanced on her, the growling a low rumble in the back of its throat.

Ella took a step backwards, then another, then one more,

backing directly against a massive tree she had stepped lightly around moments before.

The wolf growled again and shook its head, then sank back onto its haunches. As she watched, it changed, hair pulling into skin, face shortening, thickening, body stretching out, until her mate crouched naked before her. He stood, massive thighs flexing invitingly, then wiped the mentholated cream away from his nostrils, flaring them as he took a step towards her.

"You baking cookies, Ella?" he asked, his voice a low, sexy rumble.

She flushed hotly and looked down. She wanted to own the part of her that was completely turned on by the fact that he was a *shiften*, able to transform into a massive killing machine with huge claws and teeth at just a thought, but she still blushed whenever he noticed.

He always noticed. Sometimes he didn't call attention to it, but she could always see flat approval and appreciation on his face when her scent shifted for him.

She pressed herself against the tree as he stalked towards her, a thick erection growing at his middle. "Could you smell me?" she asked.

"Not until I wiped the cream away. I can smell you now." He kept walking as he spoke, his massive form coming closer and closer.

She felt herself bloom for him. Would he take her right there, on the bed of fallen fall leaves? God, she hoped so.

He reached her, and she watched the muscles in his shoulders and chest flex as he took her right wrist and deliberately placed it over her head, grabbing her other hand and raising it, then tucking it in with the first, holding both with his left hand.

Her arms raised over her head, completely and totally helpless, one hundred percent his, she looked up into his eyes. She could smell him now. Firewood and forest leaves and wildness. Pure male possessiveness. He dipped his head and his eyes roamed down her neck, as if he was deciding where to bite her first.

She moaned thickly, impatience driving her. She couldn't wait, but she wanted to wait a hundred years. The feeling was so divine, the plump, anticipatory tingling in her heavy breasts and swollen lips. If only some part of him would touch her other than on her wrists.

He did, then, his lips pressing to her neck and his right hand first lightly skimming her breasts under her jacket but over her dress, then dipping down to lift the skirt and slip through her folds. Just that one touch was enough and she cried out into his chest as her orgasm rocked her, jerking her hips forward, completely lost to her own sensation.

When it was over, and the sweet waves of pleasure receded enough that she could open her eyes, she found him smiling at her. A knowing, clever smile, that said she was his so completely, she might as well tattoo his name on her neck. *Property of Trevor. Keep back if you like your head attached to your body.*

"I thought you might like this game," he murmured, pressing his body against her. "I just didn't know how much."

Ella pressed her eyes tightly shut, hoping he wouldn't mention that she wasn't wearing any panties. She might die of embarrassment if he did. She'd tucked them into her shoes when she first entered the woods, hoping to entice him to do exactly what he was doing when he caught her.

She pulled weakly with her arms, wanting her hands free,

wanting so badly to touch him, to try to get him under her or over her.

"Mmmm," he murmured, clamping his massive hand down harder on her wrists, holding her easily, finding her mouth, teasing her lips and tongue. Her body responded immediately, like it hadn't known his touch for a lifetime, like it wasn't still shaking from his earlier attention and skill.

He pushed the skirt of her dress up and pulled back so he could see her body, spanning her belly and hip with one hand. The touch of his work-roughened skin on her midsection made her catch her breath. She had no idea what he was going to do next and it was maddening. Her hips bucked forward of their own accord, making him smile.

"You smell sweeter every day I know you, Ella." He licked his lips and looked her in the eye. "Being with young agrees with you." He caressed her still-flat lower belly as he said it. Well, flat was a relative term that she could only use when she thought about what was coming, but he never seemed to mind how soft she was there, or the way her thighs and hips flared. He relished it, actually, and she could see from the way his eyes traveled down her form that he was looking forward to the day her middle swelled, heavy with his little ones. She knew he would find her no less desirable when it did.

Part of Ella's mind tried to clamber about all of that. That she was almost three weeks pregnant and hadn't seen a doctor yet. That she couldn't even go to her obstetrician because the babies could come out as wolves. That she would have the babies at home with only men in attendance. And maybe Lorna. Hopefully, Lorna. That she was taking standard prenatals and had no idea if they were a good idea or not. That she didn't even know if she would have one baby, or maybe two, or four, or six. Six!

Trevor stretched and bent to plant a soft kiss on her belly, pulling her mind away from the worries she had months for.

She watched her mate's face as he pulled back and ate her up with his eyes, then reached a hot hand around her to caress her hips, thighs, and ass. Tingles raced up her spine, making her moan lightly. He drove her absolutely out of her mind when he did that.

"Sweet Ella, what would you have me do now? What should the big, bad wolf do to you?" he murmured, peeking alternately from her face to her mostly still-covered body.

She moaned, but didn't answer. "Take you? Eat you? Carry you back to my bed, like some hard-won prize?"

"Take me," Ella panted.

He growled his approval and, before she knew what was happening, he'd released her hands and caught her under the knees and shoulders, picking her up, then depositing her on the ground in a bed of leaves. His skin was hot in the cool air, his naked body warming her where it touched her as he dropped on top of her, propping himself up on his elbows and nudging between her legs.

She wriggled her arms out of her oversized jacket and turned over on it, using it as a throw between her and the ground below. She lifted her hair off her shoulders, pressing her face into the soft lining of her coat, feeling her mate's body graze hers as he gazed down at her.

The growling started at once. She'd learned that, no matter how turned on he was by the sight of her breasts or ass, nothing compared to his furor when she bared that spot where her neck met her shoulder, that spot where his mark permanently scarred her skin. Would a bite there ever stop intensifying their love-making to the point where she had to scream or die? She hoped not. Nothing in her entire life compared to being taken in that manner. No meal or achievement or fun event gave her the complete satisfaction and bliss and feeling of all-being-right in her world that having her mate claim her again and again did.

Now that she wasn't facing him, she could let the filth fall from her mouth without the disquiet she felt when he could see her face. "Do it," she urged him, her lower half moving sensually of its own accord. "Take me, bite me, fuck me."

Trevor half-moaned, half growled, and then she was filled. She cried out at the sweet invasion, a mix of pleasure and slight pain filling her until she got used to him. She pressed herself backwards onto him, pulling her hair further to one side, knowing what was coming next. He bent over her and his teeth penetrated her skin, achingly slow. Even as the pain shot through her shoulder muscles, the pleasure spread through her middle. It built higher and higher as he pumped into her and held on tightly. A rivulet of her blood rolled over her shoulder and fell forward onto the jacket beneath her. She ignored it, knowing the break in her skin was only temporary, but their connection was forever.

Ella threw her head back, crying out, as pleasure so great it couldn't be imagined or even fully remembered when it was over pushed through her. Trevor moaned louder at her neck and his thrusts into her intensified, pushing her higher and higher until her own sweet wave broke and finally began to recede. A moment later, Trevor's pleasure rolled through him, causing him to stiffen. She collapsed and felt more of his weight drop onto her, then he gently released his grip on her shoulder.

Ella placed her head on her stacked hands and relaxed, her body wrung out, used up, completely satiated. Trevor pulled out of her, then rolled onto the ground to her right, completely ignoring the dirt, bugs, and leaves there.

"I hope I die just like that," he said and she heard the rasp of his hand against the scruff around his mouth.

Ella didn't even have the strength to argue with him, that if he did, she would be left with a two-hundred-and-forty-pound corpse on top of her. The cool air kissed her buttocks where her skirt was still pushed up around her hips. Her eyes drifted closed as she listened to her mate's recovering breaths next to her. Her shoulder didn't hurt at all, and she knew from experience that the wound there had already closed up.

"What's on that hill?" she asked softly before she forgot, before she drifted off into sleep on the hard ground, knowing she was safe with her wolf next to her.

He looked up. "It could be a house, if I finished building it. Not sure why I ever started." His voice sounded uncharacter-istically soft and far away, as if he were close to sleep himself. She wondered where his clothes were, and if he would sleep naked. She tried to worry about bugs, but couldn't do it. She was too relaxed.

A howl sounded to their left and Ella jerked her head up, looking that way, her reverie broken.

"Trent," Trevor whispered. "He needs something."

Trent's deep rumble filled their heads. *The honeymoon's over, kids. Wade wants to talk to you both. He'll be here in twenty.*

Ella dropped her head to the forest floor, then rolled onto her back and stared at the trees spreading their protec-tive canopy above them. Trevor kissed her one last time and stood, pulling her up with him.

"I'm going to take you on a real honeymoon someday, you know."

Ella didn't answer. She knew the implied ending to that sentence. Someday, when this was all over.

If it ever was.

CHAPTER 3

*H*eather Herrin walked down the steps of her doctor's office to the parking lot, holding one hand to her stomach, as if she were going to puke. She wasn't, but she couldn't seem to let go.

She sleep-walked to her car, her doctor's last words playing inside her mind over and over.

Schedule the surgery with the receptionist. I think it's important we take it out soon.

She had done no such thing, though. She'd walked past the receptionist, her face pointed in the opposite direction, every cell in her body screaming NO.

When she reached her tiny, secondhand Kia Rio, she dropped her head and stared at the door handle for a good five minutes, her mind on vacation, possibly sipping mai tais on a beach somewhere, leaving her unable to function.

A horn blaring on the street beyond the office made her

jump. Oh, yeah. Car. Drive. Home. Somewhere. Function. Sure.

She punched her key into the lock and twisted it weakly. Somehow, she made it home without running into a ditch, or perhaps just up on the sidewalk, although she couldn't have said what streets she chose or what anything looked like on any of them, or even if she'd happened to run over any pedestrians on the way.

Heather parked in the driveway of her tiny double-wide with the decent yard and hurried inside, feeling a bit of the horrible news fall away as soon as she closed the door behind her and entered her own space.

The warmth and humidity hit her in the face, making her suck in a breath. She crossed the small living room quickly, only wanting to forget, to not think, to focus on anything else. Instead, she let her eyes wander over her make-do lizard atrium, covered with plants, perches, decorative hand-blown glass lizards, and basking lights along the far wall.

Thor, her latest rescue, sat sunning under the heat lamp on the far side of the room, next to a green-glass gecko mounted on the wall. His eyes rolled as he watched her. She moved slowly, not wanting to alarm him. He was a short-horned lizard, who was understandably wary of humans after being thoroughly neglected by someone who had no idea how to take care of him. She'd seen him for sale on a website, looking woefully underweight, and she'd driven out that night to Indiana to get him. His species of lizard should never be in captivity, anyway. When he was healthy enough, she would have him transported to a reptile conservancy in Arizona and released back into the wild. She knew people captured them out of the wild faster than she could ever put them back in, but that didn't matter. Not to Thor, anyway.

She checked the food bowl and the water bowl. Meal worms squiggled through the sand for her other rescues, but Thor only ate ants. She peeked into his large glass habitat with the low sides he could easily get in and out of and saw the harvester ants working heartily on the slices of carrot she had placed in there before she left. When Thor was hungry, he would have all the bugs he could eat.

A hiss, then clicking, caught her attention and she turned to the left, stepping over a baby gate and pushing her way past two potted yucca plants to find Falcon, her green iguana, hurrying towards her as fast as he could, which wasn't very fast.

She picked him up, feeling his increased weight on her hands with satisfaction. He'd been a rescue, also, but the old abscesses on his feet that had taken several toes and claws made it impossible to return him to the wild. Now he was pure pet, as heavy as a housecat, and almost as sweet. He opened his mouth and hissed again, looking at her.

"Hi, baby," she said, running her hand along his back. He stretched his neck out like he liked it and partially closed his eyes. "How was Thor today? Did you take care of him?" The iguana didn't answer. She petted him for a moment more, then put him down on his favorite rock, and went to check his living area to see what needed to be done.

Heather worked tirelessly, cleaning dishes that didn't need to be cleaned, replacing sand that had been replaced a few days before, then cutting up or measuring out a week's worth of food and supplements for all the eleven lizards in her care.

When there was nothing more to be done, she sank down onto the carpet, between the rows of plants and lights, and stared at her charges until the sun began to shine down the short hallway to her left, indicating the day was about to end.

With the realization came memories that she didn't want to deal with. *I think it's important we take it out soon.* Her doctor had said that so casually, the *it* he had been talking about might have been a seed out of a berry, or a wallet out of a pocket. Wasn't her uterus more important than that?

Near the door, where she'd dropped everything when she entered the house, she heard her phone ring. *No.* She couldn't deal with anything or anyone.

She stood and walked straight out the back door of her house into the yard, away from the ringing phone and towards the shed she'd modified to be an art studio. It had been the first thing she'd done when she'd bought the place, even before she'd brought in her babies. The need to create, the need to be around *it*, so strong it was all she had been able to think of. It had been even stronger than the need to get away from her mother.

She never understood the need, but when she fought it, she suffered, so she never fought it anymore.

The building was big for a shed, small for a studio, but just the right size to keep her torch the minimum distance away from the walls required by law.

She pushed through the door, closed it behind her, and headed straight to the torch, turning it on and lighting it with a click and a pop. It hissed comfortingly, the flame burning a bright white. Heather stared at it, hearing her mother's scolding about eye protection in her head for just a moment, before she slammed the lid on it.

She turned her attention to the containers of glass tubing, staring at them, although she knew exactly what she was going to pick. Two reds, two whites, and a clear, just like she had for almost a year now, without fail.

The glass tubing felt good in her hand, cool and smooth,

and she just knew that today was the day. Everything else had gone so crappily that this just had to go better. Today would be the day the dragon would come out perfectly.

She sat in front of the torch that faced away from her, staring liquidly at its perfectly controlled flame. Her thoughts fell away and her vision sharpened. Her breathing came quicker and her hands raised, dropping three of the tubes to her fireproof work surface but keeping ahold of the two red tubes, one in each hand.

She brought the red tubing to the flame and watched the colors shift before the tube penetrated the flame, and again after. Her breath caught at its beauty. She could see the dragon as it should be, now if only her skill were up to the task of teasing it out of the glass.

Time sped up, then slowed down, then ceased to exist as she heated up the tubes, connected them, twirled them and used them to manipulate the glowing, molten glass in front of her.

Red back legs formed, then met at powerful haunches and elongated into a thick and spiny tail. Each muscle and scale and spine had to be perfect. The studio fell away. Even her own breathing seemed not to exist to keep her body alive, but rather, to assist her muscles in holding and relaxing in perfect timing to create the dominant form she saw so clearly in her mind.

The body elongated, then red wings with a white underside began to take form as she pulled and swirled to create perfect flutes and embossments. She put down one tube and picked up her tweezers to crimp and fashion, then put that down to pull out a tiny, deadly claw on the tip of one wing, using only fire and the glass tube she had retrieved.

Perfect.

Corralling her breathing, which wanted to increase in anticipation, Heather finished the other wing, then moved on to the front legs, the neck, and finally the head. Two hundred and thirty-two tries ago, the tail and back of the dragon had been a mess. Now, they were perfect. The front legs she got right most of the time. The head and face had always eluded her… until today.

She gritted her teeth and concentrated harder, her shoulder and upper back muscles screaming. She put them on mute and touched the tubes together again, teasing what she wanted to see out of the glowing glass.

Until the door to the studio slammed open, hitting the wall behind it with a crashing noise. The glass tubes rattled in their containers, their sound rather musical.

Heather jumped, her concentration completely blown. She knew who it was immediately, even though it should not have been possible. Only one person would dare make an entrance like that.

"Oh my God, you're ok!" her mother wailed, then ran across the room toward her. Heather could hear her shoes slapping on the concrete floor of the shed.

"Mom, no, I'm—" She might as well have not spoken. Her mother barreled across the room and tried to grab her around the shoulders in a passive-aggressive hug. Heather saw the hands coming and did what she had to do to protect her mother. She dropped the glass tubes, with the dragon still attached, onto her work surface, flung her arms wide to catch her mother's arms, and pressed her body backwards, trying to keep her mother from being burnt on the torch.

Her mom's weight toppled her, though, and she leaned forward involuntarily, her sweatshirt catching on the flame and a hole burning in it immediately, but not spreading. She jerked her body backwards, pushing her mother with her, putting her hand down on the board in front of her for leverage, unwittingly smashing her still-glowing dragon.

"Damn it, Mother, you can't do shit like this! How many times do I have to tell you?" She stood, pushing her mom away with one hand, while turning off the torch with the other hand, that felt strangely gummy.

Her mother gasped and stared at her hand. Heather looked down to see part of the glass she had been working with cooling on the outer edge of her palm.

"Your hand! How many times have I told you not to do this kind of thing! You're bur—"

Her mother's sentence cut off and she looked into Heather's eyes, a heavy, unspoken accusation cutting through the air between them. Heather stared at her mother's perfectly coifed hair, her smart afternoon suit, and her perfectly lipsticked mouth, and finally realized that her mother would *never* change. No matter what Heather said or did, her mother would always be exactly the same. The realization held so much weight, it flattened her.

Heather moved her body between her mother and her mother's view of the worktable and wiped the cooling glass off her hand. "I'm fine, Mom," she mumbled, her thoughts whirling as she tried to figure out what the realization meant.

She turned back to her mother, who took a shaky step backwards, then seemed to gather her courage and speak. "Yes, you're fine. You're careful. I didn't do anything. And it wasn't on there for long, right? It's just a small burn, right?"

Heather hid her perfectly unblemished skin behind her back. "Just a tiny one mom. I'll put some cream on it. It will heal quickly."

Judith Herrin nodded smartly and looked down,

speaking softly. "You didn't answer your phone. For two days now. That's why I had to come over here."

Heather spoke just as softly. "How did you find the address?"

Her mother smiled brightly and laughed. "You gave it to me. You know that."

Turning quickly, so her mother wouldn't see the incredulity she couldn't keep off her face, Heather faced her workbench and the lumpy mess that should have been her beautiful dragon. She shook her head, both at the wreck behind her and the one in front of her. She double-checked that her torch was off, then picked up what was left of the dragon and placed it in the bin of vermiculite to cool slowly. She couldn't salvage it, but she would still examine it, see if there was anything to learn for next time.

She turned, still hiding her hand from her mother, then nodded toward the door. Judith pulled it open and headed outside easily, happily, her head bobbing slightly. Heather bit her tongue. She didn't want to move out of this house, but she had to put a lock on her studio door, maybe rig an alarm to tell her if anyone pulled in the driveway. Mommy surprises were never a good thing, especially when Mommy's sense of boundaries was eroding more each day.

"Heather, dear, I don't know why you have to have all those *animals* in your living room. How do you expect to have guests over?"

So, she'd been in the house. That's what Heather got for leaving the door unlocked in her safe neighborhood. "Guests over for what, Mom?"

"I don't know, boyfriends maybe, doesn't your generation do that kind of thing? Netflix and relax? Don't you need a couch and a TV for that?"

It's Netflix and chill, and that means fuck, Mom. We only do that at his place. The retort sprung to her lips but she bit it back. The joke would get her days, maybe months, worth of grilling about who *he* was. Judith staunchly refused to believe there was no *he*. Never had been.

"Anyway, I had to come ask you if you were coming to dinner tomorrow. You didn't answer me on Saturday and you haven't answered any of my phone calls since. Your father wants you there. He has something to tell you."

Heather stared at the back of her mother's head as they walked across the lawn, knowing that was code for, *I have decided to meddle in your life, but I want you to think it was your father's decision.*

Her mother walked through the sliding glass door she had left open for some reason, even though it was October and relatively cool, then pushed quickly through all the plants and past Falcon, who blinked warily at her from his perch. Heather knew her mother didn't see any of the green anoles in the branches above her head, or she'd be screaming.

Internally, Heather sighed heavily. There was no sense not going to dinner, especially now that her mother had her address. Besides, it would be nice to see Jimmy.

"Yeah, Mom, I'll be there." From near the door, her phone started ringing and she hurried past her mother to get to it, glad for the reprieve. "I've been waiting for a call, Mom. You should probably go. I'll see you tomorrow."

She pulled the phone out of her bag and clicked the answer button, opening the front door for her mom and trying to usher her that way with her body. "Hello?"

"Mrs. Herrin?" a deep and somehow provocative male voice said.

"This is Heather Herrin," she said, frowning, wondering if whoever it was really wanted her mother.

"Who is it?" her mother whispered, standing on her tip-toes to try to see the portion of the screen that wasn't pressed against Heather's face.

Heather shook her head and opened the screen door with one hand, pushing her mother onto the porch with the other. "Not now, Mom, it's important. Iloveyoubye," she said, closing the door in her mom's face and locking it.

"I'm sorry, what did you say?" she said into the phone.

"Are you the herpetologist?"

Heather frowned and looked at the phone. Blocked number. She held it back to her ear. "No. I'm not."

The man sounded flustered, but still the overt sexuality in his voice was there. Almost like he was purring at her. "Oh, I'm sorry. I'd heard—"

She interrupted him, not liking the way he sounded. She'd never met him. He had no business talking to her like she was the most delicious donut in the box. "If by herpetologist, you mean a zoologist who studies reptiles and amphibians, then no, you've got the wrong gal. I'm no zoologist and I don't follow amphibians. I do, however, rescue reptiles and know quite a bit about them. But I don't have any degrees to pro-fessionalize me."

"Oh, that's fine, I just need a bit of advice on a, a reptile issue I'm having. I got your name from Dr. Caledonia, the vet over on 5th street."

His voice hadn't cooled at all with her clipped tone and harsh explanation. Maybe he didn't even know he was doing it. She sighed and softened a bit, but just a bit. "And you are?"

"Doctor Remington Gilman."

She frowned and searched for a pad of paper and pen to

scribble that name down. She knew all the veterinarians in the area, even the ones who worked only on farm animals and she'd never heard of a Dr. Gilman. "What can I help you with, Dr. Gilman?"

"I've got a, well, a type of dragon here, and he's not doing well. He's in a bit of a coma, and we've been taking blood from him—"

She interrupted again, anger rising. "What type of a dragon?"

"Well, I'm not exactly sure. One of the big ones, but—"

"You can't possibly mean a Komodo Dragon? Is this a pet?"

"The ah, the owner didn't say, and I don't have the experience to know, and, well, I just need to ask you a few qu—"

"Send me a picture of it. Right now."

"No, well, I'm afraid that's not possible."

Heather took a deep breath and tried to keep herself from yelling at the man. He clearly had no idea what he was doing, but he couldn't possibly have a Komodo Dragon, one of the deadliest lizards in the world. She needed to back off a bit and let him speak, get more information from him. "Ok, tell me what's wrong with it, what you need to know."

His voice warmed to the point that she almost couldn't stand to listen to him. "He's unresponsive. And his blood is turning green."

Heather pulled the phone away from her ear again and stared at it. Biliverdin overload in a Komodo Dragon? Or any type of pet lizard? She spoke automatically, bringing the phone back to her face. "It could be some sort of toxin overload," she said slowly. "But I've never heard of such a thing domestically. What is the icterus index?"

The other end of the line was silent for a long moment,

and Heather pressed the phone to her ear harder. She could hear a cat meowing in the background, so she knew he was still on the line. If he hadn't determined an icterus index, he was a complete and total amateur. Maybe even an imposter.

"Dr. Gilman, I must see this lizard. I can help it, I know I can, but only if you let me see it. I-ah, I won't report you, or anything."

She heard a click in her ear as the line went dead.

CHAPTER 4

*E*arly the next morning, Heather drove down the residential street, looking for the address her little brother, Jimmy, had found for her by working some sort of magic she didn't understand on his computer. She *got* lizards on a very deep level. She got fire on maybe a deeper one. Most of the rest of the world was a puzzle to her, and what Jimmy could do with a connection to the Internet definitely qualified as the latter.

The address loomed on her right and she slowed to a crawl, passing by it once, trying to formulate a plan. It wasn't a vet's office, unfortunately. Or maybe it was. The two-story, white-panel house with the large porch looked just sanitary enough and unlived-in enough to be a business in a residential area. She passed and turned around at the end of the street to make another pass.

The asphalt driveway was widened enough to

accommodate the entire front of the house so that four cars could park side by side, but there were no white lines and no signs announcing a business. Heather parked on the street and watched the place. No movement in the windows, no car in the driveway, no signs of life at all. Oh, except a black and white cat sauntering down the front porch steps and disappearing under a hedge. That meant nothing, though. Vet's offices frequently had live-in cats. To the left of the house, a worn path led to what looked to be more woods than backyard. There were houses on either side, but nothing behind.

She twisted the keys to turn off the car. She had to at least try. If Doctor Gilman really knew someone with a Komodo Dragon, they had to be warned it was deadly. She'd never rescued a Komodo before, but she'd be happy to help. Maybe even thrilled. Even if it wasn't a Komodo, she wanted to get a look at it, offer advice. Fix it, if she could.

Heather got out of the car and walked into the driveway, nervous tension biting at her midsection as the cool fall air whistled against her face. What if he called the cops on her? A run-in with the law was something she did not want to deal with, especially with her nocturnal … issues lately. She pressed her lips together and pushed that out of her mind. The last thing she needed right now was to admit she was probably as crazy as her mother. Ah, genetics, what a fun kick-in-the-ass by nature.

As she got closer, she could tell the screen door was closed, but the heavy door inside was open. So, someone was around. She took a deep breath and stepped up onto the porch, all the way to the door, then knocked heavily.

Nothing. No one moved inside. Something rustled behind her and she turned to see an orange tabby cat dart across the steps and disappear. Ok. She knocked again. "Dr. Gilman?"

A low, deep, rumbling moan sounded from inside the house, startling her. She jumped, then chastised herself for it as she leaned forward and tried to see inside. That had been a man. Maybe someone was hurt?

A large room opened up, looking like something her late grandmother would have loved. A lovely and expensive-looking grandfather clock stood against a wall to the right of the room. An immaculate fireplace graced the back wall, and a horrifically ugly flower-patterned settee sat directly in the middle of the room. Other than that, two uncomfortable-looking wooden benches along the left wall were the only other places to sit. There was no TV, no books, no coffee table or magazines.

She craned her head, trying to see what was along the front wall. A table with colorful brochures? Ah, so it was a business. Could she just walk in? She grasped the door and pulled it open, stepping inside, meaning to call out again as she did so, but the draft of the door opening pulled with it the loveliest scent she'd ever smelled in her life, momentarily disarming her. Red hots and cinnamon, mixed with the smell of seasoned black-cherry wood on an open fire. She stopped and took a deep breath through her nose as the screen door slammed behind her.

It smelled wonderful, but didn't make her think of food, like good smells frequently did. Instead, an image of her snuggling with a man in front of an open fire came to her. He was big and he had his arm around her. He turned to her and whispered in her ear, his breath tickling the fine hairs on her neck, and she laughed in her imagination and tried to catch his mouth with hers because she just knew he would taste spicy and sweet and oh-so—

A meow from outside brought Heather back to the present. What in the hell was she doing? Going all day-dream-zombie in some stranger's house/business/whatever?

She clasped her hands into hard fists to try to steady herself. "Dr. Gilman?" she called again, weakly.

That deep, rumbling moan sounded again and she spun to her right, where she heard it from. A partially-closed door blocked her view of whatever was in there, but she knew at once that was where the smell—that heavenly smell she wanted to taste—was coming from. She took a step, then another, acutely aware of her right hand as it reached out to push the door open.

A man lay in a hospital bed, breathing shallowly and much too quickly. She could see his chest rising and falling so fast he seemed in pain. But he was still the most gorgeous and distinguished-looking man she'd ever seen. The bit of silver and gray at his temples and scruff, plus the lines on his face, told her he was probably close to her father's age, which made him forty-five or fifty. Dark tattoos like spiky vines on his left arm and swirly flowers on his right caught her eye, intriguing her, almost overwhelming her. She took another step forward, willing his closed eyes to open. Wishing deeply that he would look at her, talk to her. A need to know him intimately filled her so deeply she physically balked, but pushed forward anyway.

He was huge, and not wearing a gown or shirt. She could see his bare shoulders and part of his chest before the sheet interrupted her view. She didn't know men like this existed in real life. His chest looked like he'd spent a lifetime lifting heavy things, possibly heaving them into space. Even with how muscular he was, though, she could tell he was sick, or injured. His skin lay loosely over his muscles, and he seemed to have no fat between the two, like maybe he hadn't eaten in too long? Even while she thought that, she realized he didn't have the look of a man who was sleeping, but rather a man who was unconscious.

But how could that be? The lovely smell was coming from him, she knew it, and it wasn't a sickly smell. It was robust, inviting, and exceedingly healthy. It made her think of sex and babies and—her heart skipped a beat at that last word and her stomach turned slightly. No babies for her. But still she couldn't tear her eyes away from the beast in the bed. Boy, did she mean that as a compliment!

She wanted to lean forward and sniff him, see if he was wearing cologne, but she settled for reaching out her hand slowly, watching it go out from her in the same way she'd watched it push the door open. His own hand, thick, veiny, and strong-looking, lay on his chest, the fingers slightly curled and tense. She had to touch his skin. Felt like she would die if she didn't know the relative smoothness of it.

A yellow spark of static electricity jumped from him to her. She saw it in slow motion, like a tiny bolt of lightning reaching up for her, honing in on her, claiming her. The spark didn't hurt, no, it soothed, calmed, and she felt the flickering sensation spread through her hand, then up her arm to her neck and head, then envelope her entire body like a cold flame. She shuddered as it dissipated, feeling a lovely heat in her core that made her shift her legs and notice a hot throbbing that hadn't been there before. Like her entire being had been instantaneously sexualized in a way she'd never experienced.

Her mind took all of this in as her hand continued the descent of the last few inches to reach his. Heat bloomed from his skin, warming her, even though she always seemed to run hot. She gasped, still reeling from the spark, the added pressure of this new sensation threatening to knock her to the ground. Her fingers curled around his involuntarily, as if to keep her grounded, and he moaned loudly. His eyes opened, once, twice, fluttering, and she saw they were multi-colored, with reds and yellows converging like a campfire at twilight. She'd never seen eyes like that before, but when she looked closer, she swore he recognized her. His lips curled into a ghost of a smile and his eyes slipped closed again.

His lips moved as he murmured something. Heather stood stock-still, refusing to breath, so she could hear what it was.

"Ta ma hurry, chi annit," he whispered, or at least that was what it sounded like to her. Like no language she'd ever heard before. It had been thick, throaty, and guttural, and she so wanted to hear it again.

Heather leaned over him, wanting to speak to him, but she noticed immediately that something was different. His shoulders, tense before, had smoothed out and relaxed, and his breathing had slowed. As she stared at him, he took a great shuddering breath and blew it out, then tucked his chin, that tiny smile still on his face.

Now he looked more asleep than passed out, and she didn't have the heart to wake him, no matter how much she wanted to. The connection of their hands called to her and she stared at it, strange feelings flitting through her center. A deep longing balanced exactly with a feeling of sublime satisfaction. Like she was exactly where she should be but things could go so much deeper for her. Like something she'd wanted all her life was at her fingertips, close enough to reach, but still not certain.

The feeling brought desire. Desire she let run wild inside

her own mind for the first time in her life, instead of clamping down on it with everything she had. She wanted to watch something burn. She wanted to feel the heat of fire on her skin and the glow of it in her eyes. She didn't care what burned, the house, the forest behind, the neighborhood. She just wanted to be there if it went up. *When* it went up.

The slamming of the screen door from the other room startled her, and she almost cried out. She looked around wildly, smashing the lid shut on her fire-lust in the way she had a thousand times before. To her left, a form passed the partially-closed doorway. She saw only a glimpse of reddish hair on top of a tall, broad figure. Heather held her breath at the sound of footsteps crossing the room to the back, then sounding quieter and quieter until they stopped. Like the person had gone into an unseen room in the house.

Heather pulled her hand back, her heart twisting as she lost the connection with the man in the bed, then she walked out of the room as quickly as she could. The thought of being caught in that room made her feel sick to her stomach. She knew no one could read minds, but it was bad enough that *she* knew what she'd been thinking. She had to get out of there. Had to get away.

Without looking around, Heather walked quietly to the screen door, opened it without making a sound, and slipped outside, not breaking into a sprint for her car until she was off the porch.

She fled like a criminal, all thoughts of why she'd been there in the first place driven completely from her mind.

CHAPTER 5

*T*roy left the house through the small wolf (*doggy*) door behind the couch, biting his tongue as he pushed through the plastic flap, not quite hard enough to draw blood, but hard enough to deflect any bitter thoughts that might try to force their way into his head. He'd never minded his lot in life too much, until now.

Behind him, Ella trilled laughter and Trevor growled something unintelligible. Case in point. In another half a minute, Trevor would probably throw her over his shoulder and carry her up the stairs, and no one would see them for an hour or two. Then they'd come back down, flushed, happy, eyes only for each other, feed each other strawberries or cake or pita-fucking-pockets for all he knew, drink tea and beer, and do it all over again. Troy did not want to be around for it.

He was thrilled to see Trevor in love, and having Ella join the family made his heart glad. She softened daily life, smoothed rough edges between him and his brothers, and he was beginning to enjoy being petted behind the ears for the first time in his life.

So, why did he feel like such a dick?

Because he was jealous. Not only was he jealous of his brother's new romance, new mate, and all the time he spent with her, but he was even more jealous because that would never be him. Ever.

And he had no one to talk to about it. He'd tried to talk to Trent a few times, but Trent had a firm no complaining rule, making Troy break off before he ever really got started.

Outside, in the crisp autumn air, he shook his head, making his ears fly. The reverberations cleared his thoughts, so he scented to see who was on the protection detail. Harlan. *Good.* Beckett. *Good.* Mac. *Eh.* Mac wasn't near as much fun now that he'd calmed down a bit on the Trevor-hating. Ever since Trevor had offered himself up to Khain as a trade for Ella's life, Mac had barely given him any shit. Sure, Mac was still a pompous blowhard whose intellect was rivaled only by the garden tools in the back shed, but he'd been different lately. Troy hadn't had a reason to chew on him in weeks.

Two more scents hit his nose. A *felen*. Nalan, Troy thought his name was. Decent enough guy for a cat, not that Troy minded cats too much anymore. Smokey only paid attention to Trent, but Chelsea was ok. She was soft and smelled interesting and hadn't tried to steal Troy's food or his breath once. The other smell was a *bearen*. Troy hadn't met him yet, but he recognized him as the same *bearen* who'd been out more regularly than any other in the last couple of weeks. *Bearen* were a mystery. Kind of slow, it seemed. Even standoffish. They usually scented like they thought they were superior to *wolven*, although Troy hadn't gotten anything like that from this fella yet.

Troy walked down the dirt driveway to the tree the *wolven* liked to congregate under, while the *felen* and the *bearen* usually smoked and joked on the other side of the driveway, under a green tarp Trevor had brought out for them.

Harlan and Beckett sat on one side of the picnic table under the tree, while Mac sat on the other, all dressed in response outfits; dark cargo pants and dark long-sleeve shirts, their badges and guns at their hips. Beckett wore his trademark camouflage ball cap, the one Wade couldn't break him of wearing no matter what he did. Their voices were pitched low enough that Troy couldn't hear them yet, but he didn't need to. Their scents and the thoughts he caught told him they were talking about the boxes and tunnel found in Ella's old house.

Mac's voice reached him. "They're all in code," Mac kept his voice pitched low and cast a disgruntled glance over at the two males under the tarp across the way. "Six boxes full of nothing but hundreds of pieces of paper, all handwritten, all completely in code. Jaggar is trying to break it now."

Beckett snorted, and when he spoke his southern accent was stronger than usual, telling Troy he was upset or irritated. "I tell you what. That fucker, Grey, he was into some shit. We should find him and force him to talk, the way he used to force us to kiss his ass."

Harlan noticed Troy approach and sit down next to the table. He nodded to him, then held up a hand, looking at Beckett. "Wait, wait, wait. Grey? You mean the *citlali* who ran the war camps on the East Coast? What's he got to do with this? And I know Trev had some run-ins with him, but why do you care about his standards?"

Beckett leaned forward, his face in a snarl. "He didn't run just the war camps on the East Coast. He came up with the entire *idea*. He started the first one based out of New York, and then he started setting them up all over the country, and traveling to them to make sure they were up to his standards. I dealt with him plenty, and if I saw him today, I'd shove his standards right up his ass."

Harlan shrugged. "What's the problem? The war camps were a brilliant idea. With all the females ..." He stumbled over his words and Troy watched him closely, amazed that his grief was so strong after decades. "With all the females gone, the males with pups still had to go to work. It's not like you all could have just gone to human daycare. You'd be even more useless than you already are."

Mac chuckled and leaned back in his seat until Harlan sized him up. "That goes for you, too, Mac. Where the fuck were you gonna learn advanced battle techniques if Daddy dropped you off with the human kiddies shitting in their diapers for twelve hours a day? Huh?"

Mac flipped him the bird. "I ain't arguing with you, old-timer. I'm agreeing with you."

Harlan snarled at Mac, then turned back to Beckett. "So, what's Grey got to do with it, anyway?"

"You haven't heard? The tunnel in Ella's old house? It goes to Chicago PD. They put it in fifty years ago when Grey was the deputy out there, and they left it because that was his home base."

Harlan whistled. "Eighty miles of tunnel? I didn't know we even did that." He looked sideways at Beckett. "Wait. Grey lived in Ella's house? What does that mean?"

Mac shifted in his seat and his scent changed. Troy watched him, wondering if he'd been told not to share that they were looking into whether Grey had been shacking up with Ella's grandma. And maybe her aunt, too, after her grandma died. Ella was embarrassed that she didn't know who her grandpa was, since her mother never shared anything with her, and if it turned out that Grey had been her grandpa? That just opened up a whole bucket of slimy stuff.

Mac ducked his head. He smelled like he was dying to share, but he didn't quite dare. "Who knows." He threw Troy a glance and lifted his lip. Troy lifted his back. His teeth were much more impressive.

Harlan looked up at the house and changed the subject. "So, I've only got duty out here once next week. I'm surprised Wade's whittling it down to one KSRT member a shift and bringing patrol out instead. And I'm surprised Trevor's ok with it. He doesn't trust too many *wolven* around his female."

Troy whined lightly. Too bad none of them spoke any more than rudimentary *ruhi*, if that. He wanted to join this conversation.

They all looked at him. "What, Troy?" Beckett said, pushing his cap up off his forehead and standing up. He paced for a second, then walked over to Troy, looking at him.

"Sit the fuck down, hayseed, you don't know what he's saying," Mac snarled, not unkindly, picking a splinter off the table top.

"I can speak *ruhi*, a little, if it's strong," Beckett said, his voice sounding hurt. He bent at the waist and stared Troy in the eyes. "What?"

Troy chuffed. He hoped that was true. He fixed a picture of a monster lightbulb with legs, wearing a camouflage cap in his head. *Anyone ever told you that you have a head like a lightbulb?* he sent to Beckett as hard as he could.

Beckett pushed his cap back farther, scratched his head,

then pulled it back down over his forehead. He looked over his shoulder. "I think he wants to say something about Grey."

Mac and Harlan looked amused. Troy rolled his eyes. Beckett wasn't a bad guy. He was a hard-worker, tough, mellow, and he was the only cop in Serenity who could rival Mac when it came to picking up females. They liked his smile or some shit. But he didn't have a bone of sophistication in him. Partying, working, listening to country music, that was about the extent of what he thought about.

Troy tried again. This time he pictured Beckett in his normal off-duty outfit of camo, jeans, cowboy boots, and more camo. *All that camo makes you look like the redneck from hell,* he sent, giggling a little. Lightbulb-head was better, but Beckett had a thing about being called a redneck. If he did catch it, he'd be twitching.

Beckett just screwed up his face. "Ah, crap, I don't know." He rubbed the back of his neck absently, then pulled his cap down lower over his eyes. "Sorry, Troy," he said, walking back over to the table.

Troy's stomach lumped up. It was no fun ribbing someone if they didn't know it and they were just gonna be nice.

A voice filled his head. *You want me to tell him?*

Troy looked over his shoulder, knowing immediately it was the *bearen* who was talking to him. *Felen* didn't sound like that, all gruff and tough. *Felen* were more sexual, they purred everything, even the males.

He turned around and looked at the *bearen* across the driveway. *Nah, it was a lame joke anyway.*

The *bearen* snorted and bobbed his head. He was lumberjack big, like all *bearen*, but he looked more intelligent than Troy had found them to be in the past. *I'll be happy to translate if you need me to.*

Thanks, ah…

Bruin, my name's Bruin. You're Troy. Nice to finally meet you.

Troy nodded, thinking maybe he'd go have an actual conversation, even if it was with a bear, but then Beckett said something to Harlan that caught his attention. *Thanks, you too,* he sent back, then turned to the males at the picnic table.

"So what's it like, anyway?"

"What?"

"You know, Trevor, how he's so caught up in that female he can't even stand for other males to be around her?"

Harlan stared at him hard. "Are you asking me what it's like to be mated? I was mated only for a day."

"But you loved her."

Harlan growled deep in his throat, a reverberating warning that preceded his threatening scent. "Yes, I did."

Beckett didn't notice or didn't care. He stared at Harlan openly, innocently. "What was it like?"

Harlan's face twisted and a strangled noise came out of him. There was that grief again, flooding Troy's nostrils. It almost made him glad for a second he would never have the opportunity to have something that precious to him taken away .

"Never mind," Beckett said quickly.

Harlan looked at the sky for a second, then back down to Beckett and Mac, who was also watching him closely. "Loved her? I did more than love her. She was my everything. She fucking owned me. Looking at her, touching her, hearing her voice, was like breathing, like eating. It was everything."

He stopped talking and his gaze dropped to the table, then over his shoulder to the house where Ella and Trevor were. His voice lowered till Troy had to strain to hear him.

"For the short time I had her, I woke up with a smile on my face every day."

Mac looked away while Beckett clapped a hand to Harlan's shoulder. "Sorry, I didn't mean to bring it up."

Harlan was about to speak, when the air shimmered beside the table, closer to the tree.

All four *wolven* jumped to their feet as the scent of strong disinfectants and ammonia pushed away the scent of despair and a female appeared as if from nowhere, her hand on the tree to brace herself. The air still shimmered behind her and a dim view of a stark hallway shone there, obscuring most of the view of the tree itself.

Troy ran in her direction, baring his teeth, looking behind her for some sign of danger, some indication of Khain. The female herself did not look dangerous. She looked scared, and sorrowful. Her hair was long and dark and hung stringily around her face. Her skin was a deliciously creamy caramel and her features made him think of coconuts and balmy beaches, but he didn't have time to analyze that.

She threw a terrified glance over her shoulder as men in hospital uniforms appeared at the end of the long hallway and approached her slowly, hands up, as if she were dangerous. Only then did Troy notice she wore a plain white gown with tiny flowers or butterflies or something on it, like a hospital gown. Her feet were bare.

Troy stopped within two feet of her and stared as her eyes marked him, then slid off him. She looked at each male in turn, but her gaze stopped on Harlan. She held up a hand to him.

"Harlan, they say you're not real," she said to him, almost in a whisper. "Is it true?"

Troy looked at Harlan, noticing in the shifting scents

around them that Bruin and the *felen* had run over to join the strange party.

One of the men in the hallway that could not possibly exist in the middle of the Illinois field sprinted quietly up behind the female. Troy barked once, warning her, then tensed, ready to leap on the man. He didn't know what was going on, but he had taken sides already. Too late, he saw the needle in the man's hand as it entered the female's shoulder.

Three things happened almost simultaneously. She made a tiny sound like a whimper cut short and crumpled into the man's arms. Troy leaped. The shimmering vision, including the female and the hallway behind her, disappeared like they had never been. Troy sailed through it, his side scraping painfully against the tree. He landed roughly, glad he hadn't hit the tree muzzle first.

He turned around and glared at Harlan, as Mac rushed over and looked up and down, even looking behind the tree. Nothing.

Mac whirled on Harlan. "What was that?"

Harlan shook his head. "I don't know."

"She knew your name. Tell me you know who she is."

Harlan sank back down onto the picnic table, staring off into space, his voice far away when he spoke. "I told her my name a long time ago."

"What the fuck are you talking about? How long ago?" Mac snarled as he pulled his phone out of his pocket and started firing off texts.

"Forty years," Harlan said, the clouds reflecting in his eyes.

"Good night," Beckett whispered and Mac's head snapped up.

Mac walked in front of Harlan and snapped his fingers in

front of Harlan's face. "That girl was twenty, twenty-five at the most. There's no way she was alive forty years ago."

Harlan looked up higher, anywhere but at Mac and the confused group of *shiften* around him. "I know."

CHAPTER 6

*H*eather pushed open the door of her childhood home, grimacing as the smell of mothballs hit her in the face. Was her mom going out of her mind? She walked into the front parlor and pushed open the two windows there. She wouldn't be able to eat a bite if the place still smelled like that when the food made it onto the table.

"Mom," she called towards the kitchen, trying to sound normal, even though she felt anything but. "I'm here."

"That's nice, dear, tell your brother it's time for dinner."

Heather clomped up the stairs, then turned right and followed the hallway all the way around to Jimmy's room, passing two empty rooms on the way, one of which used to be hers. Jimmy's door was partially open, but she knocked anyway.

Jimmy didn't hear her. He faced his computer, his back

to her, large headphones over his head. In front of him, lines and lines of text streamed by so fast she didn't have a chance of reading it.

She knocked louder, then called his name. He turned and his face broke into a wide smile when he saw her. "Hey, sis, good to see you." He pulled his headphones off and hung them on a hook next to him.

She crossed the room to hug him, then sat on the bed next to him. He held out his hand, palm up, like he was waiting for her to give him something.

"What?" she teased.

He scoffed. "Come on. If you don't want your cold-blooded buddies to starve next time you go out of town, you know what."

"Yeah, I know." She pulled a fifty out of her pocket and dropped it onto his palm.

He made it disappear. "You're welcome," he said, and looked back to his screen.

Heather watched his profile as he turned back to his work, thinking again how little he looked like her. Most people didn't even believe they were related. He was all dark skin and large features, lanky, with huge hands and feet, while she was slight and blond, with little button features.

He was the dead spit of their father, while she favored their mother and looked nothing like their father.

"Hey," she said, leaning towards him. "Mom found out where I live."

Jimmy snorted. "I'm more surprised you were able to keep it from her for so long." He lowered his voice and stared at her under his eyebrows. "The guilt is strong with that one."

Heather ignored him. "Did she maybe follow you when you went over last week?"

Jimmy gave her a disgusted look. "I'm sixteen, not stupid. I bet she followed *you*. You're more likely to walk around in a trance and not know what's going on around you."

Heather bit her lip. So much for hoping no one noticed how spacey she got sometimes, like her mind was not just elsewhere, but on a completely different planet. A fear gripped her, and she wanted to ask him if he'd ever noticed anything else about her, but she didn't dare.

Jimmy turned in his chair so he faced her, his expression serious. "Hey, there's actually something I need to tell you," he said slowly, and she could tell immediately it was something he'd thought a great deal about, something he was dreading talking about. She could read him like a book, having practically raised him when he was little.

"Shoot," she said, dropping her head and matching her expression to his.

"I, ah, I'm not sure how you're gonna take this, but I think you have a right to know," he said, taking a deep breath.

"Okaaaay," she said. "You're freaking me out here."

He opened his mouth but before he could say a word, their mother appeared at the door, her words clipped like she meant business. "Heather, there you are. Dinner is served. I've been yelling up for you for ten minutes."

Heather looked at her mother. "I just got here, Mom, but message received, we're coming."

Judith stood in the doorway and folded her hands, her face unsmiling. She pressed her lips together and gave Heather the look.

"Mom, just give me a sec, ok?"

"Heather, the dinner bell has rung. Wash your hands. Don't make me talk to your father."

Heather stared her mother down. Short of physically

pushing her out of the way and slamming the door, she knew her mother was not going to move until they did.

"Fine. Fine." She stood, pulling at Jimmy's sleeve. If she was heading down to dinner, he better damn well be on her heels. She couldn't face it alone.

Their mother watched until they were both within a few feet of her, then she turned and walked down the hallway, waiting by the bathroom for them like they were both five years old.

Hands washed, they headed down the stairs together and entered the dining area. Dad was already in his chair, fork raised expectantly. "Hi, Dad," Heather said, pushing into the booth seat and not bothering to try to kiss him hello. He hated any display of affection from her, always had.

Judith sat and watched as Heather and Jimmy scooched to their spots, then bowed their heads. Her dad's quiet baritone filled the room. "Bless us, oh Lord, and these thy gifts which we are about to receive from thy bounty, through Christ, our Lord. Amen."

"Amen," Heather echoed as her mother and brother did the same. She watched her father's face as he dug into his food and began eating. She would bet a hundred dollars she wouldn't hear him say another word the entire night.

"So, Heather, I gave your number to the man who cleans the windows at the retired living community my friend, Shirley, moved into."

Heather groaned out loud and held her head while Jimmy elbowed her. "Mom, you can't do that. How many times do I have to tell you not to give my number to strangers? Do you want me to end up murdered?"

Judith put down her fork and stared sternly at Heather.

"I want you to end up married. You can't have babies if you aren't married."

Heather looked to Jimmy for help but he was staring at his plate of food. Her dad didn't even seem to be able to hear the conversation. Her retort rose to her lips automatically. "I can have babies if I'm not—"

She stopped talking and shut her mouth with a snap. Actually, she couldn't have babies. At all. Ever. The visit from her mother the day before and her worry after her botched trip out to the doctor's place where the gorgeous man had been had driven that realization completely out of her mind. She'd spent the rest of the morning at work and all of the afternoon hiding in her studio again, trying to forget that man and the lapse she'd had while standing over him.

She cleared her throat, then figured she'd just say it. She had to tell her mother sometime. She wasn't telling her just to spite her. She wasn't. "Mom, I have something to tell you," she started gently. "I, ah, I went to my ob-gyn yesterday and he told me something that you're not going to want to hear."

Judith blinked at her, the blood draining from her face.

Heather nodded. She didn't care if this wasn't dinner conversation. There was never a good time for something like this. "Yeah, uh, turns out there is a reason I've never had a period in my life. Turns out the last doctor was completely wrong with everything he said. I, ah, well, my uterus is just a wrinkled mass of dried-out flesh that is never going to menstruate or hold babies and the doctor, well, he actually wants to take it out. He's afraid it's pre-cancerous and he says if I don't have the surgery, there's a 95% chance of me developing uterine cancer in the next ten years."

Judith gasped and held her hand to her throat. Heather looked down at her spaghetti and twirled some around her fork while her throat closed up. It was real. She'd said the C-word. Out loud.

"That can't be true," her mom finally managed to say.

Jimmy had stopped eating and put a hand on her arm. Her father was still staring at his plate and chewing, but his fork motion had stopped.

Heather let herself be pulled into Jimmy's arms. He didn't say a word, just hugged her. Too late, she yelled at herself for not considering him when she decided to tell their mother. Their dad was an emotionless robot, he could handle it. But Jimmy? He was sensitive, and he probably loved her more than anyone. He hadn't needed to hear it like that. At the dinner table. No warning.

"He's absolutely sure you'll never be able to give me grandkids?" Judith finally sputtered, and Heather felt her chest tighten. She never should have said a word.

She sat up and pulled away from Jimmy, then gave him a weak smile, dismayed to see the concern on his face. "It's ok," she told him. "I'm going to do everything the doctor says. I'll make sure it all ends up ok. I'll be fine."

Jimmy nodded and stared at his food. Judith started talking, mostly to herself. "You know what, it's probably a mistake. You'll go back in there next week, and the doctor will tell you that he made a mistake. He switched your chart with someone else's. It happens all the time. In fact, Heather, what's his name? I'll go see him. I'll tell him he made a mistake."

Heather stared at her mother, not sure what to do about her, about any of it. Finally, she just made up a name. She'd deal with it later. "It's Doctor Stevens, Mom. His office is by the river."

Judith smiled. "Ok, that's taken care of, then. I'll go see him tomorrow. It will all work itself out."

Heather nodded remotely. "Sure, Mom, sure it will."

Judith's smile brightened. "Good. Jack and I have something we want to talk to you about," she said, putting her hand on her husband's arm. Jack resumed eating.

Heather waited. Here it was. Her announcement hadn't changed anything.

"Jack hired that assistant he's been talking about to work under you for years now. He's an older man and you don't even need to train him. Used to work for Burns Funeral Home over in Roscoe. He's prepared to work three days a week. More if you say so. He'll be in tomorrow so you can show him the ropes."

Heather gaped at her mother and father, her eyes jumping between them. She settled on her father "Wait, are you firing me?"

"No, dear, didn't you hear me? Assistant. You're still in charge of the crematorium." Judith grimaced as she said it. She had always hated that Heather had been most at home in the furnace facility of the family-run funeral home Jack was the director for. Along with a few employees to help out, Judith manned the phones and the books and Jimmy had been running the computer network since he first installed it when he was twelve.

"I don't need an assistant," Heather said, trying to catch her father's eye. "We're always on time. Three people working down there is more than enough. We don't need a fourth."

Her father kept eating.

"Dad!" Heather almost screamed.

"Your mother's right," Jack intoned, his eyes still on his plate.

Heather shook her head, trying to clear her sudden lightheadedness. "I can't believe it. She finally talked you into pushing me out. How long until I'm completely gone? It's her way or the highway, huh, Dad? I swear, sometimes I'm embarrassed to be related to you. Even a jellyfish has more backbone than you."

Jimmy dropped the fork he had picked back up and mumbled something. Heather faced him. "What?"

He lifted his eyes to hers, his gaze scared. "I'm sure this is the exact wrong time to tell you this, but if Mom has her way, you'll never find out."

Heather tried to get her breathing under control as he wrestled with whatever he was trying to say.

"Mom and Dad met in 1995. I overheard them fighting about it two nights ago. Dad wants her to tell you now that you are an adult that you're not his. Apparently, they've been fighting about it for years."

Cue the screeching tires, the record needle scratching across the plastic grooves. Cue the liquid memories of her dad's awkwardness around her since she could remember. She swung her head towards her mother, her eyes trying to pop out of her head. They'd *met* when Heather was four years old?

"What in the actual hell, Mother?"

"Heather Herrin, swearing! Need I remind you that at *this* table, we do not swear."

Heather scooched out of the booth seat, hunched over and vowing she would never sit in it again. When she was finally able to stand, she faced her mother. "No, we just lie. For twenty-one years. Next time, swear at me, ok? It'll be less painful."

She stalked out of the kitchen, heading for the door, but turning right to head up the stairs at the last minute, the angry outburst in her head replaced by something softer, a static-y sound that overlaid any thought or purpose. At the top of the steps she turned left, towards her mother and Jack's room. That was easy. Replace the noun *dad* with the proper name *Jack*. Simple. Barely any pain associated with it. Right? As long as she didn't lose Jimmy, too, she'd be fine, right? They were still half-brother and sister, right?

She ended up in front of her mother's jewelry box, barely aware of the tears slipping down her face. Her hands reached out on their own and sorted through her mother's things. Costume jewelry, silver, just for show. She lifted out the tray where all the cheap stuff was. Ah, there it was. The gold. She grabbed the three necklaces and the two rings she saw there, thrusting them in her pocket, one ear to the steps just outside the door. No one was coming yet.

She laid the tray back in, her brain still buzzing with that strange overlay that made it hard to think about what she was doing and why. Just doing was so much simpler, and she didn't have the strength of will anymore to fight it. As long as there was no thought of starting a fire. She would fight that with her dying breath. Stealing her mother's jewelry was acceptable when you compared it to starting her mother's house on fire.

The lid on the jewelry box dropped shut as she pushed the tray into place, catching her fingers. She left them there, as a strange pulsing *thing* she could only feel called out to her. Called her by name.

Heather stared at her hand, the fingers half obscured by the lid lying on them and felt her blood pulse in time with something… something external.

She lifted the lid again, then took out the tray, but there was nothing left under it. Her fingers caressed the felt at the bottom of the box, then her hand curled into a fist and knocked there. It didn't sound hollow, but the thought wouldn't leave her brain. She put the tray in, shut the lid, and picked the box up level with her eye, then turned it around. As she moved it, one of the sides gave way just a little under her fingers. She put the box down and jiggled that side until it slid up, revealing a hidden drawer.

Heather felt her heart speed up and her mouth go dry. She pried at the drawer with her fingers, knowing there was something in there more valuable than anything else her mother owned. More valuable than the entire house, probably.

The drawer slid open, revealing a small, colorful pendant, approximately an inch and a half high, caught on a delicate chain.

Her dragon.

He was real, exactly as she saw him in her mind. Strong red scales lined a powerful body. Head kicked up in an arrogant, alert pose. Chest a lighter color than the rest of the body, maybe a yellow, she couldn't tell. Her senses clamped down and her focus narrowed to a small field, pointed at the dragon.

Without realizing she had reached for it, her fingers grazed it and an electric shock shot through her body, startling her and wiping her emotional slate clean for just a second. Her earlier sadness and frustration fell away, and the rest of her life, her *real* life, stood in front of her. A life where she mattered, where she was powerful and strong and accepted herself fully. A life in which her mate was different than all the other males that stood with him, but he was still accepted fully. A life where she could choose to drop her old life completely, with a whispered prayer of appreciation to everyone in it for bringing her to this exact point… or merge the old life with the new life.

Heather's fingers curled around the pendant and she lifted it out of the drawer, feeling power course through her hand and arm as she did so. The power felt good, but also dangerous, because she knew she had no control over it. She loved it, but she feared it, as well, especially here, in this enclosed space, this wooden house, this den of her mother's.

A pop sounded behind her and Heather whirled around to see the top of her mother's bed on fire.

"Oh, fuck," she whispered, shoving the pendant in her pocket and pressing her hands frantically to the flames, putting them out. She crossed hand over hand until the entire blanket was smoking, but no longer on fire.

Heather backed away from the bed, watching the smoke as it lazily made its way to the ceiling, to the four smoke detectors strategically placed around the room. This was bad. She couldn't be caught up here like this, in the middle of her worst nightmare. Her ass hit the dresser and she turned her body enough to put the jewelry box back exactly the way she found it, then rushed to the bed and pulled the bedspread off it just as the smoke alarms began to blare, in that room and in every other room in the house.

Heather ran for the stairs, scorched bedspread tucked under her arm, pendant and jewelry in her pockets, this time heading straight out the door, ignoring the high-pitched voices of her family in the kitchen.

For the second time that day, she snuck out of a house, hoping to keep her secret just a little while longer.

CHAPTER 7

The fire. It was so lovely. Warmth. Power. The colors of life swirling within it. She wanted it to burn. Wanted it all to burn. She would dance, frolic really, as indiscriminant flames consumed everything in their path.

Her consciousness asleep, Heather celebrated the fire in a way she would never let herself dream of while awake. Her fire-lust, as she had called it as long as she could remember, was dangerous. Terrifying on some level. Something that no normal person would ever feel. She knew how people ended up in prison for arson, though. She knew that desire to watch it all burn intimately.

The year before, someone had set fourteen fires in a desperately dry California, and, while most of the country expressed outrage, Heather had only understood, even while she hated the part of her that watched the footage on TV, and never condemned the fire-setter once.

Her hands worked while her eyes saw nothing, forming, shaping, preparing. The night wore on without her conscious thought about what she was doing and why, as she worked in the shadows.

***

A strident sound broke into Heather's consciousness and her eyes flew open. For a moment, she thought she was still at her mother's house and the smoke alarm was going off again. But no, she'd gone home, texted Jimmy to tell her mother that she'd taken the bedspread off her bed as a joke and she would bring it back in a few days, just use something different until then, then fell asleep in her own bed.

Which she was no longer in.

Heather looked around, scared, her disorientation falling away quickly, but her fear growing as she realized she was on a city street and the alarm that was blaring was either a fire alarm or a burglar alarm. She backed into the dark empty street and stared at the horrible sight in front of her.

Her stomach turned to water. Oh, God, she'd done it again. Started another fire in her sleep. This time it wasn't a small one in the woods near her home. This time, it was right in front of a building, and as she watched she could see the siding of the building melting and smoldering in places. It was only a matter of moments before the whole place went up. She craned her neck to the right, afraid of where she thought she was. Yep, at the bottom of the street, well-lit and surrounded by radio towers, less than a half a mile away, was the police station. The police could be there in moments. Hell, if any were on the upstairs floor, they could look out the window and see her.

She backed up farther on shaky legs, realizing her work had a message. How had she done it, formed the reedy bundles of sticks wrapped with rags into the letters that she saw propped up into words in front of her? Each letter burned merrily and she read it quickly but the message made no sense to her.

Heather read it again, then again, realizing once and for all what she'd been fearing for months now. She was completely batshit crazy. They should cart her off to the funny farm, the booby hatch, the loony bin. She'd have her own monogrammed straightjacket and make friends with the other firebugs. They'd form a clique and shut out anyone who didn't love to burn, like high school all over again. Her mother would visit and wring a handkerchief in her hands while crying the entire time. Maybe she would wear a veil and cry out things like, "Heather, how could you?"

Something on the ground in front of the burning letters caught Heather's attention and she scrambled forward, falling to her knees to see it, feeling the lovely warmth of the fire on her forehead. One of her mother's gold rings. What in the…? There was another, and the necklaces she had taken—had she really taken her mother's jewelry? Yes, she could remember doing so now, even though it had been hazy earlier when she'd gone to sleep, like she didn't dare think about it—and down at the end, her own gold jewelry, all gifts from her parents, in a little pile.

What had she been trying to do? She bent to gather the jewelry up, her eyes scanning it to make sure the pendant wasn't there. No, she had tucked that into her safe at home, she remembered doing it, remembered feeling like it was hers, it belonged to her, not her mother, and that was why it was ok for her to have kept it.

All at once, the sound of a siren split the air, and Heather jerked her head to the right, towards the police station. It looked quiet. The siren must be fire trucks on their way. The realization hit Heather full in the face as the flames burned happily in front of her.

She couldn't be caught there. She just couldn't.

She shot to her feet and ran, having no idea if she was running into trouble, or away from it, but knowing her simple life would never be the same again.

CHAPTER 8

Graeme moaned and twisted. It felt so good, he never wanted it to stop. Never wanted her to stop, the woman with the blond hair and the lovely eyes. He didn't even know her name, but she was working him in a manner he'd never experienced before, sliding first her hands and then that lovely, generous mouth over his cock.

The realization hit him hard, pressing fear into his insides like a knife into warm butter. He had to warn her. Had to get her away from him. His eyes flew open, even as his orgasm spilled molten semen from him, coating his leg and the bed he was in.

There was no woman. The room he'd never seen before was empty except for him… and now the fire. Graeme watched it spread for a moment, or try to spread. The mattress seemed to melt and twist wherever his ejaculate had touched it, but the sheet burned merrily on top of his body, revealing his lower half. Why in the world was he naked?

Absently, he wadded the sheet up in his hands, putting out the fire and even pulling the smoke from the air into himself. He twirled a finger around the few remaining holes in the bed that were still trying to burn, then cleaned up all that remained of what had spilled out of him. Just a bit of ash at that point.

He stared down at his body, at his wilting penis that lay innocently on his right thigh, but twitched once as if to say it could go again, and wondered why he'd had a wet dream for the first time in over nine hundred years.

Before he could wonder long, a door slammed somewhere past his little room and a male appeared at his doorway, shrewd, feline eyes finding his at once.

"Oh," the male said and stopped, his eyes crawling over the destroyed sheet and gutted mattress.

The fellow was a *felen*, to be sure. The feline eyes, the economy of movement, the utter lack of surprise, all gave him away long before his scent reached Graeme. The equipment and the hospital bed, plus a *felen*, all added up to only one possible thing.

"You're the doctor?" Graeme inquired, the real question burning behind his lips, where it would stay until he knew what he was dealing with.

"To be sure," the male said, then entered the room delicately, his feet making no noise on the floor. He took the sheet from Graeme and made it disappear, then tried to take Graeme's wrist. "Call me Remington."

Graeme pulled his arm away and swung his feet to the floor, causing Remington to back up. "My clothes," he said thickly. "I am fine. I assure you of that."

The doctor eyed him for just a moment before shaking his head. "You came in with no clothes. Naked like this."

Graeme dropped his head and checked his internal cache for clothes. They were there. He stood. "I should like to transform, sir. It is safe?"

The doctor walked to the other side of the bed and pulled the curtains closed. "Yes, we are the only ones here."

Graeme altered his cells with his mind, like he was flipping a light switch. One minute human, mostly, and the next dragon, albeit a small one. He didn't expect to have energy for a major transformation, since he suspected he'd been in this room for longer than just a day or two. But, surprisingly, power overflowed inside of him. He could have grown a hundred feet tall and smashed the entire city at that moment. Instead, he transformed again, this time, fully dressed in BDU pants, a tactical polo, and work boots, his wallet tucked into the pocket of the pants. What he had been wearing the night they had crossed over into the *Pravus*.

He caught the *felen's* eye, glad to see a hint of surprise there. Everybody loved to trip up a *felen*. They were usually so unflappable.

"Trevor Burbank, the police lieutenant, how is he?"

Remington made a show of examining the burns in the mattress as he spoke. "He's fine. He was married last week. His mate has her first appointment with me late this afternoon."

He stood straight up and stared at Graeme with a bit of self-importance. "The pups, you know. I'm glad to finally be back in the business of birthing the young. It's been many years too long."

Graeme nodded, all tension dropping from his muscles. He knew.

"What about the human? Ella's sister?"

The *felen's* eyes widened in contempt. "I know of no human."

"Of course."

Remington stared at him sharply. "Don't you want to know how long you've been here?"

Graeme grunted and ran through the questions he cared about in his mind. He would do better to talk to Wade or Trevor directly than waste any more time here with the doctor. He strode towards the door, talking over his shoulder. "Two weeks, I would guess, since you said Trevor was mated last week and I'm sure they didn't wait long to mate, but they probably needed five to seven days to put together a proper ceremony."

Remington hurried after him, pulling him around in the large room just outside of the room they'd been in. "Thirteen days, yes, is it common for your species to recuperate in a vegetative state for so long? Did the sparking indicate you were waking, because we thought it meant the opposite."

Graeme allowed himself to be pulled. The doctor had taken care of him. Done a good job too, he felt like the golden lion himself. Ready to roar, ready to pounce, ready to... wait. He didn't remember feeling this good in centuries, physically or emotionally. Maybe ever. He searched his mind, thinking deliberately about the many *dragen* he would never see again, the sad state of life as a *dragen*, his family, his lack of the things that made life something to enjoy, something to look forward to.

You know, anything that might trigger some sort of depression in him.

Nothing seemed to bother him. He pictured his mother's face in his head, the way she looked as she went to her death, half surprised he could still remember it. That had been so long ago. No, even that didn't make him wilt.

The thoughts, did, however, make him see the face of another female in his mind.

He grabbed the doctor's shoulder. "Where is she? *Who* is she?"

Remington frowned. "Who?"

"The maiden." Graeme sniffed, trying to remember her scent. A maiden she had been, yes. "The woman with the blonde hair and the soft hands."

Remington shook his head. "There is no woman here. You dreamed her."

Graeme pulled himself up to his full height, a good six or seven inches taller than Remington. "There was a woman. Dinnae think of trying to keep her from me. I can stand much maligning, *cat*, but dinnae ever believe I would not destroy you if you cross me."

Remington took a step back, bristling, but when he spoke, his voice wavered. "I swear on my life, *dragen*, I keep nothing from you."

Graeme watched him closely, not able to scent emotions like he knew some *wolven* could. But he believed this male. Behind him, he heard a car pull up close to the house they were standing in.

Graeme let go of him. "I'm sorry, sir. I did not mean to threaten you. Would that you knew who I was talking about, though. I would like to make her acquaintance."

Even as he said the words, he heard the folly in them. Because the kind of acquaintance he really wanted to make with her would leave her destroyed from the inside out.

Never.

Feet pounded on wooden stairs outside and Graeme

turned to the front door of the house, smiling when he saw who their stunned but excited visitor was. Exactly who he wanted to talk to.

* * *

Wade stared at the broad back ahead of him on the river trail behind Remington's house, marveling at the change in Graeme. He looked like he'd put on twenty pounds overnight, his skin plump and healthy-looking, his renewed strength apparent. Everything about him radiated health. Remington needed a bonus. Whatever Wade could wrangle out of the department.

The path beside the stream widened and Wade hurried abreast of Graeme again. "The sparking, why did that happen?

Graeme turned towards Wade slowly, his eyebrows pulled down heavily. "You saw me spark."

"Two days ago. Remington was scared shitless you were going to burn the place down. He thought it meant you were dying."

Graeme faced the path again, his shoulders tense, but he shook it off, turned his face to the trees surrounding them, and took in a deep breath. "Usually, it does."

Wade watched him closely. "What happened?"

"I have no idea. The cat says he dinnae do anything."

Wade chuckled. Calling *felen* cats was not considered politically correct and no one did it anymore. Wade wasn't going to correct him.

The path opened up to a small clearing, with a rough-hewn bench sitting by the water. Wade made to sit there, but Graeme seemed to have too much energy to sit still. He paced, trying to look everywhere at once, taking huge draws of air in through his nose.

Wade sat and put his hands behind his head, enjoying the *dragen's* display of renewed strength. They would need it. "Graeme, do you remember what happened when you came out of the *Pravus*?"

Graeme turned toward him. "I remember Trevor needed my blood. So did Ella's sister. Then, it's blurry. The last two weeks have been a blank."

Wade spoke softly, sharing what he would not tell Remington. "You tried to crawl off into the woods. You told us not to follow you and said it was time for you to die."

Wade hadn't known how he expected Graeme to react, but he certainly hadn't expected the smile that played over his lips. He cocked his head, the color in his eyes shifting in a way Wade had never seen before. "Do you have any idea how old I am?"

Wade shook his head.

"I am nine hundred and thirty-six years old."

Wade's mouth dropped, but before he could respond, footsteps pounded along the path they had walked. Wade scowled as Mac burst into the tiny clearing.

Mac smiled broadly at Graeme and clapped hands with him. "Fire-breath! Good to see you up and moving. Or should I call you fire-crotch? You really did a number on that poor mattress."

Wade stood and stared at Mac, ready to bind the insensitive lummox.

But Graeme only chuckled. "Ah, Mac, I've missed your wit, fractionated though it may be."

Mac stared at him for a second, then laughed and clapped

him on the back and Wade relaxed. Graeme did not seem to anger easily, and for some reason he liked Mac.

Wade glowered at Mac. "I thought you were going to wait in the Jeep so you didn't have to deal with all the cats."

Mac shuddered and paced over the same ground Graeme had been walking a moment before. "They were staring at me, jumping up on the hood and everything! I couldn't stay in that thing without doors."

Graeme chuckled. "I've heard they like their *wolven* well-done, so unless you see any of them pulling out a lighter or a flint and steel, you're probably safe.

Mac whirled on him, eyes wide, then relaxed when he saw Graeme was messing with him.

Wade stood up and approached Mac. "Sit down and shut up, ok? Graeme and I still have business and we need to be quick about it. Harlan texted me that there's something big going down with the *foxen* and we need to get back to the station."

Mac gave him puppy eyes, but did as he was told. Wade approached Graeme. "I'm afraid I know nothing about *dragen*. Is it normal for you to live that long?"

"Aye. Longer even. *Dragen* are notoriously hard to kill. Even old age never takes a foothold. I have heard stories of mated *dragen* living for two thousand years or more, back when there were more of us around."

"Do you have a mate?"

Graeme looked off into the trees as if weighing his answer. "No. I am the last *dragen*."

Wade dropped his head, feeling the sudden heaviness of Graeme's emotion. "I am sorry."

Graeme nodded. "As am I."

Wade looked up, not wanting to ask his next question,

but needing to know the answer. "I apologize if this is out of line. Do *dragen* have renqua?"

Graeme's eye color shifted again and Wade stared, fascinated, hoping the dark red hues didn't mean he was about to get flash-fried. He didn't know the *dragen* well enough to know if he was finally angry, but *renquas* were a touchy subject for most *shiften*.

Graeme sighed, as if fearing where the conversation was going, choosing his words carefully. "They dinnae. *Dragen* were not created in the way *wolven* were. Rhen did not take a dragon and put a piece of herself in it, as no such creature existed. Rather, she created us out of whole cloth, in the 30th century B.C. She came across a town that Khain had attacked, where masses of humans were burning in the earth Khain was actively scorching. She beset upon them all the power to transform into a winged, scaled creature that could resist the burning from Khain's fire and create their own fire to fight back with. The *dragen* rose up en masse and battled Khain, driving him back into the *Pravus*. Because of certain… proclivities of the *dragen*, Rhen never made any more than the three hundred or so she created that day. We thrived for a short while, mating and breeding like any other, but our species was not meant to be."

Before Wade could ask what the proclivities were, Mac snorted a laugh. "So what you're saying is, you're a bunch of inbred motherfuckers."

Wade glowered at Mac but Graeme only nodded. "That's about right." His eyes swam with fire again. "I know what you are going to ask. *Dragen* fought with each other and they hunted humans if they got hungry enough, or sometimes just for fun. No. We don't have the protection drive that you do."

Wade nodded slowly. That could change everything.

"What about the one true mates?"

"What about them? I did not come here for a one true mate. There is not one for me. There cannot be. No female alive can withstand mating a *dragen* or bearing his young."

A group of crows cawed in the distance, reminding Wade they were short on time. He had one trump card and he would play it. "May I touch you? Will you open yourself to me?"

Graeme stared at him as if he knew exactly what Wade was after. Finally, he nodded and held out his arm.

Wade steeled himself, having no idea what he would find, but trusting enough in the power given to him by Rhen after *dragen* were created to know there would be something.

He reached out and grasped Graeme's wrist tightly, curling his fingers around the skin hard. He had been smart to do so, or he would have been immediately blown into the forest. The blast of emotion and knowledge that thrust into his brain caused him to stagger and bow backwards until he was standing only on his toes, his spine in danger of snapping, his head almost upside down. Nine hundred years of personality, history, insights, and experience downloaded into him as he began to tip backwards, his head in danger of smashing to the dirt at a dangerous angle.

But Mac was there, catching him around the waist, pulling him away from Graeme, who let out a grunt and staggered backwards himself.

Mac picked him up, carried him to the wooden bench and placed him there as gently as he would a pup, murmuring to him softly. Wade felt the strength come back into his limbs slowly, but steadily, even as his mind went into overdrive. When he could, he stood and reached into his pocket, withdrawing what he had been carrying around since the night Graeme, with a bit of help, had saved the future of all *shiften*.

He held the badge out on his palm, with its special KSRT marking. "We shall have a proper ceremony if you accept. Graeme, will you officially join the Serenity P.D.? We could use a good male like you."

Graeme stared at the badge for what felt like too long. Just when Wade was certain he would refuse, he said, "Life's burden forever grows. I will give you my answer anon."

Before Wade could blink, a red dragon the size of a sparrow replaced Graeme on the dirt in front of him, then took flight, disappearing into the sky.

CHAPTER 9

revor turned left, pulling the eight-passenger van into the police department parking lot. The building looked different to him now. Not a place to do his most-important work anymore, but more of a distraction from his real life. Fighting against Khain would always be in his blood, but Ella was his world now. Ella and the young she carried inside her belly. What happened between the walls of the sterile building in front of him would never be able to compete with that.

Even as the thoughts ran through his mind, he knew that wasn't reality. He could be called to give his life in the service of the Serenity PD at any moment, and then Ella would be alone. His pups would grow up without a father, and there was nothing he could do about it.

He bit his lip, ignoring the banter of the males in the back seat, then glancing over at his mate. She looked lovely. Glowing was definitely the right term.

She caught his glance and smiled at him, then held out her hand, twining her fingers in his for just a moment before she tried to step out her door.

"Wait," he called, then jumped out and ran around to her side, helping her down.

They strode arm in arm to the front door of the department, catching up to Wade, who was also just arriving.

Wade beamed at them. "Good news."

"The *dragen* is awake," Trevor said, thinking of the best thing that could happen.

"He is. I saw him this morning."

Ella clapped her hands together and bounced on the balls of her feet. "I'm so glad he's recovered. I want to thank him properly for everything he did for us."

Her face darkened for a minute, and Trevor thought she must be thinking of her sister, who was still in her own coma in the hospital. He pulled Ella close and kissed her on the forehead.

"Come, apparently there's something going on with the *foxen*," Wade said, but before he could open the door, Harlan exited it, his head down, his brow furrowed, almost running into them. He looked up at them and frowned. "Finally. I sent the video to your computer, Wade. All three of you need to go watch it, and then we need orders."

He tried to keep walking, but Trevor caught his arm. "You coming?"

Harlan shook his head. "No, I've got to go deal with the *foxen*."

Wade looked hard at Harlan. "Wait, I thought we were here to get some big news *about* the *foxen*."

Harlan waved a hand. "You are. Go watch the video, then talk to me. I have to meet with a *foxen* representative at city hall who says he's got a group of them together demanding one true mates."

Wade scoffed. "What? We aren't doling out females here. Even if they are or aren't fated to one *shiften*, we can't decide who that *shiften* is or who the one true mates are attracted to."

Harlan leaned forward. "Beckett's already told him that, twice. The male doesn't believe it and says they are going to schedule protests if at least some of the one true mates aren't *put aside* for them. His words. That's why I'm going to meet with him in person." He looked to Trevor. "Can I bring Trent and Troy? I could use some help reading him."

"What a fool," Trevor growled. "Yeah, they are in the van with the rest of the guard."

Wade clapped Harlan on the shoulder. The male hurried away and Wade pushed in the door, holding it open for Ella and Trevor. Heads turned their way immediately as every officer in the large, open room stopped what they were doing to stare at the only one true mate found so far.

Ella scooched closer to him and curled her fingers around his arm, ducking her head behind his shoulder. He was about to whisper something reassuring to her when the applause started. "Oh God," she squeaked. Trevor put his arm around her then waved his thanks and appreciation to his fellow officers. She didn't understand what a big deal it was that she existed, but he did.

They crossed the room quickly and he felt her body relax as they entered the empty hallway that headed toward Wade's office.

Mac was waiting inside for them. "About time. Harlan said there's some video we're all supposed to see?"

Wade reached his laptop and fiddled with it. "I'm working on it," he said.

Trevor pulled over two chairs and sat Ella in the one farthest away from Mac, then bared his teeth at Mac in greeting. Mac grunted back.

Wade stopped what he was doing and looked up at them, his eyes narrowed, his voice tight. "What's up with you two?"

Trevor sighed and sank into his chair. "I'm good, Chief."

Mac snapped his fingers and popped both his thumbs up, a cheese-eating grin on his face. "Me too, Daddy-O. Right as acid rain."

Wade leaned on his desk and pinched the bridge of his nose. "You two have got to work together. You have no idea—"

Trevor interrupted him. "Really, Chief. We're good. Mac carried me out of the *Pravus*. Saved my mate. We're not ever gonna be best friends, but I owe him my life and I've told him so. We are able to work together."

"Yeah, Chief, you missed the waterworks. Golden boy got down on one knee and everything. Hell, I might have said something humble myself. I know I've let my mouth get away from me a few times in my life. You know, once or twice, three times max."

Wade looked from wolf to wolf, then his gaze settled on Ella.

Ella nodded. "I don't remember any crying, but there was a sincere attempt on both their parts to forge some sort of a civil relationship." She smiled at Trevor and he squirmed, knowing what she was going end with. "It was beautiful."

Wade nodded, relaxing slightly. "That's good. That's great. Because we're going to need it. Something big is coming. I can feel it."

Trevor shifted in his chair, pulling his posture up straighter. "About that. Do we have any idea what Khain is up to?"

"No, there's been no sign of him since the disturbance the day you were mated and nothing came of that."

Trevor shook his head, thinking. "Any chance he'll take off? Leave the area?"

"I doubt he'll ever leave Serenity as long as Rhen's body is here. Something about it seems to keep him rooted here. My guess is he's resting like he always seems to do after a major battle with us. If we could get to him, now would be the time to do it."

Mac snorted. "Or he's pouting."

Wade messed around with his laptop again and Trevor spit out his words in a rush, not wanting to leave them for later. "I think I should give up leadership of the KSRT."

Ella's hand found his and he squeezed it as Mac and Wade both turned hard stares on him. He held up his free hand. "Hear me out. The Demon Destroyer prophecy. Guaranteed it's not about me. It's about my young. And my focus is divided. I'm not going to be able to give the role everything it needs while I'm worried about Ella. I don't think I can even leave her to come to work. I don't care how many *shiften* you've got guarding her. I have to be there myself."

Wade stared at the wall over Trevor's head, his gaze thoughtful. "I think Ella can take care of herself."

Tension built in Trevor's chest. "It doesn't matter what she's capable of doing. I still need to be there."

Wade's eyebrows shot up. "You're not going to leave her side until the young are born?"

Trevor shook his head. "Are you kidding me? Once the young are born it will be even more important that I am with her every second. Her and the young. I understand it may not always be possible to be with her. But I can't imagine coming to work every day and leaving her on her own. Put yourself in my place."

He searched for more words to explain what he was feeling. "The young she is carrying are everything, Wade."

Wade was silent for a long time.

Mac cleared his throat. "Even if the prophecy is not about you, even if I and the other members of the team do all or most of the work, you're still the leader. You still need to be calling the shots. We can make it work."

Trevor couldn't believe what he was hearing. He thought Mac would have jumped at the chance to take over.

Wade nodded. "That's settled, then." He flipped his computer around so they could see it, walked around his desk, stood between Trevor and Mac, then pressed "play".

The screen showed a dark room, with a male in a chair in the middle of it, his face blank, his lips moving steadily.

"Hey! That's the guy!" Ella cried.

"Which guy?" Trevor asked.

Mac leaned forward. "The *foxen* from the *Pravus*. You were doing your impression of a fish being smothered by good old H2O." He tapped Wade. "Can you turn it up?"

Wade fiddled with the sound and the male's voice filled the room, but his words ran together too quickly for them to make any sense of what he was saying.

"TheselandswillbeourstoreignoveraslordsandourfemaleswillberestoredtousourprogenywillfloodthesoilIamthevanquisherof…"

Trevor frowned, picking out a word here and there, but not liking the way it sounded or the words he could catch. It made him think of pillagers and pirates. It went on for five minutes or more, the soliloquy from hell.

"He's crazy," Mac muttered, then froze as a female voice cut in over the syllables.

"Stop!" the unseen woman cried. "Tell me about the wolves. I only want to know about the werewolves."

The *foxen* froze and stopped talking, but Trevor could see his chest moving as he snuck tiny sips of air. His head turned slightly to the left as if he were looking at someone.

"There are no werewolves."

The woman's voice turned almost desperate. "That's not what you said before."

"Werewolves are made up. Make believe. What we are facing is much more dangerous than a werewolf."

Trevor held his breath. Where had Harlan gotten this video? Who had seen it? Any humans?

The *foxen's* reedy voice lowered. "The wolves that live in Serenity, indeed, in the entire world, are not tied to the moon in the manner of story. They run by it, mate by it, but they do not worship it or change only when it is fat." His eyes widened and Trevor saw madness there.

"Go on," the female voice said.

The *foxen* faced forward again, his voice losing any intonation. "Ohhearmethycunningandcrimson—"

"No!" the woman screamed, but this time no light returned to the *foxen's* eyes and his mutterings continued. The video ended.

Wade looked to Trevor and opened his mouth like he was about to say something, but before he could, Mac jumped to his feet and pulled Wade's laptop across the desk, his movements jerky and his breath steam-rolling in and out of his body as if he'd just run a marathon. "Who is she? I have to hear her voice again," he muttered as he restarted the video, that horrible muttering dawning anew.

"Wait," Wade said, reaching past Mac and pausing it. "There's something about the—"

Mac set his feet and shoved Wade across the room without looking at him, then started the video again. Trevor stared at the insubordination, unable to believe what he was seeing. He half-stood, not knowing what to do, while Ella curled into a ball in her chair.

"Mac! Face me!" Wade's sharp order reverberated off the walls of the office, telling Mac he had one chance and one chance only.

Mac didn't hear. He manipulated the video timeline to where he wanted it with jerky pulls of the mouse. "You don't understand. That voice. That female. I must hear it ag—"

His word cut off like he'd been karate chopped in the throat and his body froze, half-bent over Wade's desk. Trevor glanced at Wade, who was frowning, but not in effort. Trevor knew Mac was bound and could not move, could not even breathe, until Wade let him go, and it did not cost the *citlali* much effort to bind one of their own species.

Wade approached Mac. "You forgot yourself, Mac. Don't ever do that again."

But Mac was struggling against the bind. Great cords stood out on his neck as he tried to move even a muscle. Wade's frown deepened and he lowered his head and stared at Mac. Never, in all of his time on the planet, had Trevor seen a *shiften* even try to resist a bind.

Until now. With a great roar that forced a startled squeak from Ella, Mac pulled the right side of his body free and moved the mouse one more time.

Wade let him go, and he took in a gasping breath, his body jerking to bend over the computer again as if none of it had ever happened, although a vicious growling started deep in his throat.

Wade reached out and touched Mac's arm, almost reverently. Mac collapsed to the floor, unconscious, his head bouncing off the white tile with a hollow thump.

Ella moaned and Trevor took her hand. "It's ok, Wade put him under. It won't hurt him." Trevor looked to Wade. "Right?"

Wade nodded, staring at Mac, concern on his face. "I needed to make sure I could. I've never had anyone successfully resist a bind before."

"What in the hell was that all about, anyway?"

Wade motioned to the computer, his face set. "A hundred bucks says we found another one true mate. Kind of." He faced Trevor and motioned to Mac. "Another hundred says things are about to get dangerous."

A thunderous roar from somewhere in the duty room outside Wade's office shook the building like an earthquake, and Trevor shot to his feet, pulling Ella into his arms and staring at the doorway.

"Did I say dangerous? I meant deadly." Wade muttered, then touched Mac on the arm again. "Wake up, you overgrown Saint Bernard, we might need you." Males shouted and Trevor could hear people running and yelling to each other in the hallway.

Mac pushed to his hands and knees and shook his head, his mind seemingly his own again. "What's going on?"

"Let's go see," Wade said, heading off at a dead run.

CHAPTER 10

*E*lla moved closer to her mate, knowing he would protect her, no matter what was happening in the duty room.

He curled a protective arm around her shoulders. "You ok, if we go see?"

She nodded, admitting to herself that she felt more curious and excited than scared. She thought she recognized that roar.

When they rounded the corner into the large open room lined with desks and computers, she saw she had been right. But why was Graeme in the middle of the room in a fighter's stance, holding Blake and another male by their throats, while half the department circled him warily, unsure what to do? She recognized the second male as one she'd seen at the house under the green tarp a few times, which meant he was either a *bearen* or a *felen*. Given his straight-forward good looks, his abundance of dark hair and beard, and his brawn, she thought *bearen*. The *felen*, she'd noticed, tended towards more sleek and compact. *Bearen* were more like *wolven* in that the ones she had seen so far were always big.

Wade skidded to a stop a few feet from the action, Mac just behind him. "What in the hell is going on here?"

Blake rolled his eyes to Wade, clutching at Graeme's fingers, but he couldn't speak. Beckett spoke up from the other side of Graeme, skirting him to get closer to Wade. "Do you want the full version? Or the Cliff notes?"

Wade snarled. "I want whatever is going to let me understand this in the quickest way possible."

Beckett pointed to a blonde female Ella hadn't immediately seen because she was partially hidden, crouching behind a desk. "First, she came in and said she had to confess to a crime, but every time I tried to get details from her, she shut down and stopped talking. I brought her back here to process her when *he* walked in the back." Beckett pointed at the *bearen* Graeme was choking the life out of. "When he saw her, he handed me this dvd and said she started the fire last night on the hill." He gave Wade a pointed look. "You know, the one we were briefed about this morning."

Wade raised his eyebrows and nodded, watching Blake and the *bearen* as if checking to see if they were still conscious, while Graeme sucked in huge agitated breaths, his fingers curled around two throats, his eyes on the blonde woman. Wade nodded at Beckett and twirled his fingers in a little *hurry it up* gesture.

"I asked him what was on the dvd and he said "evidence", so I was going to watch it. I asked Blake to fingerprint her. He took her by the arm, and that's when Graeme came in the door." Beckett splayed his fingers towards Graeme and shook his head. "You'll have to ask *him* why he lost his shit."

Graeme snorted and Ella heard electricity crackle in the noise. "No one touches her," he yelled, his eyes traveling over every male in the room, as if daring them to try.

Wade nodded, seeming oddly pleased, but Ella barely noticed. Her eyes were glued to the female behind the desk, who was watching Graeme with eyes that held more healthy appreciation than fear. For some reason, Ella wanted to gather her up, take her into a quiet room, and just talk to her. Ask her about her life, share secrets, compare notes… just get to know her. As Ella stared, the woman lifted her head and stared back, something weighty passing between them for only a moment.

Wade addressed the officers near the back of the room. "Everybody, clear out, go back to work. Find something to do that is not in this room. We're all done here." He raised his hands to include all the males in the room. "That means everyone! Come back in fifteen minutes."

The officers in blue uniforms and dark detective outfits moved slowly, some grumbling.

"Now!" Wade roared, reverberations from the word bouncing off the walls and making Ella jump. The room cleared in under thirty seconds. Trevor pulled Ella back against the wall like they were exempt from following the order.

Wade addressed the woman. "Miss, ah, if you would, could you go stand over there?" He pointed to a far corner of the room.

The blonde woman nodded and scrambled to her feet, hurrying to near the wall where Wade had indicated, her eyes bouncing between Graeme and Ella.

Wade turned to Graeme, hands open, indicating Blake and the *bearen*. "Let them go, so they can leave. They won't touch her."

Graeme's eyes fell on Wade and he nodded. Ella half expected him to clunk their heads together, but, instead, he very gently released their throats, peeling his fingers away delicately. Both males triple-timed it out of the room, sucking in huge breaths as they did so.

"Everyone's gone," Wade said, as if he were discussing the weather, then he turned to Graeme. Ella held her breath to see what would happen. Wade was in charge of all the *wolven* in the area, but Graeme was not *wolven*.

The two males locked eyes, Wade's stance tensing, while Graeme's relaxed. Ella watched, fascinated, but nothing seemed to happen. She felt eyes on her and looked to the woman in the corner. She was tall, slim, blonde hair messy but gorgeous, no makeup, wearing an outfit that made her look like she was going hunting.

She was watching Ella.

Could the situation be any more awkward? Ella smiled and lifted her hand to wave at the woman, but, when she did, blondie's cheeks heated and she moved her gaze quickly back to Graeme.

Ella took a long moment to look over the woman, knowing as well as anyone that something big was happening, then she, also, looked back to the two males in the center of the room. They both still stood quietly, eyes locked.

"What's going on?" she whispered to Trevor.

"They're talking."

"Why can't we hear them?"

"*Ruhi* can be kept private between two *shiften* who are strong in it."

The blonde woman spoke up. "Look, ah, I don't mean to tell you all how to do your job, but, ah, maybe I should come back later? This doesn't seem to be a good time."

She stared at Graeme as she said it, and somehow Ella knew the woman didn't want to leave, but she did want Graeme to turn to her, look at her, notice her, talk to her.

Graeme fidgeted and Wade turned his head slightly, but the two males did not break their silent conversation. Graeme pressed his lips together and shook his head left and right with agitation.

Ella pulled away from Trevor. "I should go talk to her. But first, tell me what Beckett meant when he said he was briefed about a fire this morning."

Trevor caught her arm, looking at the woman as if for the first time. His mind seeming far away, he whispered, "Someone bound sticks of decorative bamboo and cloth together to spell out words that formed a message on the hill last night in front of an abandoned business, then started the whole mess on fire."

Tingles flooded Ella. "What was the message?"

"You are not the last dragon."

***

Heather stared at the two men in the middle of the room, not sure what to do. What she should do was run screaming out the door and turn herself in at another station, where the cops were not insane. But *he* was here. She couldn't ignore that kind of coincidence. If she left, she might never see him again. Yesterday, she'd thought about him frequently, telling herself she'd go back, talk to Dr. Gilman, find out who the mystery man was and how she could get to know him. A fantasy, maybe, but one that made her feel normal for the first time in months.

But since she'd woken up in the middle of the street, enigmatic words blazing jauntily in front of her, she hadn't been able to think about anything but the fact that she was now a criminal. Worse, that she'd *fled the scene of the crime*. That cops were looking for her, and when they found her they'd handcuff her and haul her off to jail. She'd never been handcuffed or arrested. Her closest experience with the inside of a cell was watching 'Orange is the New Black' on Netflix.

She'd stewed all morning, knowing she was going to turn herself in, there had never been any question about that. The only question had been when.

She'd finally gotten the courage to drive to the station and walk in the front door, but actually saying the words, "I started the fire," had eluded her. Then the fire inspector had walked in and done it for her. Then the guy from the hospital bed had come in and flipped out. Fun times.

But he looked so different! Her eye traveled over his face and body, taking in all the changes. His cheeks weren't hollow anymore and either he looked even better in clothes than he did out of them, or he'd put on twenty pounds of muscle overnight. He'd shaved and even his hair was longer. He looked good.

Good enough to forgive the little freak-show he'd pulled? Grabbing two men by the throat because... because they'd been near her? Because one of them had touched her? Could that really be why? They'd only met once, and she couldn't even call that a meeting. She wasn't even sure he remembered.

She knew she should be scared. Outraged, even. But she wasn't. Instead, some deep part of her embraced what should have scared the crap out of her. It didn't make sense to her yet, but it would, something about him told her it would.

Her eyes drifted off the two men in the center of the room for just a moment and landed on the other man standing on the far side of the large room, his arm protectively around the woman who'd looked at her a few moments before. They were having a heated conversation. The man didn't interest her, but the woman pulled her senses in similar manner that the man from the hospital bed did. Smooth black hair framed her pale face perfectly, giving her an elegant look. She was dressed in yoga pants and a warm-looking pullover, and the man next to her looked like he'd maim anyone who even glanced at her wrong. Something about her called to Heather, made her want to know who the woman was.

Their eyes met again, and this time Heather knew she was going to come over. The only thing that bothered Heather more than awkward introductions, was silence, and the silence between the two men at the center of the room was freaking her out just a little bit too much to deal with an awkward introduction, no matter how big of a pull she felt toward the woman.

"Hey, dangerous criminal over here, is someone going to arrest me, or what?" she called out loudly.

Her guy—she was already thinking of him as her guy and she didn't even know his name, her mother would be thrilled—made a noise she could only describe as a snort and broke eye contact with the other man. He faced her, eyes blazing. Uh oh. Another freak out was on its way.

But before he could lose it, the older man spoke up. "Graeme, why don't you take her out to lunch?"

Warmth billowed inside of Heather. *Graeme.* She loved it. She whispered it to herself. Graeme. Even his name was sexy. She was so totally done for. Which wasn't a good thing, since her mother actually would not be thrilled that the first man she'd ever shown any interest in was twice her age. Her mother would hate it. Hate him.

Graeme faltered. "You want me to process her?" His voice rumbled with a very slight Scottish brogue that she hadn't noticed when he'd been yelling before. It was so yummy, she wanted to eat him for dessert while he read something, anything, to her.

"No, I want you to take her out to lunch. She looks hungry. So do you." The man turned to Heather. "My name is Wade Lombard. I'm the Deputy Chief of the department. I have to apologize for everything you've been through today. I understand your situation is quite delicate, but I don't think there's any need for anything quite so formal. Would you be willing to go out to lunch with Officer Kynock, Miss? He'll talk to you about what happened, get your side of the story."

He made it sound so reasonable. Like she'd gotten in an argument with someone over a parking space instead of lit something on fire. Her stomach growled, as if to try to agree for her. "Sure," she said haltingly. She wanted to. Lord knew she wanted to go anywhere with that man, Officer Kynock. Graeme. Funny, he didn't look like a cop.

Chief Lombard beamed, but Graeme glowered, making Heather shrink a little bit. He didn't want to take her out. Heather pressed her hands to her temples. The whole situation was starting to make her head hurt.

"That's settled, then." The Chief patted Graeme on the arm. "Take her somewhere nice. Check in with me later." He turned to Heather. "What's your name, dear?"

"Heather Herrin."

Chief Lombard's face squinched up. "Heather?" he repeated.

Graeme looked directly at her, the eye contact flooring her, making her mouth go dry. She couldn't look away. A longing inside her welled up, taking her by surprise, in the exact way the fire-lust always had. Oh, God, the fire-lust was the very worst thing in her entire life. She didn't want to equate it with this man.

She tore her eyes away and pressed a hand to her mouth, looking at Chief Lombard instead. He had turned around and looked at the man and woman on the other side of the room. "Heather?"

The woman spoke up. "It's a purple flower."

Chief Lombard turned back around, a knowing, triumphant expression on his face, then practically pushed Graeme towards her.

Heather barely noticed the strange conversation. Her eyes and mind were on Graeme. He looked like he would rather run screaming out the door than even talk to her.

Big surprise. Story of her life. She didn't know how she'd been granted this intermission in the process of becoming a convicted criminal, but apparently it wasn't going to include any fascinating, sexy side-trip into daddy-issue-land for her.

Too bad. She would have given anything to have an interesting story to tell her cats when she was old and graying and alone. Would they let her have cats in prison?

His eyes met hers again and although she still saw the reluctance there, she also saw something deeper. Something behind the reluctance. An acknowledgement of her as a woman and a secret yearning she could identify with that added a dimension of mystery to what she saw as reluctance, but that could have been something much deeper.

In a dark flash, she made a decision. Fuck her jitters, her doubt and apprehension, and the fact that this was not at all what she thought was going to happen when she tried to turn herself in to the police. Fuck what her mother would think, what anyone else wanted her to do or thought she was or wasn't. She wasn't giving up without a fight. If there was even the slightest chance that she could get Officer Graeme Kynock to notice her, she was going to take it.

CHAPTER 11

Graeme stalked across the room, shame filling him, his eyes on the young woman who had started this mess just by existing. He knew what his over-the-top, irresponsible, juvenile response meant. He was staring at a one true mate. One meant for him, somehow, by all the folly of angels and deities with nothing better to do than play with the lives and hearts and souls of their creations.

He hated the game, and he, for one, was done playing it. How to get that message across to everyone else involved, though, he didn't know. Maybe leaving was his best option.

She certainly was young, though. And pretty. Fresh. Sweet-looking, like if he managed to get his mouth on her tongue or her other soft spots, the taste would overwhelm him. He could imagine it. Saliva filled his mouth as his brain told him exactly how good she would taste.

He clamped his tongue between his teeth and bit down hard. Absolutely not. He was almost a millennium old. He would not be tossed about by his hormones and the wants of his body like a babe in arms or a torrid teen.

Besides, they weren't the wants of his body. They were something planted there by some supposedly superior being who claimed to know better.

He would not be a part of any of it.

"Miss Herrin," he started as he got within a few feet of her, his words almost stuttering as he caught her scent. Roasted chicory with a hint of toasted sugar on a hot summer night under a full moon. Nights when the burden of life had not yet settled on his shoulders. Hours of freedom soaring under a heavy, welcoming sky, with nothing between him and happiness.

His knees buckled. Oh, to be that youngster again. It would almost make this world bearable.

"Please, call me Heather." She lifted her chin to look up at him, blonde wisps of hair catching in the eyelashes of her right eye.

He curled his fingers into his palms to keep from brushing the hair back into place. She was not for him and he would not act as if she was.

He walked past her on leaden legs and pushed the door to outside open, looking back at her and motioning that she should step through it.

She did, her eyes on him the entire time, her face full of something indefinable, but oh, so lovely, something he wished he could unsee. It did things to him.

As the door closed behind them and the cold outside air swirled around them, he looked into her eyes as best he could. "Why don't I walk you to your car, Miss."

She stared at him for a long moment before answering. "Didn't your boss just tell you to take me out to lunch?"

The defiant tone in her voice made his lips curl into a smile. They might all be pawns on somebody's chess board, but she was not willing to back down from what she wanted. She did not know he would kill her. He could not believe otherwise.

"He's not my boss," he said, his eye traveling over her cheekbones, the slightly upturned nose, her lithe body. He bit his lip again and looked at the pavement.

"I'm hungry," she said, simply stating a fact. No whining or needling there, her voice pleasant and warm.

God help him, he would not be impressed by her. He would not take her out. The smartest thing to do would be to take her right back around the front of the building and introduce her to some young, hulking *wolfen* who would be a perfect fit for her.

The thought made his blood heat to an almost unbearable temperature, even for him, and he looked around for someone to maul.

She took a step backwards and alarm crossed her face. Damnú! He calmed himself quickly, wondering just how high he'd turned the heat up. Words bubbled up his throat. "I don't have a car. Can you drive us?"

Something flitted across her face that he would have called embarrassment if he knew her better.

"Let's walk," she said, pointing her body toward the street. "There are several good restaurants a few blocks away. Do you, um, want to get a coat?"

Graeme eyed her light jacket. "I'm good," he said, and began to walk. She fell into step beside him as they reached the street and she pointed left. He turned that way, then looked at the bare trees, the sky, the businesses across the street, anywhere but at her, almost unable to believe he had agreed to any of this, but after a few minutes he relaxed. She had a calm spirit and it soothed him, made him realize none of this had to be a big deal. Fates could be avoided. Side-stepped. His stomach clanged solidly, reminding him of how long it had been since he'd eaten. Weeks. Lunch suddenly seemed like the best idea in the world, and pleasant company did not have to mean a mating.

Restaurants appeared along the street and enticing smells began to pull at him. Lemon chicken dripping in butter, fresh lightly-seasoned lake trout, seared steak with sauce. He could pick out the scent of every dish being cooked in every restaurant they passed and he wanted them all. Her scent mixed in occasionally with the food, enhancing it to the point where he felt starved. He plowed steadily forward, unable to suggest they stop anywhere, no matter how rude he was being.

She didn't seem to notice. "Oh, Benihana, I love this restaurant," she cried from behind him, having come to a halt on the sidewalk.

A smile tugged at his lips. "Benihana it is," he said politely and held the door open for her. The smile she gave him made his stomach stop clanging for just a moment.

Inside, a Japanese hostess with black hair down to her knees and a nametag reading Chiemi greeted them. "Good afternoon. Chef's table, or regular seating?" she said, without even a hint of an accent.

Graeme looked to Heather. He'd never been in a Benihana before, but the scents from the other room told him it was exotic food cooked on an iron grill with a drizzle of a rich oil.

"Chef's table?" she asked breathlessly.

The hostess smiled brightly. "The wait is one hour."

Heather's face fell only slightly. "Ok, regular seating then."

"Certainly, that will be fifteen minutes. Please have a seat."

Graeme watched Heather sit down at a row of chairs along the wall, then he moved in close to Chiemi, producing a hundred- dollar bill from a clasp in his pocket. "Could we be seated at the chef's table within the next five minutes?"

Chiemi smiled and made the bill disappear. "Certainly, Sir. I will be right back."

Graeme crossed the room to be closer to Heather. He wanted to see that smile on her face again.

Chiemi returned quickly. "A table has opened up, right this way."

Heather bounced up and there it was. A mega-watter that made Graeme's stomach flip. He followed her into the large open room with grills located strategically and ten diners placed to a grill, one chef behind each. Chiemi led them to an empty grill and sat them on one end of it. Graeme pulled out Heather's chair and the mega-watt smile appeared again. It gladdened his heart and he hated that.

"Your chef will be out momentarily," Chiemi said, then disappeared.

Heather turned to him, a gorgeous light on her face. "Don't you just love this place?"

Graeme struggled to keep his emotional distance. "I've never been," he said softly.

Heather shrugged out of her jacket and placed it on the chair behind her. Graeme averted his eyes from her simple, but lovely purple blouse. He searched his table for a menu, but then their chef appeared, pulling his focus. The chef was a tall, thin man, obviously not Japanese, but certainly from one of the islands off the coast of Asia. Singapore, maybe, or the Philippines? Graeme frowned and looked around. A non-Japanese chef cooking in a Japanese restaurant. He marked the other chefs, noticing several were Japanese but not the majority, and one was even a European-looking woman. His eyes slid over the diners and he found a large mix of ethnicities there, also. He looked at Heather but she didn't seem to notice anything out of the ordinary. Had the world really moved on so much in the years he'd been submerged?

Their chef introduced himself and began a practiced banter that told Graeme that, not only was he a chef, but he was also a showman. Graeme would allow it, as long as the food was top-notch. He glanced at Heather. No, he would allow it as long as Heather was happy.

She beamed at the chef, talking to him in an excited voice that told him she was happy. Graeme frowned, feeling minute stirrings of some babyish emotion in his chest. No, he would not succumb to whatever had set him off earlier. No way. Not with a human.

Chef Eugene spilled a large portion of rice onto the grill and the starchy scent filled the air as oil and salt flashed, a server brought him and Heather soup, and Chiemi sat two more people at their table. Graeme finished his scorching-hot soup in one large draught, then waited for the next course as Heather sipped hers and laughed when Chef Eugene flipped an egg into the air with a silver spatula and caught it in his hat.

Heather watched the chef, and Graeme watched Heather. Fresh was the right word for her. She brought light and joy into the room, her infectious laughter making him smile more than he wanted to.

She blushed and looked down, and Graeme's eyes shot to Chef Eugene. He was leaning forward towards her, one eye opening from a wink. Graeme played over what had just been said, the banter he'd been ignoring as part of the show.

Looking at you makes my soufflé rise, is what the chef had said, thinking Graeme wasn't really listening, or maybe not caring. Hot liquid rose in Graeme's chest like mercury in a thermometer. He held the anger in as best he could.

Heather dropped her eyes to her food and seemed uncomfortable for the first time. More heat rose in Graeme's throat, the urge to grab Chef Eugene by the throat and take him into the back for a little lesson spearing through him. He would not, though. Chef Eugene was a human and would not live through even a tiny lesson from Graeme.

Graeme stared daggers at the chef, trying to decide on his next move, as the grill sizzled and popped. It would be a disaster if Chef Eugene paid so much attention to the females at his table that all his food burned…

Graeme maneuvered his water glass in front of the grill to block the view of the people across from him, then placed a finger on the silver surface, heating it by several hundred degrees. The rice, eggs, and shrimp that had been searing nicely flash-fried, black smoke rising in lazy coils into the air.

"Oh!" Heather cried, and scooted her chair backwards.

Chef Eugene gasped and bent to fiddle with his controls, then stood sharply to pull the food off the grill.

Graeme pulled his hand back slowly and smiled. "Maybe you'd be better off flipping burgers, Chef Eugene."

But when he turned to Heather, she was watching him, wide-eyed, her eyes going from his hand, to his face, and back again. Graeme pressed his lips together, wondering what she'd seen but, before he could think of what to say, Chiemi hurried over to reseat them.

"I'm so sorry, so sorry," she repeated as she ushered them

to another grill. Graeme answered quietly, trying to reassure her, as Heather watched him with something new in her eyes. Something he couldn't identify. Maybe he should take advantage of the situation and suggest they separate. He'd send someone else to talk to her.

As he was considering, he sat down at their new grill, which was closer to the door to the kitchen and he saw a familiar face move behind the tiny oval window.

Mac. So, Wade had sent someone to watch over him. Probably at least two someones. A good idea if he went all caveman again. But the sight of Mac stirred something inside him he didn't want to face. If Mac even came close to Heather, Graeme knew he was going to make Mac hurt.

This was a game he didn't want to play. Thoughts of packing up and running crossed his tired brain again. He wouldn't even tell anyone, he'd just go.

"So, when are we going to talk about what I did?" Heather said to him, paying no attention to the new chef who'd arrived.

"What did you do?" Graeme asked, suddenly curious.

Heather blinked at him. "I started a fire."

"Really," Graeme said, fascinated. The word conjured only good feelings in his chest.

She frowned and he could see embarrassment flood her features. "And I stole my mother's gold jewelry and spread it all out in front of the fire."

Graeme dropped the fork he had picked up and turned in his chair to face her. "Really?" he said again. A fire and gold. Two things that had fascinated his kind for eons.

She bit her lip and nodded.

"Why did you do those things?" he asked, keeping his voice gentle.

She shook her head and Graeme saw tears form in her eyes. She didn't know.

"I think I might be going crazy," she finally whispered, lowering her head, like it was something she didn't want to admit to anyone, especially herself.

Damnú, Graeme cursed silently, aiming it at the gods, the angels, the demi-gods, anyone who made the beings in this world feel like they had free will, and then messed with their minds and hearts and genetic code to the point where they felt such pain at their unwitting actions. If the angel who had fathered this lovely young woman had been in front of him at that moment, he would have done his best to wring the being's neck.

For the first time in six hundred years, he would have done it because he cared about someone, and not as a bid to get himself killed.

CHAPTER 12

*H*eather fought with her emotions, trying to get them back under control. She hadn't realized she was going to say the words out loud, but when she did, lightness had filled her. She wouldn't lie to this man, no matter what.

She peeked at him through her lashes and the compassion on his face undid her. His fingers twitched and his hand reached toward her. She remembered touching him as he lay in the hospital bed and didn't know if she could bear his touch at that moment.

"Ta ma hurry, chi annit!" she blurted out, trying to get the guttural h and the accents on the words that were burned into her memory just right, although she knew she was butchering them.

His hand faltered and dropped back by his side as his mouth curled into a frown. "What?"

"What does it mean?" she asked, her voice still soft.

"Where did you hear it?" he almost growled, his voice hard suddenly.

"I saw you in the hospital bed, at the doctor's place."

His frown deepened. "I thought I dreamed you." Emotions warred on his face and she tried to place them. Disbelief seemed to be the strongest one, then something bigger, meaner, like he was at war with himself. "You were the reason I got better," he finally breathed, his eyes boring into her, his words making her gasp. "You touched me, didn't you?"

The breath squeezed out of Heather's lungs, smothering her. "Your hand. I touched your hand. Were you sick?"

Graeme looked about the room as if searching for rescue. His eyes narrowed as he looked towards the kitchen and she looked that way, too, but saw only a closed door.

The chef at their table spoke and joked and the other people they were seated with laughed. Food was piled onto their plates but they both ignored it.

Finally, Graeme spoke. "I was resting after an injury," he said in a tone that did not invite more discussion. He turned to his plate, picked up his fork, and began robotically to eat.

Heather faced her own plate, although she didn't feel the least bit hungry anymore. She pushed her rice around, speared a shrimp, twirled it, dipped it in butter, smelled the butter—garlicky—then dropped the fork again while Graeme ate everything on his plate.

She hated where they were. How awkward she felt. Like she'd done something wrong. On some level, she knew nothing was her fault and Graeme was wrestling with something, but that knowledge did not remove the awkwardness.

"Where are you from?" she asked cautiously, hoping for something to lighten the mood.

Graeme shoveled the last bit of rice into his mouth and wiped the lower half of his face with a cloth napkin, looking around as if wanting more to eat. She felt him look at her, even as she stared at her food.

"South Uist," he said, watching their new chef, then holding his flower-patterned plate up for more meat.

Heather's mood brightened immediately. "Oh, South Uist, I've always wanted to visit Scotland. That's where Remus Whitecastle vacations in the summers. He bought a house he swears Bonnie Prince Charlie once visited for a fortnight in 1745. I don't know if it's true or not, but there is a plaque on the grounds that says Flora MacDonald once owned the land. I've seen a picture and—" She broke off. Graeme was staring at her, a strange look on his face.

"Who is Remus Whitecastle?"

"He's a famous herpetologist. He directed and starred in the documentary *The Great Dragon* and founded Dragon Park."

The color drained from Graeme's face and he grabbed his water glass, scooped the ice out of it, dropped it on the table, then sipped the water slowly while staring at her.

"What?" Heather whispered, nervous.

Graeme put his water down. "The Great Dragon? What, ah, what exactly is that about?"

Heather smiled, unable to help it, as the image of a heavy, lumbering Komodo Dragon filled her mind. "Komodo Dragons, they are a huge monitor lizard found in Indonesia. In fact, they are the largest lizards on earth. Not the largest reptile, that's the saltwater crocodile, and it can grow up to eighteen feet long. The biggest Komodo Dragon is only about ten feet long, but still, that's pretty long, don't you think?"

Graeme was staring at her, a complete lack of expression

on his face, and for a moment her nervousness returned. But then he threw back his head and laughed. Warmth danced up Heather's spine at the rippling, masculine sound, making her shiver. On her other side, the chef finished his show, thanked her and everyone else at the table, bowed, and disappeared. She tried to smile at him and tell him thank you, but the truth was, her attention was mainly on Graeme, and had been for most of the afternoon. Just before the first chef had charred their food, she'd thought she'd seen Graeme reach out and deliberately press his finger to the grill, which was impossible, of course, but at that exact moment had been when she'd felt the blast of heat from the thing. It had reminded her exactly of the heat she'd thought she'd felt come from Graeme in the parking lot of the police department.

Both incidents must have been her imagination, she knew that, just part of her taking a slow trip to the funny farm, but part of her didn't believe it. Part of her thought it was more likely that she was caught up in something she didn't understand. Some secret that was both unlikely and impossible, but still true. Her chest tingled in anticipation of the moment when that secret would be revealed to her. Somehow, she knew that the more time she spent with Graeme, the closer that moment came.

Graeme stopped laughing and smiled broadly at her, the first genuine smile she'd seen that was all for her, that she hadn't surprised out of him, and it made him impossibly handsome.

"You like reptiles, don't you?" he said.

Her eyes widened and she didn't know what to say. Ordinarily that was something she would hide, because she'd been called a freak one too many times in her life not to.

He shook his head. "I don't even need to ask. Of course,

you do." He leaned forward, his expression mischievous. "What do you think of dragons? Not Komodo, but the village-clearing, fire-breathing types of legend?"

She looked at him aslant, trying to decide if he was making fun of her, when his expression turned sad. "It doesn't matter, anyway," he said curiously. "I really should be asking you what you think of wolves." He faced her squarely. "Wolves are kind of cool, right? Mating for life, alpha males, and all that?"

Heather rubbed her forehead. The man sitting next to her was handsome, distinguished, and eloquent, but confusing as crap. "Wolves are ok, I guess. I've never really thought about it."

His gaze snapped to the kitchen again and his eyes and voice turned mean. "You really should think about it. For your own sake."

***

He held the door open for her as they left the Benihana and Heather was surprised to see it was getting dark outside already. She pulled her jacket tighter around her, zipping it up and shoving her hands in her pockets. "How long were we in there?" she asked quietly, not expecting Graeme to hear her.

They'd moved to regular seating and Graeme had ordered another full meal. After a bit of mostly normal conversation, she'd been able to eat her sushi and rice, spurred on by Graeme's expansive appetite. She'd had green tea ice cream for dessert, and he'd had two servings of the banana tempura and three of the fresh pineapple boat. She'd learned he was a helicopter and a small plane pilot, he'd just transferred to Serenity from Scotland, and he hated ice cream. On her part, she'd tried not to share too much. She'd mostly talked about her brother, Jimmy. He was normal. They hadn't talked about her crime at all, and she was trying not to let that weigh on her, but now their interlude was over. Back to real life.

He turned back towards the police station and she thought about her tiny sedan with the half-eaten protein bar on the passenger seat, the lizard bedding spilled all over the back seat, and the massive dent in the rear fender. She'd held her own over the last few hours and didn't think she'd come off too strange. She didn't want to ruin any positive image he might have developed of her by letting him walk her to her car and get a good look at the state of it.

"You know what, Graeme, I think I'm going to walk home. It's a nice night. I'm only about a mile this way. I really wanted to thank you for lunch. It was wonderful, and I enjoyed talking with you." She stood stock still as she waited for him to make the next move. He was old enough to be her father, but she'd flirted with him enough, or tried anyway, once she got over her nervousness, that he should know she was interested. But was he? He hadn't flirted back, she didn't think, but he'd smiled a lot. Maybe men his age didn't flirt. She should ask him how old he was.

He nodded in the direction her house was in. "I'll walk you."

Heather turned that way and put one foot in front of the other, her heart doing somersaults in her chest. Was he just being polite? Or was there to be something between them? What if he wanted to come in? Her house was clean but the lizards! She grimaced, knowing in her heart that if he wanted to come into her house and take her on her living room floor while every reptile in the place looked on, she would let him. She barely knew anything about him—just his name, his occupation, where he'd been born, and something he liked to do for fun, but it didn't matter. She would have climbed into that hospital bed with him if he'd opened his eyes and asked her to, climbed up there and ridden him like a horse. She bit down on her cheek, hard, and curled her fingers into her palms, the nails pressing into her skin like punishment as she berated herself for being crude. She bet he wasn't crude. She bet he was a perfect gentleman with the women he slept with. She snuck a glance at him and wondered how many women he had slept with. A dozen? A hundred? Women probably threw themselves at him all the time.

She turned left, then right on auto-pilot, barely noticing the roads they covered as her mind spun on and on in overdrive. They neared her road as darkness began to fall in earnest and she unzipped her coat. She felt comfortable all of a sudden, like it was late summer, instead of late fall. Warm air bathed the left side of her face, the side Graeme was on, while a bit of coolness still nipped at the right side. Her thoughts finally slowed down a bit and she looked at him again, realizing he hadn't said a word the entire time they'd been walking, and neither had she. He didn't seem bothered by it. He seemed relaxed, content even, his face turned up towards the sky, a slight smile on his lips.

They entered her street and Heather could see her double-wide three houses down. She sighed. This was where he realized she was not successful or glamorous. Just a working girl doing her best to make it month to month in the family business. She steered him towards her house, strode up the walk, and stepped a foot onto the bottom step, before she turned around to face him.

"This is it," she said, giving him a chance to clear out of there, but desperately hoping he didn't want to.

He smiled absently. "Your home is lovely. May I come in?"

Her heart triple-timed in her chest and her breath caught, until she realized what he'd actually said was, "I'll wait until you go in."

"Right," she mumbled. "Thanks again."

"Heather," he called, his voice deep and gorgeous.

She turned back. "Yes?"

"Don't worry about the fire. I'll smooth it over with the Chief."

"Thanks," she tried to say, unlocking her door quickly and pushing inside, ready to head for the mint-chocolate chip ice cream in the freezer.

But she didn't make it there. She closed the door behind her, her back against it, and slid down it to the floor, fat tears rolling down her cheeks.

She knew he hadn't been interested in her. Of course, he wasn't. She was a baby. A freak. A-a-a. Her mind ran out of insults, but she didn't feel any better.

She'd only just met him, but it felt like her life would never be the same without him in it.

CHAPTER 13

Graeme watched the closed door for a long time, his gut twisting and rolling. He hadn't wanted their evening to end and he could tell she hadn't, either. But smart was smart, right was right, and wrong was wrong. Them being together would be wrong for so many reasons. It would never happen.

He turned on his heel and strode purposefully across the street, down three houses, then ducked behind a large bush and transformed quicker than any eye could track. To anyone watching, it would have seemed like he just disappeared.

Smaller than a bird, about the size of a dragonfly, he flew like an arrow back to Heather's front porch, his thick body and leathery wings hidden in the darkness. If he were going to leave, he'd have to make sure she had ample guard first. He would not leave her to be picked off by Khain.

He set down on her windowsill, but could see nothing of

her house, so he flew to the backyard to try to see in those windows. There she was, just inside the door, sitting on the floor with her head in her hands, her shoulders shaking with sobs.

Even in *dragen* form, the sight of the maiden overcome with sorrow hit him in the head like a brick, making him long to put an arm around her, pull her into his chest, and whisper, *You're safe. I'll stay with you. You're not crazy. None of it is your fault or your doing.*

Graeme's tiny *dragen* chest cramped with the futility of it all. He soared straight up, over the house, and turned in tight, angry circles over the dark shingles, the moon ignoring him, and him ignoring the moon. It wasn't right. It wasn't fair.

After much time had passed and Graeme's anger had cooled to a dull roar, he settled on the front porch again, tucked his wings, and stared out at Heather's neighborhood. He would keep watch all night and decide what to do in the morning.

The scent of *wolven* reached him, stirring his ire again.

Who is there? he shouted in *ruhi*. *Reveal yourselves!*

Wade's voice entered his mind, sounding tinny and far away. Geographical distance was not an impediment to *ruhi* with two beings who were emotionally close, but Graeme had kept his distance from everyone, especially Wade.

It's Mac and Beckett and a felen. *They are going to watch over her for the night.*

Graeme gnashed his jaws together. *I will watch over her.*

Wade didn't say anything for several minutes. When he finally did speak, his tone was gentle. *You could be inside, you know.*

What makes you think she would have me?

In his head, Wade chuckled, and Graeme felt a rush of affection for the old *wolfen*.

You're right, did she spend the four hours while you two were at Benihana telling you how ugly she thought you were?

This time Graeme chuckled. He settled in lower on the corner of Heather's windowsill and pulled his neck in closer to his body, wishing for a cup of tea. *She didn't throw herself at me.*

Of course she didn't. But don't lie to yourself. She's feeling the pull as strongly as you are. If you shut her down like I think you did, she's probably holed up inside crying right now.

Graeme didn't answer, but his old companion, guilt, pulled up a seat beside him on the sill.

Look, Graeme, I know you have your reasons for refusing what most shiften *would kill for, but have you ever considered just letting them go? Just giving in?*

You've been in my head. Would you let it go?

Graeme, you could be wrong.

Aye, and I could be right. I've made my decision.

They both fell silent and Graeme watched the street, the cool night air caressing his cheeks. He knew Wade was still there. Searching for just the right thing to say. He spoke first. *Wade, what will you do when all the members of the KSRT have mates to watch over? You will run out of males to do the watching.*

So you think the KSRT will get mates first?

Don't you? It makes sense that the strongest and smartest would be given the chance to create young first, especially if the young are really the end-game.

Wade was silent for a long time and Graeme wondered how much thought he had put into the young that would come from the one true mates. Too much, probably.

Finally, Wade made a statement. *You believe they are fated.*

Yes.

Is Miss Herrin fated to you?

Graeme growled deep in his throat and mind.

Because if she is, then she can mate with you. And if she is, you are hurting her if you don't go to her.

Graeme stood, ready to fly, his body shaking. *She can take another mate. She can bear the young of a* wolfen *or a* bearen *or a* felen. *You told me Crew said the one true mates could take any.* He forced the words out in *ruhi*, even though the thought made him feel like tearing out someone's throat.

Graeme, what if your young, dragen *young, are needed to end it all. The whole thing.*

Graeme leapt into the air and flew straight up, trying to work off some of the fury settling in his muscles. *I will never put a bairn through that,* he said, and shut down his connection to Wade.

But two words still got through. Two words said with a depth of sadness that Graeme thought only he was intimate with.

I know.

CHAPTER 14

*K*hain floated a half-inch above the ground, eyes rolled back in his head, his thoughts living things that raced around in his overgrown, bleach-white skull. With Boe not around, he needn't disguise his true form, but that was the only good thing about Boe being gone.

His one cloven toe on each foot bounced against an outcropping of rock, scraping at the bone there. He didn't notice.

A *dragen*. A *dragen* had come to him. That had been the one sticking point in the signs for him. The one sign that he thought would never, ever come true, because he had been convinced that all the *dragen* were gone. Dead. Rotting.

So, when Boe first recited the 777 signs to him that would lead to the *Vahiy*, the Day of Reckoning, the Death of Rhen, he had never fully believed. Many of the signs had already happened. Some he could force, given the time. But he never thought he could force sign number 665. He had it memorized and he heard it in his mind, recited in Boe's voice.

A fight will come to the Pravus, *a dragen with two lives will breach the walls. The Destroyer will lose the battle, but gain the air to win the war.*

But he'd known the second he'd seen the *dragen* flying at him in his own home, that they'd always interpreted that one wrong. It really was the heir to win the war, not air.

He smiled, his jaws eating most of his skeletal face, his jagged teeth scraping against each other. He laughed, pulses of air pushing out between his glaringly white ribs.

A *dragen*. And an heir. The energy was moving faster. His time had almost come.

He needed Boe back. There was so much to be done. Boe had been right about consuming the angel for the energy. His sleep had been short after the *dragen* had appeared and the wolves had injured him, because he'd taken a tiny chunk of the angel into himself. He would not take much more until he was certain he had no more use for the angel, and he could not know that without Boe.

Khain dropped himself to the ground, put his human-like covering over his real body, and flipped into the *Ula* for just a moment, not caring where he ended up over there.

The fetid air of the *Ula* greeted him at once and the foul light of the moon shone down on him. He would pluck that lighted monster from the sky when Rhen was dead.

He opened his senses to the *felen*, searching for them, listening to them. Yes, they could feel him. He examined their thoughts and conversations, sifting for exactly what they could determine about him. They sensed where he was, but he was faint, fainter than the last time. *Yes!*

He flipped back to his home, cutting off the senses of

those nasty felines like severing a rope. Something about the angel was indeed changing his relationship with them. If he consumed the angel completely, would he be able to walk among the humans with no *felen* ever knowing? If so, would it be short-lived? Would it be better to consume large pieces of the angel but still keep him alive? Khain sighed, too high from the angel's energy to feel very down, but wishing he knew the answers to those questions.

Boe. He needed Boe. Without Boe, his connection to the *foxen* was so weak, it barely existed. He would have to try something else.

Khain strode into his home and reclined in his favorite chair Boe had handmade for him. He would try again. If he couldn't connect with the *foxen*, there had to be some being in the *Ula* that would accept him. He had done such, centuries ago, before the *foxen* had been created. The small creatures of the *Ula* could not resist him. The creepies and the crawlies, of which he used to have a favorite...

He cast his mind back to those days and tried to remember what the creature had been. They were plentiful. Small. Fast. Vicious. They existed upon every corner of the earth. Their eyesight was poor but their other senses heightened. And humans hated them, which was the best part.

He relaxed and sought that miniscule connection that would allow him to find a way into the *Ula*. When he had found his wayward son, he would bring him back. If there was mischief to be waged in the search, all the better. He was feeling up for a bit of good fun.

A small part of his consciousness sought one of the many cracks between dimensions in which to make its entry into the *Ula* without the flip of his body that alerted the *felen*.

He found one near his larder, no bigger than the hair on a spider's leg.

Ah, yes. He shivered in delight when he realized he had remembered the name of the creature he had always favored inhabiting.

The spider.

CHAPTER 15

*G*raeme blinked as the sun came up on the far side of Heather's cozy home. He stood and stretched his body, while making himself smaller still. He hadn't slept. He'd slept enough for the last six hundred years that he didn't care if he ever slept again, or at least not until he fully handed over watch of Heather to the *wolven*. When that would be, he hadn't decided. He turned, walking delicately along the windowsill, seeking a crack in her drawn shades to peek in. The front room of the house that he could see looked empty.

He flew over the roof, checking all the windows in turn until he found her. In her bed, sleeping on her side, covered with a golden bedspread, one creamy arm and leg punched out from under the covers.

He stared for what seemed like minutes, but was much longer. His eyes traced the bare limbs, then her face, her hair, her form under the gold coverlet. She was lovely and innocent and if only she were truly his. He would give all the treasure he owned, everything he had to give, to touch her just once. To know the softness of her, the sweetness. To take the innocence. Such an act could live in memory forever, even after death.

Graeme shook himself and forced the thoughts out of his head. He turned and stared out at the yard, resolute in his decision.

As the sun rose over the buildings, he heard a horrible blaring sound coming from the room. He turned and pressed his tiny, scaly face to the glass and saw Heather rise, then slam her hand down on a small brown square, which cut off the noise. She moved slowly, stretching and yawning. Graeme took off, flying back to the front of the house, where he would stay. He would not violate her privacy and at the front of the house he would know if she left.

Which she did, about an hour later. She walked out her front door, pulled it shut and locked it, then walked down the steps of the porch towards the street, without looking around. Her lovely scent of roasted chicory with toasted sugar surrounded him, making him take a deep breath through his nose. She was dressed in a much warmer jacket than she'd worn the day before, plus a purple stocking cap that came down over her ears and cheeks to tie below her chin. Even the breath coming out of her mouth, visible in the cold air, looked unbearably cute.

Graeme waited for a few minutes, then flew from tree to tree on the street, knowing anyone who saw him would dismiss him as a bug. He followed her that way, only sparing a momentary thought to whether the *wolven* knew they were on the move or not. Of course they did. That was their job.

Twenty minutes later, they neared the police station. She was going to get her car. Good. She would go about her life like normal. He would wait for a good moment to hand off the guarding of her to the *wolven* (and insist Wade send more than two *wolven* and one *felen*) and then he would leave. Where? Who knew. Out of the United States, certainly. Back to the watery loch which had not the power to kill him? Eh. He no longer felt so much like dying. But he could not stay near the maiden. He had so little control of himself when she was around.

He landed in a tiny, leafless tree on the edge of the police station parking lot and watched Heather make her way towards the station. Too late, he realized she wasn't going to her car, after all. She pulled open the door to the receiving area and walked inside. *No!*

He tried to be glad. Tried to tell himself she would find a *wolfen* in there who would be thrilled to show her the ways of mating, to plant his young in her belly, but his stomach rolled and his wings trembled. Sour bile forced its way up his throat, as his legs quaked with his attempt to hold himself in place.

He couldn't do it. He dropped out of the tree, flew behind a fencing unit that separated the parking lot from rows and rows of squad cars, transformed in the air and fell to the ground running. Back around the fence at a full sprint toward the receiving area.

Even as he ran, he knew the only answer was to leave. Go somewhere, anywhere that he wouldn't be able to see her and react to her. Which he would do. That evening. He swore it. No more excuses.

He reached out with his mind. *Wade, I need help. She's back at the station and I don't know if I can control myself.*

Where?

Receiving desk.

I'll be right down.

He could see her through the glass doors of the station, standing at the receiving desk, waiting for the Desk Sergeant to get off the phone and talk to her. Graeme hit the doors at a run, slamming them open, which caused her, and the seven people sitting in chairs in the waiting area, to look at him, alarmed.

He took a deep breath and strode to her, gauging her reaction. Shock at the sight of him. Maybe some indignation, also?

"What are you doing?" he said when he reached her. "I told you I would take care of it."

She turned up her nose at him. "And that, Officer Kynock, is what is wrong with the world today. I don't want it to be *taken care of.*"

Graeme winced at the official title. He must have hurt her as much as Wade said he had. He leaned forward. "You want to be arrested, then?"

"I do."

"Fine."

He turned toward the door that led to the inner workings of the department, glad to see Wade already striding through it.

She's insisting on being arrested.

You do it. I'll put you in a private room.

Graeme nodded and motioned for Heather to follow him through the door Wade was now holding open for them. She smiled warily at Wade, then slid her hat off her head, stuck it in her pocket, and followed.

Graeme steeled himself against the inner urge to maim any male that came near them, glad when Wade opened a door to their right without them meeting anyone. He ushered Heather inside the tiny room with one desk and a shelf covered with forms and other things he didn't recognize, then told Heather to take a seat and take off her coat. Wade closed the door and disappeared, but still spoke in Graeme's head.

Find the Form 5150 and fill it out. Ask her the information. Then fingerprint her. That's it. Then take her out again. I'll help you get out of the building if you need it.

Graeme walked to the shelf and began pulling out forms. He found what he was looking for and grabbed it, looking around for a pen. It had been fifty years since he'd written anything down and even then he'd only signed his name a few times. How much had changed? Thank goodness Wade hadn't tried to set him up with a computer. He found pens in a drawer, grabbed one, and sat at the table across from Heather. He could do this.

He made the mistake of lifting his eyes to meet hers and all he could do was stare. The cold air and walk had flushed her cheeks, and her irritation with him had given her a haughty look that he found irresistible.

His struggle with himself intensified.

***

Heather waited for the big cop to do something, anything. Anything besides stare. She finally blushed and looked down. It was almost like he could read her mind. If so, he was getting an earful, because she hadn't wanted to see him again. When she'd finally cried herself to sleep the night before, she'd been convinced that she never would. That he'd make sure of it, avoid her.

So now that he was here again, going out of his way to be the one who arrested her, she didn't know what to think.

He cleared his throat and seemed to just notice the piece of paper in front of him.

"Right, then. Full name?"

"Heather Herrin," she recited, then spelled it for him.

"Date of birth?"

Her birthday fell out of her mouth easily, as did everything else he asked, until he got to, "Ever been arrested before?"

"Ah, no," she said, almost remembering something important, but it slipped from her mental fingers too quickly. She shook her head and focused on the form he was filling out. His handwriting was gorgeous, a swirling, flowing script that always ended with a flourish. She stared at it as he wrote in the synopsis box, *Started a fire.*

She frowned, thinking that didn't sound very official, or complete.

He pushed the paper and pen to the side of the desk and stood. "Ok, Hea—, I mean Miss Herrin, I'll need to finger-print you."

Heather sighed. It wasn't his fault if he wasn't interested in her. You couldn't help who you were attracted to. "Please, call me Heather. I'm sorry I snapped at you earlier. I know you were just trying to help me."

The smile he gave her warmed her from the inside out, pushing her dangerously close to that edge she had sworn to stay away from with him.

"Step over here, that's right, now—"

He fumbled with the equipment on the counter, opening and closing lids and pulling out paper, then pushing it back. After a few moments, he seemed to get what he wanted. An inkpad and a roll of paper on a block she recognized from TV. She would have thought all of this would be digital by now.

He looked at her and held out his hand. "Your hand, please," he said in a low, quiet voice.

She lifted her hand and he took it gently. His fingers were warm and strong, and she sucked in a breath at the feel of his skin on hers.

"Just relax, let me do all the work," he said in a low voice she thought was unbearably sexy, running his other hand down her arm to her elbow and pulling her forward slightly. The scent of red-hots filled her nose and saliva squirted into her mouth.

Heather shuddered and took the step forward, feeling the warmth from his skin spread through her body. She fought letting her eyes roll back in her head. Just a simple touch. Nothing sexual about it. And all she could do was wish he would touch her all over her body in that exact same way. She could see it in her mind, his fingers dipping under her shirt, gliding across her belly, sliding around to her back, going lower to cup her buttocks—

She bit the inside of her lip and tried to get herself under control as he looked her in the eyes, his expression confused. Her eyes found his mouth. Would his lips be soft? Would his manner be harsh or commanding? Or would he be gentle? They stood, locked like that for a moment, until he cleared his throat again and maneuvered her hand so her thumb touched the ink pad. The cool wetness of the ink shocked her slightly, pulling her back to herself. He moved her hand so her thumb touched the paper and he rolled her thumb so that, when he pulled her hand back, a smeared thumb print was left there. She thought he would want to redo it but no, he began moving through her fingers quickly until he let go and asked for her other hand.

When it was all over, he stepped away from her quickly and offered her a towel to wipe her hands on.

She took several slow breaths and stared at the floor as she cleaned the ink from her fingers.

"That's it," he said, his baritone voice cutting through the haze in her mind.

She looked up. "I'm arrested?"

He nodded. "Aye."

"What now?"

He didn't answer for a moment and she got the strange feeling he didn't know. But then he spoke.

"You'll get a court date in the mail."

"Then what?"

Again, that small pause. "You'll want to get a lawyer. If you can't afford one, you can ask the court to appoint you one."

"Oh," she said. This was all becoming too real. "Will I go to jail?"

Another pause. "The judge will sentence you. Most likely you'll get community service since it's your first offense."

She nodded like it all made sense. "Ok. I ah, I can go, then?"

He pointed to the door. "I'll walk you to your car."

"Ok, right." *Why?* she screamed inside her head. If he didn't like her, why was he walking her to her car? She was certain no other officer would do that.

Within a moment, they were outside in the parking lot. She headed towards the area she remembered parking in the day before. It didn't matter what he thought of her or her car now. She knew he wasn't interested.

But he is, a small voice inside her whispered, punching her in the gut. He walked next to her and one step behind her and as she really thought about it, she knew that voice was right. He was interested, he was just holding back for some reason. The age thing, it had to be.

She didn't care about his age. He shouldn't care about hers. They could get over that.

She stopped walking and faced him. "I never properly thanked you for lunch yesterday. Can I take you out when you get your lunch break? I'll pay."

He didn't look at her, but instead his attention was pulled by two large officers near the door that led inside. His eyes narrowed and he answered while looking at them. "That would be great. Benihana again?"

"I was thinking of something more simple."

He looked at her then and his smile almost knocked her over.

"I adore simple."

CHAPTER 16

Graeme strolled along the river path, bouncing lightly as he walked. He would be miserable in another six hours, but for now, his world was the best it had ever been.

The sky was overcast, but the expanse of the river made up for it, reflecting the silver clouds in a manner that made the day seem brighter. Heather walked to his right and her manner was easy, happy.

"Aren't you cold?" she asked him, pulling her hat out of her pocket and putting it back on her head.

"I dinnae get cold much," he admitted, turning up his thermostat a tiny bit, just enough to warm her. He hated the thought of her uncomfortable for even a second.

She looked ahead of them on the path. "There he is. Jim's Hot Dog Cart. I hope you don't mind hot dogs. His are amazing, especially the chili and onions dog, and it's early yet so we won't have to wait in line long."

Graeme looked where her attention was fixed. A small, boxy, white vehicle was parked along the path and queues of people radiated out from a window on the side. An enticing smell of salty meat and fried vegetables reached him.

"Smells good." He would try anything once, but he hadn't realized the people in Serenity actually ate dogs, if that was indeed what was in a *hot dog*. He wondered what the *wolven* thought of that.

They waited their turn, Heather alternately smiling at him and looking down at the ground. His mind cast back to the feeling of her skin when he printed her fingers and how much pure will it had taken not to slide his hand around her neck and take her mouth with his own.

"Don't you have work today?" he asked, realizing he didn't even know what she did. If she had to be somewhere that afternoon, it would be time for him to make his exit.

She peeked at him under her lashes. "No, I took a few days off."

He grunted. That plan was no good. "What do you do?"

Her face flooded with crimson. "I run the crematorium at my father's funeral home."

He stared at her, a new appreciation blooming in his chest. He knew she was fiery, feisty, and everyone he met in this new age was interesting to him, but she had an added dimension, didn't she? "You burn the dead bodies?"

She made a show of studying the menu on the side of the tiny vehicle so she didn't have to look at him. "Honestly, all I do is run the furnace. I have assistants who prepare the bodies."

He watched her face closely. "Is it a big furnace?"

She was able to look at him then, and her eyes lit up with as much love for fire as he'd ever seen in any *dragen*.

She told him the statistics for her furnace like another

woman would recite the birth weights of her children, but she was interrupted by the man in the hot dog vehicle asking for their orders.

Heather ordered automatically. "A chili dog with extra onions and a hot tea."

"Got it, and you?" the man said, turning to Graeme.

"Make it two."

The vendor nodded and disappeared into his vehicle.

Heather pulled some bills out of her pocket and put them on the counter in front of them. "What about you? Do you have any family in Serenity? You don't seem like you've been here for long."

Graeme shook his head. "I had two brothers, but both are gone."

"Oh, Graeme, I'm sorry."

Graeme looked out at the river. "Thank ye."

The vendor brought them their dogs and they found a bench to sit at, balancing their tea on the seat between them. Graeme sniffed his dog and frowned. "This is cow."

Her eyes flicked upwards. "All beef hot dogs. Do you not eat beef?"

"I eat any meat," he said, then tried a bite of it, taking care not to spill any of the chili or onions piled high on top. Excellent. A flavor combination he'd never experienced before. He would go back and order more if he could dissuade her from paying for him.

He finished his 'hot dog' in two more bites then turned to Heather. "You work with your father?" he said, knowing he shouldn't be asking, but wanting desperately to know more about her.

She grimaced strangely, then looked at the river as she answered. "We all do. Mom and my brother, too."

Graeme watched her eat her food slowly and plied her with questions about her family, wanting to hear everything about her life. He would remember the sound of her voice and the cadence of her words for a lifetime.

She ended up telling him about her mother in the stilted way that people do when they want to be kind even to someone who doesn't deserve it.

"She sounds quite formidable," Graeme said.

"Formidable? I guess. I would describe her as mean and controlling. Sometimes I think she hates everyone."

"She loves you."

She looked at him with her eyebrows tight over her eyes. "You call that love?"

He shrugged. "Sometimes when one has been hurt, their love can be painful to bear."

She didn't say anything for a long time so he changed the subject, which she went along with easily.

They sat on the bench alongside the river for the rest of the afternoon, in simple conversation that made him long to be someone—something different.

***

Heather threw her head back and laughed. Graeme's humor was aged, but much more refined and witty than anything she'd ever heard her father say. She couldn't believe they'd been on the park bench for so many hours. They'd gotten up to walk down the path a bit, then returned to the bench to talk more. He seemed endlessly fascinated with popular culture and the little things she liked, including what kind of food she liked to eat and her hobbies. She hadn't mentioned her pets but told him all about glass blowing.

Lunch had come and gone, and the park had cleared out like it was bitterly cold. She could see ice forming on the edge of the river but the afternoon felt unseasonably warm to her. Maybe it was the low cloud cover. She'd taken off her hat and unzipped her jacket hours ago.

Even the hot dog vendor had disappeared. She looked around. "We're the only two left out here."

He nodded. "Darkness will come early tonight. Snow will fly soon. People are bedding down early for the winter."

Heather looked up at the sky. She couldn't tell if snow would fall or not, but for some reason she believed him. She looked at him shyly. Was she brave enough to invite him to her place yet? She wanted to desperately.

As if he sensed her intention, he stood and waited for her to stand, too. When he spoke, his tone was stilted, his voice guarded, "Thank you again for the most *lovely afternoon* I've had in many years. I should get you home now. The hour is late and I have somewhere to be."

Heather stared at him. It was a dismissal if she'd ever heard one. He hadn't even asked for her phone number. Her throat closed up almost completely and she fought with her frozen vocal cords to speak. She thrust her hands jerkily into her jacket pockets. "I don't need to be walked home. I'm a big girl. Good-bye."

She turned on her heel and blinked furiously to keep the tears at bay. She didn't even know what direction she was headed. Away from him, that was all she cared about. She didn't even care if she was overreacting. She was done with him. It hurt too much.

She heard footsteps behind her and she stopped, turning to face him. He was right behind her. "That was not a request. Don't follow me." Her voice was sharper than she wanted it to be, but it made her heart glad to see him wince.

He held up his hands and tried to say something but Heather plowed right over his explanation. She'd had enough. "You know, I'm not sure what I did to deserve being led on by you, but here's a little lesson for you. It's not nice to mess with people's emotions. I don't know what kind of issues you've got, or exactly what your problem is, but next time you want to just have a lovely afternoon with someone, don't send all the signals you've been sending since the first time you saw me. It's just mean."

She turned again and stalked off, the blood in her ears pounding so hard she couldn't tell if he was following her or not. It really didn't matter, though. She was done with him. She got too loopy around him to keep hanging on, waiting for him to throw her a bone.

The park ended, but the wide asphalt path continued through the forest, the beginning of Big Claw Woods. Ordinarily, Heather would not have walked that path alone, but there was no way she was going to turn around and face Graeme. She knew a side path that would get her into the residential area next to hers. Then she could go home and have another good cry. Do her best to forget the sexiest man she'd ever met even existed.

After ten minutes of hard walking, her head began to clear a bit. She *had* overreacted. But she didn't care. He had dismissed her, she knew he had. He was interested in her, but he just wouldn't let himself go for it for some reason. If only she would have been nicer to him, maybe someday he might have gotten over whatever the issue was and—No! she cut off that line of thinking. This way was better.

A screaming sound to her right stopped her in her

tracks. It sounded like a wild animal caught in a trap, but also strangely human-like. Her heartbeat sped up as adrenaline dumped into her bloodstream. She knew there were mountain lions in Big Claw Woods, but she'd never heard of one so close to the city. She looked behind her, but the path that way was empty. Just when she could have used a police officer the size of a football player, he finally decided to listen to her and disappear. Great.

"Hello?" she called. "Do you need help?"

She felt ridiculous, calling out to what was probably a wild animal, but she had to be sure. The scream sounded again and this time it had an element in it that made her think of a child. A young girl, maybe, lost and afraid. She shook her head, knowing there was no young girl out there. But also knowing she wouldn't leave the area until she was certain.

The forest was dark, the canopy of trees thick over her head. She looked down at her feet, realizing she had already strayed off the manicured path into the underbrush. She took out her phone and turned on the flashlight, trying to think if she knew anything about mountain lions. Would noise scare them away? No, that was bears. Some bears.

"Hello?" she called loudly again, taking a few more steps over needles and wispy weeds. "Is anyone there?"

A slight whisper of a voice startled her, making her step backwards. She couldn't tell what had been said, but she thought the voice was male. A dank, unpleasant smell hit her nose, making her wince. A deep fear shot through her, intuition telling her there was something very wrong going on in the woods. A vision of a kidnapping or something worse shot through her mind so quickly she almost choked on it. She turned her phone to her face and pressed the picture of the old-fashioned handset, her hands shaking. "I've called

911!" she screamed into the gloomy forest. "Cops are going to be here any second! You better stop whatever you're doing!"

A hand fell on her shoulder and she whirled around, biting back a scream.

CHAPTER 17

*G*raeme held up his hands. "It's just me. What's going on in there?"

Heather sagged visibly. "Oh, thank God. I don't know. I thought I heard someone screaming. It might be a wild animal but I couldn't take that chance. It feels wrong."

Graeme nodded. She had good instincts. He'd smelled Khain as soon as he'd gotten close to where she'd stepped off the path, but his intuition said Khain was not there. But something bad was definitely going on. Maybe he'd just left. "More officers are on their way."

"Thank you," she breathed, and turned back to the forest, holding up her light. "Ew," she said.

"What?"

"Look, there, see all the spider webs?"

Graeme looked where she was pointing her light. Huge webs were strung between dozens of trees as high as a man's head, webs with strands as thick as string, like the spider who had made it was as big as a horse. He tried to pull Heather back to the path. He knew what was responsible for the scene. He'd experienced this before.

She shook him off. "I've never seen anything like it," she said, walking farther into the forest.

A soft mournful sound came from their left and Heather swung her light that way. "Oh!" she cried, then rushed forward and knelt on the ground, pulling a small kitten out of the web it was caught in.

She turned with the kitten in her arms, her face full of concern, trying to rub off the cobwebs that had shut the kitten's eyes. "How did you get out here, little guy? Where's your momma?"

It was a pitiful little thing, mostly white except for a bare patch of light skin on its right shoulder, and another on its left, plus tufts of black hair on both ears. It yowled and trembled in her arms.

"There's another," Graeme said, pointing just behind the first web.

Heather shuddered. "Look at all the spiders!"

The ground seemed to be littered with them, moving and breathing with them as they climbed over each other to get nowhere. Their sharp, leggy boundary stopped a few feet from where Heather stood.

"Yuck," she said, clutching the kitten to her chest. She looked at Graeme. "This is impossible, you know. A spider can't catch a kitten in its web."

Graeme pointed again, then picked his way over the spiders, watching them scurry away from him. "How about a full-size cat?"

"Oh!" she cried again. "How many are there?"

"I don't know. Four? Five?" They didn't look good, either. Graeme poked one with his boot and it opened its eyes to look at him, then shut them again.

He took Heather's light from her and held it high. "Is there such a thing as an animal rescue in this city?"

Heather shot him a strange look, then nodded, still trying to pull the cobwebs off the kitten in her arms. "I can call them. But not in here. It's too creepy."

He got in front of her to guide her to the path, then handed her phone back to her.

She pulled up her contacts and clicked one button, then held the phone to her ear, speaking after someone answered. "Dahlia, I was hoping I would get you. We need help."

***

Thirty minutes later, the lights of the ASPCA vehicle came smoothly down the path, lighting up the forest behind Graeme and Heather. Graeme had told Wade to cancel backup but have them wait close-by, just in case. They'd left the cats in the spider webs but stayed close-by and checked frequently to keep any spiders off them. Even Graeme shuddered to think of the size of the spider who must have spun those webs.

As the white, covered pickup truck pulled close, Graeme read the words on the side. *Serenity ASPCA.*

Heather saw him looking. "American Society for the Prevention of Cruelty to Animals," she said. "They mostly deal with dogs and cats but will try to find help for any animal." Heather waved as the truck pulled past them and she saw her friend in the front seat.

Graeme looked on, thinking of the woman's name. "How do you know her?"

"Oh I don't know. We just became friends over the years, I guess. The ASPCA calls me when they need help with more, ah, exotic animals. I foster them sometimes."

Graeme half-smiled. "Reptiles."

Heather fiddled with the kitten's ears and shot him another look.

He shrugged. "Naught but a guess."

The woman in the truck got out and slammed the door, looked over her shoulder, then ran up to them. Heather gave her a one-armed hug, introduced her to Graeme, and explained what was going on. While they were talking, Graeme looked her over. She could be twenty-five. She was young and fresh-looking in the same way Heather was, with long brown hair that framed her face and intense, haunted eyes. Graeme stepped away from the two of them, not wanting to catch the woman's scent. If she was someone's one true mate, he didn't want to know if she was a virgin or not.

Dahlia shone her high-powered flashlight jerkily into the forest, then swung around and shone it straight in Graeme's face. "Are they all bobcats?"

"What?"

Dahlia nodded at the kitten in Heather's arms. "That's a bobcat. See the tufts on its ear points and how short its tail is?"

Heather froze and looked at Graeme with wide eyes.

He tried to soothe her. "Shh, don't worry. It's not dangerous. If mom were around, we would know it."

Dahlia looked at both of them, then swung her flashlight around in a wide arc, then stopped, seemingly completely unsure of what to do. "Ok, I'll head in, then," she said, her eyes bottomless.

Graeme started forward. "We'll go with you." She was a nervous little thing, always looking over her shoulder like someone was coming after her, and he wasn't going to make her go into the forest alone. But he wasn't leaving Heather alone either.

Graeme grabbed two cat kennels from the back of Dahlia's truck in each hand, Dahlia grabbed two, and they headed into the forest.

Dahlia screamed at the first sight of the spiders. "Oh! OH! Sorry. I couldn't imagine there could possibly be so many."

"You and me both," Heather muttered, staying far away from them. "I'm just glad they seem to stay in one place.

Graeme went straight to the first cat and bent to pull it out of the web. It didn't even look at him, but it's fur was warm and there was some resistance in its muscles, so he knew it was still alive. Dahlia worked on the one next to him, while Heather held the light for them with one hand.

"Goodness gracious, this is so nasty," she said as she tried to brush the web off of the cat's fur. "I've never seen anything like this. Do you think the poor cats were bitten by the spiders? Do you think there are bigger spiders around here? Oh, my God, I can't believe we are doing this. Someone should call an expert or something and have them come look at all these spiders. Or the cops. Or somebody."

The first time she asked a question Graeme had opened his mouth to answer, but when he realized she was just talking to keep herself from screaming he let her rattle on. Within a few moments, they had all the cats in crates.

Heather swung the light in a circle, then cried out.

"There's one more! See it? On the other side of the spiders. Oh no, I think it's bleeding."

Graeme stood up tall and looked that way. He saw the blood too, but he didn't feel the same concern Heather did. Life was hard. Always. One more reason to reject the role he'd been forced into.

"I don't think I can," Dahlia muttered under her breath. "I want to, but there's so many *spiders*."

"I'll get it," Graeme said. He wasn't letting either one of those females get any closer to the spiders than they already were. He sent his senses out into the forest to make sure there were *wolven* around, in case things went bad. There were. Three, no, four, surrounding them in a half-circle. Good.

He took a step towards the carpet of spiders, half-expecting them to part before him like the Red Sea before Moses. They didn't. He took another step, then another, and still they didn't move. He dangled his foot above them, watching to see if anything changed. When it didn't, he dropped his foot down, beyond caring. The spider's bodies burst under his work boot in a horrid crunching he tuned out as he walked swiftly to the last cat.

But was it a cat? As he drew close, he could see where the blood was coming from, a shallow cut on the animal's side. "I think it's a marmot," he called over his shoulder, pulling his shirt off his body and using it to wrap the animal and pick it up.

Dahlia's eyes were on it as he carried it back. "Woodchuck," she said.

"Will you still help it?"

"Of course." Dahlia took the animal from him, wrapping it tighter in his now-bloody shirt and made a beeline out of the forest. The light from the flashlight found its way to the center of his chest and stayed there as he walked towards Heather, then bent to pick up cat kennels. He couldn't see her face behind the light, but something in her scent and the way she stood shifted slightly, making a deep desire flood through him. He cut it off and lifted his chin. "Go out to the path."

The light bobbed, then turned as Heather seemed to flee out of the forest.

CHAPTER 18

As Graeme stepped up the tiny embankment to the path, Dahlia pulled her head out of the back of the truck and started grabbing kennels from him. Each time she grabbed a kennel and slid it in its spot, she stopped and swung her gaze around the forest for a moment before repeating the procedure.

When all the cats were stacked in the back of the truck, she looked him over, a frown on her face. "Aren't you cold?

"No," he replied simply, dismissing her to listen to Wade in his head.

Mac, Beckett, and Harlan are in the woods. Crew is on his way. Do you need more?

I dinnae think so. We are leaving soon. When we go, they'll want to look through the area and see what they can find. Does Crew know how to find dimensional cracks? Or do you know any felen *who can? Because I think there's one buried under all those spiders.*

I don't know. What can be done about them?

Graeme sighed. *Nothing, but they should be mapped and watched.* He wasn't surprised Wade didn't know about such a thing. Historically, *wolven* had very little knowledge of any other worlds or how to travel between them. The *felen* would know, but they had never shared their secrets easily.

Dahlia stood close to Heather and very carefully took the bobkitten from her arms. Graeme saw a change come over her at once when she did. Her shoulders relaxed and her mouth curled into the first smile he'd seen that night. A tiny *oh* escaped from her mouth as the little thing opened its eyes and mewled at her. She stared, transfixed, then turned and walked to her truck with the kitten in her arms, not saying a word of leave.

Graeme walked up to Heather. "Is she always like that?"

Heather glanced at him, her face unreadable. "What? Intense? Yeah, that's Dahlia."

Graeme forgot himself for a moment. "She has the look of a traveler. One who doesn't know she's been traveling."

Heather expression contracted in confusion. "What?"

"Nothing."

They heard the clunk of the truck being put into gear. Graeme pulled Heather far to the side of the path as soon as he saw the truck reversing their way. From his height, he could see Dahlia had the tiny white kitten on her lap as she drove, one hand in its fur.

Heather lifted a hand to her, but they were blinded by the headlights and could not see if Dahlia returned it. The lights faded until they disappeared.

Heather's scent shifted again and Graeme looked at her,

not able to identify her emotions by scent yet. Her face wore a determined look. He knew he was about to be told off again.

But then he saw something drop into her hair from the evergreen tree above them. Eight legs big enough that he could see the hairs glistening on them. She felt it as he saw it and her face contracted in disgust. He reached out to flick the spider away, as she whipped her head back and forth and screamed, her own hands flying up to squash it.

When her hand hit it, instead of mashing into spider guts, it grew in size until it was as big as a mouse, then a rat, then a Chihuahua.

Promised an awful voice whispered in his head.

Heather screamed again and Graeme grabbed the spider around its hairy middle and flung it into the trees, then spun Heather behind him so he was between it and her. It continued to grow as it flew through the air, until it was the size of a Great Dane. It landed, bounced, and rolled into a tree, then faced him, eyes staring, two front legs pawing at the air between them.

"*No!*" Graeme roared, and he transformed, even as the spider grew to the size of an elephant. In one great outbreath that sounded like a locomotive train screaming down shaky tracks, he directed a stream of fire directly between the front fangs, both of which dripped poison in a steady stream onto the ground in front of them.

The spider didn't so much explode as it incinerated, its body surprisingly liquid. Graeme didn't stop until it was entirely gone, its poison nothing but a waft of nasty-smelling steam.

Graeme turned his scaly head to be sure there were no more spiders, then planted his feet and turned slowly, certain, based on the absolute silence behind him, he would find Heather flat on her back in a dead faint.

But, when he turned, she was standing, a look of wonder and joy on her face. She lifted her hand, placing it directly over his heart, curling her fingers around the edge of one of his scales. He'd never been touched with affection in his dragon form before. It felt unimaginably good.

"You're real," she whispered. "Exactly as I've always seen you in my mind."

Beckett and Harlan exploded out of the forest behind her and Graeme stepped closer to her, then transformed to give them a fighting chance if they came too close and he lost it. Heather's hand stayed on his chest and when she realized it was a human torso under her fingers, her scent shifted, deepened, and she licked her lips. Graeme had to catch himself from falling as his knees buckled at the sight of that pink tongue wetting those amazing lips.

He passed a hand in front of her face and sent a stream of energy toward her, hating himself for doing it, knowing it wouldn't work, anyway. It didn't. She glanced into his eyes before looking down at his chest again, but that was all.

"What in the cornbread hell is going on here?" Beckett shouted from the other side of the path as Crew and Mac emerged from farther down, both with their fangs visible in their mouths. Graeme couldn't help but notice Crew looked like death eating a cracker. His cheeks were hollowed and black purses stood out under his eyes. All the males were rubbing their clothes like they had the heebie-jeebies and Graeme could tell they had needed to run through the spiders to get to the path.

Graeme grasped Heather's upper arms and looked over

her shoulder at the males. "The spiders. Khain is controlling them."

Mac nodded, then called out to Beckett. "Get us some *bearen*. We're going to do a little slash and burn." He turned back to Graeme. "Unless you care to do the honors for us, Sparky?"

Graeme looked back at Heather, who stood compliant in his hands, her fingers still grazing his chest, her expression jubilant, but dazed. "I've gotten a better offer."

Mac nodded curtly and frowned when he got a good look at Graeme. "What happened? Burnt and Scaly run out of your shirt size?"

Graeme ignored Mac and leaned in close to Heather. "You want to go to my place?"

Her eyes found his and she nodded, her smile widening.

"Climb on," he said, then transformed, kneeling so she could clamber up onto his back. He waited until she felt solidly on his back, her fingers curling around his wingmounts, her knees grasping his sides, and then he looked up into the sky. Mostly clear. No matter, he had a bit of magic that would keep them dim when they needed it.

Hold on, he sent in *ruhi* and leapt into the air using his legs, then unfurled his wings to catch an updraft. He beat his wings hard, grabbing the atmosphere mercilessly until he owned it and they were a thousand feet above the ground and climbing.

You ok back there? he said, not surprised at all when he heard her voice in his head.

I'm in heaven.

CHAPTER 19

Oh God, Oh God, Oh God. Heather looked down at the ground again, then pressed her face onto her dragon's warm back. Graeme, she had to remind herself. Her dragon's name was Graeme, and he was also a human man. Combining the two into one being took a surprising amount of work in her head and she gave up, instead directing her gaze at the sky. They seemed to be flying directly into the moon at a speed that was dizzying whenever she looked at how quickly the ground was slipping beneath them, but seemed just right if she stared up or straight ahead.

Below them, bright lights caught her attention. Chicago, it had to be. Yes, there was Lake Michigan. She trained her eyes on it and tried to tell how fast they were going by how quickly it disappeared behind her. Faster than a plane, for sure. And higher too. Much higher than a plane.

The chilly night air breezed softly by her in a way she

never could have imagined if she ever had tried to conjure this moment in her mind. Her dragon was warm, comfortable against her body, and if she felt chilled, all she had to do was lean against him and rest first one cheek, then the other on his smooth, strong scales. She did so, holding on to him with one hand as she traced the diamond shape of his scales with the other, one finger running along the edge.

Mmmmm, he rumbled in her head, and a sweet tingle ran between her legs. *Oh God, oh God, oh God.* The voice was a man's low purr that she associated strongly with Graeme, the human. The man. She flattened her hand against his back and remembered what his chest had looked like as a man. The tattoos. The sculpted muscles. The perfection. *Oh God.* Her tongue snaked out and lightly tasted the scales of the dragon, only because she was convinced she was dreaming and she wanted to see what it (he) would taste like.

Nothing. Maybe a bit of salt. Ok.

She looked down again. Was she dreaming? Yes, she was dreaming. She had to be. Chicago disappeared behind them and another Great Lake came into view. She didn't know which one it was. Erie? Ontario? She didn't know any other names and that bothered her. She should know the names of the Great Lakes!

But then big city lights came into view and she forgot about the lakes. *What city is that?* she sent to her dragon. Dreaming, definitely dreaming.

I dinnae ken the names of your cities, lass.

Heather replayed the words over in her mind. His accent was so much stronger in her head, and his choice of words seemed different, too. But still so sexy it had her squirming. Dreaming. She had to be. The city seemed as unimportant as the lakes now, although she knew it had to be Detroit, or maybe Cleveland.

She wanted him to say more words, she didn't care what they were.

We aren't going to your place in Serenity, are we?

I dinnae have a place in Serenity. I slept in the woods.

The city slipped behind them and a few smaller ones dotted the landscape.

How do you go so fast?

Magic.

She could hear the grin in his voice and she smiled too. Wetness touched her cheek and she wiped at it, not knowing why she was crying. She'd never felt so happy, so *free* in her life.

A larger city loomed on the horizon, and past it she felt a gulf so large it threatened to consume them, even from as far away as they were. She took her eyes off it and focused on the city, watching as the lights twinkled to their right, then came in to focus, revealing how large it really was.

"New York City," she breathed but the wind ripped her words away from her.

Her dragon's trajectory changed slightly and they steered away from the city. Smaller synapses of light popped up here and there, but forest seemed to dominate the landscape. The yawing of the Atlantic Ocean began to creep into her consciousness again and she dropped her head to her dragon.

Be not afraid, lass. I've flown this route a hundred times before. The water will not have us.

She peeked over the side of her dragon and saw only water below them, but within a few seconds, an island appeared. Newfoundland. She knew that because she'd studied the reptiles of the island after an imported species of garter snakes had been proven to survive one winter in the wild there.

The island passed quickly, and then it was only water. Chilled suddenly, she pressed into her dragon.

Are ye cold?

Aye, she told him jokingly, her tongue clamped between her teeth.

He chuckled and another spurt of happiness flooded her and suddenly she wasn't cold anymore.

She didn't ask him where they were going. She knew. Of course, she knew, and she didn't want to ruin the magic of the moment. She reminded herself to text Jimmy when she got there and ask him to check in on her babies until she told him otherwise. He would just assume she was off on a rescue. He always came through for her when she had to leave for a few nights.

She peeked over the side, but the water looked just as unfriendly as it had a moment before so, she settled in on her dragon, laying her head against him, her eyes watching the wisps of clouds they passed and the light of the moon on her dragon's wings. She let her fingers relax, knowing even if she were to fall, he would catch her. He would never let her drop.

The sound of the wind and a thumping she realized to be her dragon's heart lulled her, wiping the memory of the awful spider that had touched her from her brain, beat by beat. Her body relaxed until she felt as one with the beautiful beast beneath her. Flying. She was flying. Dreaming. But what a dream. She wanted to live in the dream forever.

***

Wake up, lass. You'll want to see this.

Heather opened her eyes and blinked. Had she fallen asleep during her dream? She curled her fingers around the place where her dragon's wings met his body and looked over the side.

"Oh," she gasped. It was so beautiful. Magical even. She couldn't explain the difference in how the land below her looked and felt from what she was used to, even to herself.

Land covered with synapses and neurons of connected lights stretched out as far as she could see, but the forest and fields closest to them caught her attention the strongest. As they got closer, she could tell her dragon had slowed his speed immensely. She peered around his head. *Is that an island coming up?*

Aye, that's South Uist. And North Uist above it. The big one below them is Ireland.

He banked slightly and Heather felt a giddy laugh bubble up from her chest. She could almost believe it was her flying.

We aren't stopping there, are we?

No. I don't live there anymore.

Heather watched as the islands slid beneath them. A droning sound that got louder each second caught her attention and she looked around. A large plane passed not too far overhead, startling her. She looked down again, realizing just how much they had dropped. Her dragon seemed to be angling for the very center of a forest on the largest island that had to be the UK. The forest stretched for hundreds of miles in each direction, no lights to be seen.

Cairngorms mountain range and, more recently, national park, her dragon rumbled in her mind.

She watched, glad to be able to put a name to the place, as the trees grew bigger and bigger in the moonlight and her dragon dropped lower and lower. A thought to be nervous crossed her mind but she ignored it. She trusted her dragon more than she trusted any airline pilot in the world. He would take care of her completely. She knew that, somehow.

They dropped so low she dangled her feet over the side and leaned left to see if she could graze a treetop with her toe. Her dragon jostled her weight back to center.

No stunts, or Morag will get you.

Heather pulled her toe up so quick her knee popped. Graeme chuckled in her head and she settled down again.

Morag?

A loch monster, like Nessie.

They dropped into the trees, and Heather held on tight as her dragon dodged two of them, then landed lightly on the ground. He shook his head, stretched his wings wide, then knelt.

We're here.

Heather slid off and took a moment to admire her dragon from the ground. His lovely yellowish chest, his shimmering scales, his proud, strong jaw line, muscular neck and legs. Everything about him was perfect.

She stretched a bit herself, and turned to the tiny clearing between the trees, wondering where 'here' was. She turned back to her dragon and there was Graeme, standing tall and strong and staring at her with hooded eyes, his torso still naked.

She smiled at him in the moonlight. "Thank you for the flight. I've never enjoyed anything so much in my life."

"The pleasure was mine."

She walked in a small circle and raised her face to the treetops, smelling the pine scent of the forest, taking it deep into her lungs. Facing away from Graeme, the air felt much cooler, and she even saw a smattering of old snow in a few places the sun had never been able to reach to burn it off. When she finished her circle, she faced him. "Are we at your place? I expected a house, I guess."

He nodded over her shoulder. "Look again."

Heather did and was shocked and surprised to see a tiny cottage where no cottage had been before. Dreaming. So totally dreaming.

"It was there when you looked before, you just didn't see it. Dragon tricks."

"Are those like ancient Chinese secrets?" she said softly, staring at the cozy, square building that looked like it was made entirely out of river rocks. Had someone hauled all of them by hand?

He chuckled and she looked at him, then back at his place. *Please don't wake up.* She took a step forward, shy suddenly, but wanting to see the inside of his house. The sound of his feet on pine needles behind her spurred her on. She felt like she had hours left to dream. Surely, she could get him to kiss her in that time. If only he would open the door for her, invite her inside…

***

Graeme passed Heather and pushed open his door, scenting deeply to make sure no one had been inside, then throwing it wide for her. He recognized the smile she gave him in return. It said she was completely and totally his, and that made his guts coil into a hard little ball. He would never take her up on her silent offer, but he would do what he could to soften the blow of his refusal.

His eyes flicked around the one room, as Heather took

it in for the first time. He saw the years of caked dust on every surface, and his footprints through the dust on the floor, framed by fat drop-shapes he knew had been water from his journey in and immediately back out a few weeks before. He didn't even know exactly how long it had been. It didn't matter. The only thing that mattered to him was enlightening the lovely female in front of him to what she really was, and breaking her heart as gently as he could.

She walked to his fireplace, coat still on but unzipped, and gently touched the inches of dust there, then turned to his reclining lair. He shook his head. She would call it a couch, not that she would want to sit on it with no cushions.

He left the front door standing open and walked to the back, throwing wide the windows there to get the stale smell out, then grabbed a piece of cloth and began wiping up reams of dust. She tiptoed through the room, picking up items from his log tables and rock counters, examining them, and laying them back down. Once, his collection of Scottish antiquities had been his pride and joy, but now it could burn, for all he cared.

She finished her circuit of the room, then came close to him. "There's no bedroom."

"No," he said. "Come." He took her hand and led her outside, around to the back of the cottage and showed her where he slept.

She eyed the roughly beaten down circle of dirt under the eaves of the house. "Is it a nest?"

"Not exactly. But I prefer to sleep outside."

She looked at him curiously. "Even as a human?"

He looked off into the trees. "I rarely sleep as a human. I would say never, but you saw me sleeping as one, did you not?"

He caught her nodding her head in his peripheral vision

and he looked back to her. Her attention had been pulled, and he watched closely, wondering if she really was that strong, that in tune with *dragen* life.

She bent at the waist, turning her head like she was listening to the ground, then stood, then crouched and touched the rocks at the very bottom of the house. "There's… something below us. What is it?"

"What does it feel like?"

She dropped to her knees and ran her hands through the pine needles and leaves, over the ground itself. Graeme saw dirt collect on her fingers and for some reason he felt a stirring in his groin at the sight. She was unlike any female he had ever met, in so many ways.

"It's a circle. It's… calling to me."

Graeme said nothing. He knew exactly what she was feeling. Had it been a mistake to bring her out here? Would he find himself tricked or forced by magic into something he knew he didn't want? He would be on his guard. Always.

She continued on her hands and knees for a short way, then found herself back at the house. Her hands ran around the dirt in a large rectangle, pushing the leaves and needles out of the way. She turned to him. "It's a door. Right here. Why can't I see it?"

Again, Graeme said nothing. She stared at him, her lip quivering, then turned back to the door that was not there. He saw her gather her energy as she stared at it, then she walked from one side of it to the other. Finally, she dropped to the ground and drew a circle in the dirt exactly where he knew the door pull to be.

The circle of the door pull appeared, and the wooden door leading into the cellar appeared just below it. She shot to her feet and clapped in delight. "I did it!"

She turned to him suspiciously. "Did you help?"

"No."

"You don't seem surprised."

"I'm not."

Graeme licked his lips and pondered what he had just seen. He knew she wasn't totally human, and angels had their own magic, but still, that had been *dragen* magic. He'd felt it. Did that fact change anything? He didn't know. No. It couldn't. She was still mostly human, with soft, vulnerable skin and organs.

She pulled on the door but it wouldn't budge. He went to her and helped, because she'd earned a look at what was down below.

The door creaked and cracked but the wood held firm. It was strong. He'd rebuilt it every fifty years for the last six hundred or so, resurfacing long enough to inspect his house, take care of the maintenance, check in with the police chief, see what the latest news was, what had changed, and if there was anything dangerous he could do. Sometimes he stayed out long enough to play with the toys of the age, like his helicopter and airplane, but always, he eventually returned to what he hoped would someday be his watery grave.

He heaved the door open and laid it on the ground opposite its hinges, then grabbed the lantern just inside on the first stair. He held his fingers to the wick until it lit.

As he lifted the light high and entered the cellar stairs in front of her, he felt a weight roll onto his heart.

Something was coming. Something that would challenge all his plans and decisions.

He pressed forward, because there was no other choice.

CHAPTER 20

Heather descended the stairs slowly, watching the muscles in Graeme's torso bunch every time he lowered his foot. It was almost enough to make her forget the pinging, calling sound of the… whatever it was. She had no clue. Only a sort of coldness in her head like a fish hook embedded in her brain. It wanted her. It was calling her. The only thing she knew for sure was it was not bad or evil… and it was circular, or it's call was.

The stairs went on for what seemed like a half a mile, the air cooling more with each step she took. She'd fallen behind Graeme, and she hurried to catch up with him to take advantage of his heat, her footfalls echoing off the walls and ceiling of the stair corridor.

The calling became louder in her head and she opened her eyes wider, trying to see beyond Graeme. Surely they had to be getting closer to it.

"Almost there," he said softly and she heard a curious catch in his voice. His foot reached the bottom, a dirt floor that stretched out beyond where she could see. She took the last few steps herself and stood next to him.

The room opened up into what she could only describe as a cavern or cave, with a lofty dirt ceiling and tiny roots piercing it here and there. But, oh, the treasure! Piles of gold coins higher than her head littered the room. She counted them. One, two, three… seven. Seven piles that had to be worth a few million each just in the gold! It was no Scrooge McDuck swimming pool of gold, but more a Pirates of the Caribbean treasure room, with clear demarcations of gold coins, gold bars, gold jewelry, gold statues, then everything else. The silver and gems were piled together more haphazardly on the other side of the cavern, like they weren't as important.

Heather walked through the maze of riches, grazing one hand along a stack of gold bars here, then a pile of gold coins there, her mind barely able to comprehend what she was seeing. Graeme did not follow her.

Near the back, she found a large stack that looked different, and then she realized that there was gold, silver, and other metals and gems all mixed together.

The circle was still calling her, but in her wonder, its signal was muted. She turned on her heel and strode back toward Graeme, stopping at a small chest to open it and peer inside.

"Is it all yours?" she asked, eyeing the crowns and headpieces inside the chest.

"Not all. Some is Rhen's gold. Some gifts for other deities. I guard it here."

"Rhen? Deities?"

"Ah yes, that is a conversation we must have."

Heather saw a small, neat stack of gold bars with red flakes on it to her right. She brushed at them, wondering what they were. If she stared close enough, she might think they were dried blood. She grimaced and looked up at a golden chalice holding a dozen golden swords. A human hand with attached arm bone lay below the chalice as if discarded there.

She backed away, thinking of the stories of dragons she'd heard her entire life. "Is—is it stolen treasure?"

Graeme did not answer for a moment. "Aye, dragon treasure is oftentimes come upon in violent ways. I have not stolen it myself, though. Most of this has been passed to me by my family and mates as they died. I am the last dragon, so I have the keeping of all of it, until I die, and then the Scotland Police will decide what to do with it."

Heather turned to him slowly, her chest tight.

He took a step back when he saw the intensity of her gaze. "What?"

"Don't you know what my fire said?"

"Your fire?"

"My fire! I—it's not important exactly what I did, but somehow I lashed reeds together to form letters and placed those letters into words. There was a message. No one ever told you what the message was?"

He took three steps forward, eyes blazing. "Tell me."

"You are not the last dragon."

An amalgamate of emotions passed over his face, too quickly for her to identify them all. Confusion. Fear. Disbelief. Anger. Then, something stronger. Not terror?

He transformed. One minute a man standing with a lantern in his hand, the next a great dragon, just big enough to barely fit up the stairs. The lantern crashed to the floor, but didn't break or go out.

Heather cried out and took a step backward as her dragon whirled around with a great roar and ran up the stairs like the world's largest and scariest horse with wings and scales.

Heather scooped up the lantern and followed him at a run, tucking her elbows into her sides and putting her head down for more speed. She did not want to be left alone in the treasure room. But more than that, she worried about her dragon.

When she reached the top, and burst out into the cold night air, she stopped. It was completely silent, and so much colder than she'd felt before. She took a few steps, cocking her head towards the front, trying not to breath so she could hear better.

No insect droned, no animals called. She tried to remember back to when they'd arrived. Had it been this silent? A sudden fear wracked her. Her dragon wouldn't leave her alone in the woods, would he? She put the lantern down long enough to zip her coat, then bent and killed the light. It made her feel like too much of a target. As her eyes adjusted to the dark, she stared into the trees, trying to see if her dragon was there.

A sound like a great scream in front of a freight train erupted into the night and her dragon appeared above the tree tops, its mouth open and hurling fire below, away from her. Woody explosions crackled and popped and trees flared and burned like matchsticks.

Heather stared, wondering only for a moment about forest services, until she saw that her dragon pulled the resulting smoke into himself as he swooped, dipped, and twisted angrily through the air. Another jet of fire cut the night in half and more trees incinerated.

Even from as far away as she was, she could see the pain

on her dragon's face and feel the warmth of the fire he created. The two acted in opposite ways on her, one depressing her soul, the other lifting her spirit to heights it hadn't reached since childhood. She gave herself over to both sensations and raised her arms to dance in the moonlight as heavy tears rolled down her face.

Graeme, she sent to him. *I'm sorry. I didn't mean to hurt you.*

He didn't respond.

Heather danced until her legs were sore and cried until she had no more tears, glad each time her dragon swooped her way, checking on her. When she could stand no longer, she dropped to the forest floor to rest and wait for him to be done.

The burning stopped, and still her dragon flew in lazy circles far above her head, until, finally, hours later, he dropped wearily to the ground near her and transformed into a man, standing in the center of the clearing, just staring.

Heather stood and walked to him. "That looked like therapy," she said, keeping her voice low.

After many moments of silence, he spoke and she could smell smoke on his breath. "*Dragen* love to burn. It is always soothing."

Heather held back the comment that rose to her lips automatically, then realized if there were anyone she could share it with, it was him. "Me, too. I mean, I love to watch things burn. Sometimes I ache to start fires, which isn't good in my world. I call it the fire-lust."

Graeme looked at her for a long moment before staring into the trees again. "We call it Grádóiteán, which translates roughly into *love of fire*. It is natural for dragons." He turned to face her and his dark expression held secrets. "Have you always felt that way?"

"Yes, as long as I can remember."

His eyes flashed. "Can you start fires?"

Heather almost laughed, until she realized what he meant. She looked down at her hands, then rubbed them on her coat like they were dirty. "What, you mean, like—like you can?"

He nodded solemnly. Seriously. For the first time since they had landed, she wondered if she were dreaming again. Her brain felt curiously hot and on the edge of some sort of overload.

She held her hands up in front of her and looked at them. "I-I don't…" In her memory, flames burst from behind her mother, from their living room couch, from a roll of toilet paper. The thought filled her with a coiling black dread she could not hold and she began to make a soft noise, pulling her hands into her chest. She shifted from one foot to another, feeling like she was a little girl, so little, and something bad was about to happen. Something worse than a spanking. Worse than having her toys taken from her. So bad. *No, mommy, no! I don't want to go!*

Her muscles tensed and her arms extended and she slammed her palm into her forehead at the temple, over and over, trying to stop the horrible pain there—

Graeme's hands caught hers, holding her so she couldn't hit herself again. "Shhh, lass, shhhhh. Don't think about it for a second. Just let it go. I will not ask ye to think about it again."

Heather burst into tears and let him pull her into his chest and comfort her.

CHAPTER 21

They stood that way for a long time. An owl hooted somewhere in the forest and for the first time, Heather wondered if Graeme had unwittingly killed any animals with his burning. Her mind was coming back to normal, allowing Graeme's words to soothe it.

He separated them slightly and stared deep into her eyes. "I cannot hypnotize you, but I can relax you and sometimes that can be the same thing. Would you let me try?"

Her eyes narrowed. "That's what you tried to do to me in Serenity, after I saw you as a dragon the first time."

He nodded. "Aye."

"You would have taken that knowledge from me?"

"Aye, if I could have."

"It would have driven me insane."

He pulled her hands up to her chest and cradled them

between them. "I know that now. I promise to never try again without your permission."

She stared at him a long time, then gave him a curt nod. "Please do."

He smiled and dropped her hands. "Wait right here."

He strode a few feet away and made a pile of needles, sticks, and other forest debris, pushing it all together, then he turned his back to her and bent over it. Within a moment, a tiny bonfire was blazing merrily, then he returned to her and sat cross-legged on the ground, holding out a hand to her.

She dropped to her knees next to him and he positioned her until she was lying stretched out on the forest floor, her head in his lap, her eyes toward the fire. The forest floor heated up underneath her to a comfortable temperature.

Graeme ran the pad of his thumb gently over first one of her eyebrows, then the other, over and over, then pulled his fingers through her hair so lightly it sent tingles all through her body, then he returned to her eyebrows. Her eyes drifted closed, but she could still feel the warmth of the fire on her face and hear its soft popping and crackling.

Graeme spoke to her, his voice soft and soothing, lulling her. "When I was a wyrmling, my mother would do this to me when my brothers had tormented me before bed, saying the dragonslayers would get me while I slept. Dragonslayers hunted us because of who we were, never guessing we were also like them, so they did not find us easily. For *dragen*, fire is a difficult thing. We cannot live without it. Cannot take a vow of abstinence and say we will never start another. It lives too strongly in our bones. We need it too much. It would be like saying we will never take food or drink into our body again. Such a thing would kill us. But with the lure of fire comes shame too, as it is a powerful thing, and no one who wields fire like we do can escape hurting another. So my mother would take my head in her lap and rub my eyebrows and tell me this."

Graeme waited a moment, then his voice changed slightly, became higher. "Fire is the giver of life, the bringer of heat and succor. There is nothing wrong with fire, and there is nothing wrong with *dragen*. You cannot fight who you are. To do so is madness. But like a great wolf, fire can overwhelm you. You must always be the stronger, the one in control."

Heather took a deep breath and let Graeme's mother's words wash over her. She wondered what his mother had looked like. What her name had been.

"Then my mother would sing me this song, over and over, until I fell asleep. In the morning, I would always feel better."

Graeme gathered himself, then recited what sounded like a nursery rhyme.

The water is wide, but I can cross.
For I have the wings to fly.
I shan't need a boat that can carry two,
For we can soar aloft, my love and I.

I leaned my back up against a young oak
Thinking it were a trusty tree
But first it bent and then it broke
Thus my strength slayed me.

O love is sweet and love is kind
The sweetest flow'r when first it's new
But love grows old and waxes cold
And fades away like the morning dew

Heather shivered at the words, then opened her eyes. "Ask me again."

"Can you start fires?"

"Yes, I used to when I was little. With my mind, and my hands."

"How little?"

"Three, maybe. Four and five. Maybe younger." Heather's voice broke and she realized she was crying again.

"Why did you stop?"

"My mother took me to a doctor and he—he fastened electrodes on my head and sent electricity through my brain."

Graeme's hands faltered, stopping their rhythm, then quickly started again, rougher than they had been before. Heather let out a great sighing sob and half-sat up, then leaned to the right, waiting for a sudden nausea to pass. It did, quickly, but she stayed that way and spoke into the dirt. "Oh, my God, my mother gave me shock treatment when I was a little girl. I haven't started a fire since. Not on purpose anyway."

Graeme pulled her hair through his fingers, still trying to soothe her. After her mind had quieted again, he spoke. "I think you should start a fire. Here. Now."

Heather lifted herself onto her elbow and stared into his handsome face. "You're right." She curled an elbow around his neck and pulled herself up to him, not giving either one of them a chance to think, then pressed her lips to his, her mouth open slightly, seeking him, inviting him.

She wanted him to respond more than she wanted anything in the world.

CHAPTER 22

Graeme groaned into Heather's mouth as the tip of her tongue touched the tip of his, sending waves of pleasure through his body. He pulled her into his arms, then bent to lay her out flat on the ground and cover her body with his. Why had he refused this for so long? The kiss was everything. Better than the hottest fire or the highest flight.

Their bodies rolled over the forest floor as she wrestled to be on top, grabbed his head and pulled herself in closer to him, then he had to be the one with the leverage to get them even closer, the fire and the moon giving him plenty of light to see her by.

She squeaked and moaned against his lips, and he took the chance to kiss down her neck, making her shudder and throw her head back. She climbed on top of him again and unzipped her jacket, then threw it onto the ground, dropping her mouth to his as his hands grasped her breasts. So perfect! So soft and yielding, even through her bra. Like nothing he'd ever touched before.

Their kiss lengthened and he began to heat up uncontrollably. He took his hands off her breasts and curled them around her back, tucking her to the ground and rolling over her again, kissing her neck, trying to get his temperature under control again. The shift in her scent was not helping. It had deepened until he could almost taste it. Rich chicory tea heaped with toasted sugar and warm milk. A sweet, hot drink he desperately wanted.

"Graeme, let me…" she said, trying to get her hands between them. He propped himself up, and she pulled her shirt over her head, revealing what had been hidden before. Lost! He was lost at the sight. He would burn straight through the mountain if he got any hotter. He dipped his head and suckled her hard nipples through the fabric of her red, lacy bra that called to him like a bull in a ring. He felt his erection grow and strain against his pants, but he ignored it. This would never be about him. It would be ok, if it were not about him.

He slipped a strap down off her shoulder, then moved to kiss the creamy skin there. Lovely, she was so lovely. The most beautiful being he'd ever seen, in the air or on land.

Somehow, she made the bra disappear. Her breasts lay bare before him, calling to him in a voice he could not resist for a second. He dropped his mouth to first one pink, peaked nipple, then the second, his hands covering the one his mouth was not on. Oh, the sweetness!

"Heather," he murmured into her perfect skin. "I burn for you. I would slay a hundred demons, incinerate a thousand villages for you."

"Yes, yes, I want to see them burn," she cried underneath him, her back arched to expose more of herself to him.

He groaned and kissed the skin of her stomach. She would be the death of him. His death. Something he'd wanted for so many years, but didn't anymore. He could be happy forever if she were with him, even if they could never properly mate, as long as he could kiss her, worship her, just like this.

She rolled again and he went with her, letting her climb on top of him, her legs straddling him, until her hands went to his pants, grasping what had grown there.

He grunted and rolled her again, pinning her arms to her side, kissing her mercilessly, covering every exposed inch of skin with his mouth.

"Graeme," she cried, bucking underneath him. "Please, I want you so bad. I've wanted this since our first meeting."

"Aye, you shall have what you need, I promise you."

He let go of her arms long enough to remove her pants, staring at the simple fabric that covered her when they were gone. Like a gift, she became more beautiful with every piece he unwrapped. Slowly, he pulled her panties down her legs, taking it all in. Gorgeous. Perfect.

He looked up at her eyes and she was watching him, her hair a halo full of forest needles. He smiled. "So bonnie, you are. All of you."

She smiled back shyly and reached for him. He took each of her hands and kissed the palms, then pinned them to her sides again as he nudged her knees apart so he could give her what he would allow himself to give.

He breathed hard on the downy curls he found, heating them, making her moan. Then he moved below, readying her with his breath before he began to kiss her, to ply her with his tongue, moving slowly enough that he could gauge her reaction to his every movement. Her taste was as divine as he knew it would be, deep, robust sweetness, better than the finest tea or cocoa.

He watched her face, watched the movements of her body as she stiffened and her breathing came faster. Yes, right there. He found the spot that she reacted to the most and played with it, touching it gently and kissing around it, then he slid his tongue up it until it swelled, plump and ripe. He slid his tongue back down and she cried out, lifting her hips as her cry rolled away down the mountain.

Graeme teased his way around the sweet spot again as she tried to speak but couldn't get the words out.

"Please," she finally cried and he could refuse her no more.

He latched on gently, taking her into him, using his tongue as it came to him, gratified when first her legs began to shudder, then her entire body. Her hands fisted, pulling away, but he held them firm as she lifted her hips and cried out in a way he'd never heard before.

When he was certain of all her pleasure taken, when her body had relaxed and sunk to the ground, he kissed her a few more times, then climbed to lie next to her, nuzzling her shoulder with his lips, directing his body heat towards her as she caught her breath, eyes closed, full lips parted, chest heaving.

Around them, the sounds of the forest started up slowly. No bugs, too cold. But the hardiest birds chirped hesitantly, then more strongly, and small mammals rustled in the leaves and the trees, calling warnings to each other. He looked around, realizing the night was receding. The sun would greet them soon.

"Graeme," she said without opening her eyes. "I don't really want you to burn any villages for me."

He laughed, an open easy sound in the crisp air, feeling his heart leave him and go to her, ignoring the part of him that wanted more than he would ever give it. "I know, bonnie, I know."

She reached for him then, and he forgot himself for a moment, allowing her hand to roam over his erection, losing himself in the incredible sensation. Too quickly—not quickly enough he came to his senses. *No!*

He jumped up, wishing he had a shirt to take off to cover her with. He began to gather her clothing, not daring to look at her face, to see the expression there.

"Come, my leannan, my bonnie, my lovely," he said, still facing away from her. "Let us return to my cottage where I can take care of you properly."

CHAPTER 23

*E*lla skipped down the stairs, pausing at the first landing to look out the window at the males in the driveway. Her mate was there, locked in conversation with Mac and Harlan. Harlan stood on tiptoes and held his hands over his head, as if indicating how big something was. Mac spit in the dirt and shuddered, a frown on his face. So, that was why Trevor had left their bed early. She would have to think of a way to get him back up there before their day properly started.

She continued to the bottom and found Trent and Smokey facing each other, nose to nose, tails held high, Smokey's tail twitching at the very tip. Ella stopped, watching, trying to catch any thoughts in the air, but there was nothing.

Smokey's tail twitched a final time and then he broke contact with Trent, running over to sniff at Chelsea, who was sitting on Trevor's chair, waiting.

Ella caught Trent's eye. *Were you talking?*

Trent's deep rumble in her head made her smile, as it always did when he spoke, because it was so rare to hear it. It made her think of mountains and glaciers and planets. Consistent. Unmovable.

I don't know if Smokey can communicate in that way. I've never heard him say a word.

What were you doing?

He wants to do it most mornings. I'm not totally sure why. Sometimes it seems like he is memorizing me in a way that goes deeper than sight or scent. Like he will someday need to know me by feel alone. Trent sighed. *Or maybe I'm just being philosophical.*

Smokey finished with Chelsea and ran out the wolf door. They both watched him through the window as he disappeared into the forest. They knew by experience he wouldn't return until nightfall.

Trent sat on his haunches, his expression stoic. *I don't know where he goes, but he makes me want to wander sometimes.*

Ella panicked a little at the words and the tone. She sank down to her knees and ran her fingers through Trent's fur, staring in his eyes. *You aren't thinking of leaving us, are you?*

Trent didn't answer for a long time. When she thought for sure he would not, he rolled his eyes to look at the sky out the large front window. *It's hard to have a foot in two worlds but belong in neither. Sometimes I do wonder if I would fit in better in the other world.*

What other world?

Trent rolled his eyes back to hers. *The world of the wolf.*

Ella bit the inside of her lip, then saw Trent had looked away from her again. Now he seemed to be watching Troy, who was outside in the driveway speaking with Bruin, the big *bearen* who held watch most days at their place. Her stomach rolled. *Does Troy feel the same way?*

Trent licked her arm, then stood and headed outdoors himself, although she knew he would not be conversing with any of the males in the driveway. He would head into the woods, just like Smokey, but stay much closer. Before he pushed his way out the door, he spoke to her one last time. *You must trust your own thoughts on that, Ella. I may be biased.*

Ella stared after him, thinking she would definitely talk to Trevor, maybe to Wade. She hated to see Trent unhappy, and until today, she hadn't thought of him as such.

She wandered into the kitchen to see what there was to clean up before she began breakfast for herself. If she didn't eat soon enough after waking, and if she didn't eat enough, Trevor would start trying to feed her grapes or ice cream or chocolate or sausages, or anything, really. Remington had said her pregnancy looked perfectly normal and healthy, but she wasn't far enough along to know how many young her belly held, and in case it was more than one, she needed to be extra sure to get enough protein and vitamins. Trevor pushed food on her at every opportunity.

Behind her, the front door opened and closed and she knew it was her mate. She looked around frantically for a hair tie. Finding one on the kitchen windowsill, she put her hair up in a quick bun on top of her head, then pulled the strap of her pajama tank top to the side slightly as she heard Trevor enter the kitchen. It worked, he started growling immediately, then crossed the room in two long strides and buried one hand in her hair, the other around her waist, pulling her to him.

She let her head fall to the right side, exposing the mark he'd left on her skin even more, and he dropped his mouth to it, nibbling her lightly, sending sweet arrows of pleasure down her body.

"I think someone wants something," he murmured into her ear, as he followed the curve of her neck with his mouth.

"Is there time?"

"Always time for you," he rasped. But then his phone buzzed in his pocket. He swore and pulled it out, reading the text there. "Wade wants us at the station, now."

"Ok," she said, trying not to feel disappointed. They stayed connected during their day better when they started the morning off with attention to each other, and she would miss that if it didn't happen.

He turned her in his arms and the phone had disappeared. "We can make up time on the drive in," he said, then bent and picked her up, throwing her over his shoulder.

She shrieked and laughed as he ran up the steps, with her in a fireman's carry.

She hoped their relationship never changed, although she knew in her heart it would have to, once the young arrived.

***

Forty minutes later, Ella had to jog to keep up with Trevor and Wade, who were taking large, swift strides through the tunnels below the police station, past the prophecy room, past a grand, ornate double door she'd never been in but she knew led into the great hall. They turned into a tunnel she hadn't been down yet. Far ahead of them, Crew was striding just as fast, his head bent, his back bowed. Ella watched him, wondering how he was doing. From the back, he looked tired, worn out.

Wade was speaking quickly, telling Trevor all the places they'd found masses of spiders and what Graeme had said it could mean.

"We don't know where Graeme is. Mac says he took off with the woman, Heather, on his back, heading northeast. I can only guess that he took her to Scotland, which is bad, because I called the police Chief there who originally contacted me about him, and he says Graeme doesn't own a phone. He just shows up occasionally. They know about where he lives in the forest, but he won't send anyone out there to talk to him. He says it's dangerous to approach a *dragen's* home without an invitation and he won't risk any of his males."

Trevor held out a hand. "Wait, doesn't he have control over Graeme?"

Wade shook his head. "I've been meaning to tell you, but it's been crazy over here and I haven't gotten around to it." He stopped in the hallway and faced Trevor. Ella had to turn and come back to them when her momentum carried her past. For just a moment, she watched as, ahead of them, Crew stopped and opened a door to his right, then disappeared inside. She turned her attention back to Wade.

"I haven't told anyone this, but you need to know in case something happens to me."

Trevor scoffed. "Nothing's going to happen to you."

Wade shook his head. "I'm getting old, Trevor. For the first time in my life, I feel like my time to return to The Light is closer than it is farther away. I can't ignore that."

Trevor reached out and grabbed Ella's hand. Ella squeezed it hard.

Wade began his story again. "I learned a few things about

Graeme the day he woke up. He never was a police officer. He's more of a hired gun. He's been showing up at the Chief's office for over two hundred years, out of the blue, asking if there's anything they can't handle. They've had him do normal stuff, like infiltrate drug rings, but they've also asked him to do stranger stuff, like investigate tales of monsters in the forest and the lochs. He's always come through for them, and they have great trust in him, but they've never had any control over him."

Trevor stared off down the tunnel. "I wonder if one can control a *dragen*. They aren't *wolven*."

"Exactly. But I have to tell you, I asked him to join the KSRT. We need him. I'm certain he would have said no, flat out, except for one thing."

Ella felt tingles march up and down her spine. She knew what that thing was. Love. True love. She got the feeling if anyone deserved it, it was Graeme.

Wade glanced at her, like he could read her thoughts. "The woman, Heather, who was in the duty room the other day. It was not the first time he had met her. She came to him at Remington's place. I don't know how or why, but she touched him then. He didn't believe it, thought he dreamed her, but the touch set off the same cascade it did with you, and until he mates her, he will be dangerous to all of us."

Ella shuddered, remembering how big the *dragen* could get, and how far he could shoot fire. Was he more deadly than five or ten *wolven* put together?

Trevor rubbed his chin. "Maybe they will mate while they are in Scotland. We should let them be."

Wade nodded. "That would be ideal, but I am afraid it won't happen. In fact, I'm surprised he took her there at all."

"Why?"

Wade lifted his face to the low ceiling, then back down. "Trevor, what do you know about *dragen*?"

"Nothing."

Wade sighed and forced his words out, like he was sharing something he would rather hold back. "They aren't like us. They weren't made to protect humans. Graeme has three major reasons why he is determined not to ever take a mate, and one of them is because he doesn't think he's worthy." Wade dropped his eyes and stared at the floor. "Half a millenium ago, he killed humans, many of them."

Trevor's eyes narrowed. "You know this but you still invited him into the KSRT?"

Wade nodded. "I was able to see inside his heart. Something major changed him, five hundred or so years ago. He has devoted his life to protecting humans since. It's like he's had two lives. One… I don't want to say evil, because I will not judge him in that manner, but I will say the life he has lead since then could be called good by anyone's standards. If he takes a mate, he will be doubly determined to stay the course of Rhen, the course against Khain." He leaned forward. "You know how I know we need him?"

It came to Ella. Slammed into her like a concussion. "Because if we didn't, he wouldn't have a one true mate just for him."

Wade nodded at her. "Right."

Trevor snapped his fingers, about to ask another question, but Wade's phone began to buzz uncontrollably. He held up a finger and looked at it, scrolling through message after message. "Damn. I gotta go." He looked up. "That video? The one with Boeson on it?"

"Boeson?"

"The *foxen*. The video went viral and now our *foxen*

population here in Serenity, maybe the entire state, is revolting. Go talk to Jaggar. He'll tell you who Boeson is and what exactly he was saying, then you'll get it. Oh, and check on Crew, I'm worried about him. He was out all night killing spiders and he doesn't look good. Then come find me."

Before he could run off, Ella grasped his forearm. "Wade, ah, I haven't had a chance to talk to Trevor about this yet, but is there any more work that Trent and Troy could do? I'm afraid they are getting bored just watching me all day."

Wade looked at her appraisingly, his phone buzzing relentlessly in his hand. "There will be a lot of work for them in the coming months and years, I'm sure. They and Mac and your mate are the only *wolven* who have ever made it out of the *Pravus* alive. I'm afraid we'll be going back there in the future and we will need their experience. Do I need to talk to them?"

Ella nodded, knowing he understood.

"Will do." He turned and left, running back the way they had come.

Trevor kissed her on the nose. "I love you for loving my brothers."

"I do, you know," she said, as they headed back down the tunnel again, her chest aching. "More than you know."

CHAPTER 24

Trevor pulled Ella down the hall. There was much to be done, and he loved having her with him. He felt like she softened the team, gave them a focus they'd never had before. As long as he could keep her safe.

"Let's check on Crew, first," he said. "I saw him go into his office."

Ella nodded. They stopped in front of the door and knocked on it. No answer. Trevor knocked again, calling out for Crew. Still no answer.

He tried the knob and it turned, so he pushed open the door. The office looked like a tornado had ripped through it. One desk sat in the far corner, covered with papers and folders so high, Trevor wondered how Crew could possibly find what he needed. A black leather couch was to their left, against the far wall, and every surface of floor and table in between the two was stacked high or just strewn with books and folders. Trevor took a step into the room. "Crew?" he called out, then bent to pick up a book.

He showed it to Ella, then paged through it. It was 'The Lion, the Witch, and the Wardrobe', and from a glance, every chapter had a few passages highlighted.

"Did you see him leave?" Trevor asked.

"No, he didn't leave. I would have noticed."

"Yeah, me too."

Trevor picked his way across the room to the other side, looking under the desk and behind a chair while Ella picked up more books to look at the covers. Much of it was non-fiction. *How to Understand the Fifth Dimension. Space and Time Warps. Time Travel, Four Ways in which it Could be Possible.*

Trevor walked to the couch and seemed to sniff it, then lifted the cushions off it, and even moved it to peek behind and under it. Ella turned and looked behind the door, reading a few of the titles she found there. *Daughter of Smoke and Bone. Outlander. Into the Abyss. The Traveler.* Ella frowned. Crew had a serious obsession going here.

"This is the last place in the room he was," Trevor said, holding two couch cushions in his hands. "His scent is still warm."

Ella turned in a circle. There were no windows, no more doors. "I'm kind of freaked out."

Trevor nodded and reached for her hand. "Me, too. I'll forever be grateful to Crew for helping me save you, but he gives me the creeps when he does this."

She looked at him. "This?"

Trevor nodded, looking around at the piles of paper and books around their feet. "It's happened before. I follow him into a room, and he's not there anymore. Then he walks out of a bathroom or a closet or something, like nothing ever happened. Once, we couldn't find him for a week, but Wade would never let me discipline him."

Ella shuddered. She wondered if even Wade knew where Crew went when he disappeared.

Trevor pulled at her. "Come on, let's talk to Jaggar. His office is the next one down."

Out in the hallway, Trevor knocked on the next office door. "Yeah," a male voice called from inside. Ella put on a polite smile. She hadn't officially met Jaggar yet.

Trevor pushed open the door and entered the office, holding Ella's hand. Ella got just an impression of the exact opposite of Crew's place, a neat and tidy space with computers lined along one wall and a large weight rack on the opposite wall, with a mural of the forest painted behind it. Then she saw Jaggar and she gasped. He paced in the middle of the room, an electronic tablet in hand, not looking at them.

He was completely naked.

"Jaggar! Get some clothes on!" Trevor roared, backing up into the hall and fumbling with the door, trying to pull it closed, dropping Ella's hand to do it. Ella covered her mouth and tried not to giggle, looking at the ground.

Trevor finally got the door closed and turned to her. "Fuck, I forgot he did that."

Ella couldn't stop the smile from spreading across her face. "Did what? I didn't see anything."

Trevor shook his head. "Walked around naked. He says it helps him think. The first time I caught him in a debriefing naked, sitting in a leather chair with one leg thrown over the arm, I lost it."

Ella couldn't help the giggles then. They streamed out of her in a liquid rush. "Where does he keep his gun?"

Trevor grinned. "I'm trying to save the world with a bunch of misfits working for me," he muttered, but Ella thought she heard affection in his voice. He faced Ella. "I shoulda told you about him, anyway. He's our code-breaker, and, ah, did you see his face?"

Ella shook her head.

"Don't stare, whatever you do. He doesn't like that. He's half-*felen*, half-*wolven*, and he looks different."

Ella stared at the door as if it would open and Jaggar would appear. "How is that even possible?"

Trevor shook his head. "No one thought it was. He's the only one there's ever been, as far as I know, and before you ask, no one's ever seen him shift, he won't even say if he can. But both his parents were big deals, his mom had Wade's job before she died. Plus, he's wicked smart about Khain. He's earned his position."

Before Ella could respond, the door flew open, and there stood Jaggar in camouflage pants and an olive-green shirt, his eyes on Ella's feet. "Sorry, I didn't know you had your female with you."

Trevor stared at him. "Even if I didn't, nobody needs to see you airing out your balls. Put some pants on before you answer the door."

"Whatever you say, LT."

Jaggar backed into the room without looking at Ella. Trevor tried to introduce them, but Jaggar kept his head down, raising a hand to her from a few feet away, which let Ella study him. His face was hard, with lines around his mouth and between his eyes, but his hangdog expression and apparent shyness softened it. His coloring intrigued her the most, with the right half of his body lighter, and the left half darker, but no matter how she stared, she couldn't see the demarcation on his face or chest, it blended together so well.

He spoke to Trevor. "Sorry, but I don't have any more intel on the boxes from your mate's old house. Each box is in a different code. I've broken one and can confirm the contents seem to be from something Grey was working on, but he's disappeared from his position in the Chicago PD and we can't ask him about it. Top said I had to put it aside for now and work on this *foxen* thing."

As he was speaking, he looked up for just a second a few times and Ella could see that one of his eyes was much lighter than the other, but he never let her look for long enough to determine the exact colors.

"Who's Top?" she whispered to Trevor.

"Wade," he whispered back, then spoke to Jaggar. "It's cool, Jaggar. I'm here about the *foxen* thing. Tell me everything."

Jaggar nodded, still looking at the floor, then turned away from them to walk to his desk. "You've heard the video?"

"Yeah."

"I've analyzed it. Want to hear what it really says?"

Ella remembered that video, the one where all the words ran together and didn't seem to make any sense.

"Tell me," Trevor said.

Jaggar picked up a piece of paper from his desk. He cleared his throat and began to read slowly, like reading out loud was not something he did often or well. He broke for so long between each paragraph that Ella could almost visualize them as stanzas, or verses.

Oh hear me, thy cunning and crimson

The angel has spoken, and his words fall on the side of our father

Claimed are those who witness and follow and heed the

call of the new world. For when the Vahiy *has come, it is us who will rule*

I am Boeson, sending this to the seven corners of the earth, calling all faithful seven times, until the seven nights of Vahiy *fall upon us*

Our father, The Destroyer, the Vanquisher, the Demon, and the Great Matchitehew, *he who will bring the glory to us*

And lead us into righteousness and power

These lands will be ours to reign over as lords and our females will be restored to us. Our progeny will flood the soil

"I am the Vanquisher of the unworthy," says our Father, the strongest of all beings. "Follow me, and your future is certain."

I, Boeson, your pack mate, share your disquiet at having been misjudged, mistrusted, and mistreated by those who think they are better

I have been called to spread the word as the Destroyer's trumpet. I did behold a vision straight from The Light, *who proclaimed he would restore our father to his rightful place when the world had been cleansed and readied*

The voice of The Light *spoke to me over seven nights, clear and strong, proclaiming how we will prove the progeny of the* deae *unworthy*

He told me I must record his words, must spread them, and that all believers will enjoy the Ula *forevermore, when it has been wiped clean of the ungrateful and the unworthy*

We, the crimson, the cunning, the quick, and the children of the chosen shall usurp them

The coming of the 777 secret signs will signify our father has risen up and is prepared to vanquish the deae *forever*

The greatest being showed me how this will happen. He showed me a vision of the new world, and how our father will beget it to us

Ella's stomach twisted and a lump formed in her throat. Could she be interpreting what she was hearing right?

Jaggar stopped and looked up at Trevor for a second, then dropped his eyes again. "It goes on like this for a bit longer, but it's all the same and doesn't say anything new. He starts reciting the 777 signs, but only gets a few of them out and then he does a little hiccup and starts over at *hear me, thy cunning and crimson*. I think he's batshit crazy, but there's a lot of ways this message could blow up in our face if it gets out."

Trevor shook his head. "Wade just said it went viral."

Jaggar finally stared right at him, his eyes blazing. One was light blue and the other a deep chocolate brown. "Oh boy, the *foxen* are going to lose their shit. This is bad."

Trevor nodded. "You think there's any truth to it? Like Khain can really bring about the *Vahiy* by making all of these 777 signs happen?"

Jaggar nodded, then shook his head. "The ones I heard have already happened. Example. Eradication of the great lizards who walked the earth, and two wars in which every country in the world took part. I've got Sebastian trying to figure out if Khain could have had a hand in either of them. I need to hear all of the 777 signs to give you my opinion on the truth or falsity of the rest of it."

Trevor grunted. "We need to get our hands on that *foxen*."

"Yeah, before Khain does. We have no way of knowing if he's aware of the signs, or if he can accelerate them. Plus, if we don't know what the signs are, we don't know if there's any way for us to stop them."

Trevor stared straight ahead for a long time, and Ella leaned into him, scared for him, for their future. She dropped a hand to her belly and rubbed it softly.

Trevor's phone buzzed. Ella read the text over his shoulder.

We need you and your crew. Command post at Elm and Locust.

He nodded at Jaggar. "What's your next action?"

"Sebastian and I are scouring the prophecies, trying to find any other mention of the signs, while we wait for someone to find Boeson. We also have several *citlali* sitting in repose, seeking answers."

"Good. Contact me at once if you find anything."

Jaggar nodded, making sneaky eye contact with Ella for the first time, then snapping his gaze back to Trevor. "Oorah, LT."

"Oorah," Trevor parroted, then pulled Ella out into the hall, his face grim.

Only when the door closed behind him and they headed back out of the tunnel, did she feel she could ask him, even though she probably knew the answer already. "What is the *Vahiy*?"

"The end of the world," he said, his voice and expression tight. "Or, to be more exact, the Death of Rhen, which is supposed to trigger the end of the world as it is now."

CHAPTER 25

*H*eather lifted her face to the rising sun, her heart soaring, her dragon's hand in her own as they walked slowly toward his cabin. Or rather, Graeme's hand in her own. Idly, she wondered about the time difference, as the night had seemed short. She felt wide awake though, and ready for whatever was coming. Her entire body thrummed in time with her heart, which had eyes only for Graeme. Whatever he wanted, she would give herself to him fully.

She'd never had a man. Never been interested before, not like she was in Graeme. She wondered if he knew she was a virgin. They'd never discussed it, but could he tell? There was so little that she knew about him, but none of it seemed important until they took care of this one little detail…

In a few short moments, they were back at his place. She was surprised to see the door to the stairway that wound down to his underground treasure was gone again. Disappeared. Did that mean it was shut? She put it out of her mind, focusing instead on the tall, broad man next to her and what she anticipated they were on their way to. Her heart beat hard and her being soared, her shoes barely touching the ground. She cared what happened later, but she couldn't control it. All she could do was open herself fully to this experience, here, now.

He preceded her into the cottage, then walked to a cabinet set into the wall and retrieved some sort of a sleeping roll, or mat, unrolling it on his stone couch in front of the fireplace.

"Would you like a fire?" he asked, and she sensed a distance between them that hadn't been there in the woods. He was manufacturing it, creating it, she knew that. What she didn't know was why.

She went to him, pressing her body into his, looking up into his face, trying her best to erase that distance. Before, she'd thought she was too young for him, but maybe that wasn't it at all. Maybe she was too human for him. But why would he have brought her out here if that was the case? Her heart tried to whisper to her that if he was protecting himself, she should protect herself, but she ignored it completely. This was what she wanted. Exactly this, in the stone cottage on the top of the mountain with the man who was also a dragon.

She wouldn't leave him any room for wondering what she was looking for. "I want you."

He stared into her eyes for a long time before inclining his head and kissing her. *Yes.* She ran her fingers over his chest, feeling heated contrails follow her hands. Everywhere she touched, his skin heated. Up his pectorals, tracing his shoulders, down to his elbows, that fire followed as surely as gunpowder followed the barrel with the hole in it on the cartoons she used to watch on Saturday mornings.

Emboldened by his body's response to her, she swirled her hands down his torso until she reached his belly, but before she could go lower, he caught her hands again. She groaned in frustration, but he moved both hands behind her back and held them there with just his left hand, freeing his right to move up to her hair, to catch it and pull on it slightly as he deepened his kiss. Her groan shifted from frustration to a yielding passion. Yes, yes, yes! She couldn't get enough of his gentle domination and the way it made her forget everything but the feel of his lips on hers.

He laid her down then, repeating his acts in the forest until she felt like a goddess being worshiped as a ritual act. The reflection jerked her back to reality. She thought she'd closed the emotional distance between them, but had she been wrong?

But when Graeme's hot mouth found its way to her softest skin again, she forgot the question or even that there had been a question. She forgot everything, save for the sweet wave of sensation that erased all worry from her mind, leaving her naked and panting in the dragon's den.

***

Heather opened her eyes slowly, her body feeling groggy, her mind slow. Had she napped? She looked around in the small cottage and didn't see Graeme anywhere. A fire burned low in the fireplace and the light from the window looked different, as if the entire day had passed.

She held the soft blue blanket that had been laid over her to her chest as she swung her legs to the floor and sat up.

Graeme was not in the room. But she could feel him. He was outside, not far away.

Bending to gather her clothes, her temper began to flare slightly. Had he done something to her to get her to fall asleep? She hadn't wanted to sleep, but rather had wanted him to take her. Hadn't he known that?

She shook her head, trying to remember exactly when she had fallen asleep. It didn't matter, anyway.

Once she'd pulled on her last boot, she hurried outside, finding Graeme a few feet from the cabin, no shirt still, apparently about to head inside. In his hands, he held a clay pitcher and a small red container.

He smiled broadly, but there was something guarded in it. "Ah, leannan, how did you sleep?"

She scowled at him. "I didn't want to sleep. Did you put me to sleep somehow?"

His smiled turned mischievous. "If you mean did I do something besides relax you with what looked to be a very satisfying orgasm—make that two orgasms—then no, I did not."

He passed her, that grin still on his face. Heather's slight anger leaked away and she turned to follow him into the cottage. Inside, he placed the pitcher on the table and held out a glass for her. "Fresh water from the purest stream on the planet."

The second Heather had the glass to her lips, she realized how thirsty she had been. She drank two glasses, her stomach clanging loudly for food, too.

Graeme lifted the lid off the red container and a lovely smell filled the room. She peeked in. Roasted... something. Maybe a rabbit? She'd never eaten an animal straight out of the forest before.

Graeme reached in, tore a bit of the meat off a bone, and put it in his mouth, his expression amused. She watched him, then tried it herself. *Divine!*

"Mmm, yum. It's so good. How did you cook—" She cut herself off from asking the stupidest question in the world. "Never mind," she mumbled, then shoved more meat in her mouth.

Graeme chuckled and held out his hands. "It's all for you, leannan."

She scowled at him again. "That word, what does it mean?"

"It's a Scottish word for sweetheart."

"Oh." She lifted her shoulders a bit. That was ok, then. The rest of the rabbit, or whatever it was, disappeared quickly. Graeme found her a towel to wipe her hands and she did, then looked around the room again. *Crud.*

"Ah, Graeme, I, ah, need, ah…"

He smiled and looked out the window. "I'm afraid the forest is the only loo I have."

Great. "Ok. You stay here, all right?"

He smiled again. "You sure you don't want me along to protect you?"

He was teasing her now and she grew hot as the word crossed her mind. She'd show him what teasing was. "Just because I can't turn into a big scary dragon doesn't mean I can't take care of myself."

"I don't doubt it."

She stared at him for a moment. He was so handsome her fingers itched to touch him. After. "I don't suppose you have any toilet paper."

His smile didn't change. "Sorry."

She frowned, then grabbed the towel and the pitcher of

water and took off out the door. She wandered a few feet into the forest and did her business, then cleaned up as best she could.

She took a deep breath, looking around, wondering if anyone actually lived like this anymore. Could she do it? Fetch water from a stream? Kill or grow all her food? Nothing to do but take care of your property, maybe knit in the evenings and make love when the nights grew long?

Which reminded her… She marched back into the cottage and found Graeme putting away the mat he had laid on the couch before her nap. She met him at the cabinet and waited for him to stand straight, then put her hands around his still-bare waist, snuggling into him.

His eyes darkened. "I brought you out here to tell you something, Heather. Something that's going to change your life forever."

"Is that all you brought me out here for?" she asked, trying to inject a bit of sexiness into her voice and feeling like a fool, instead. But when she felt his skin heat up, the feeling turned triumphant. She ran her fingers around his pecs again, looking for the heat contrails that had fascinated her earlier. Outside the window, darkness crept over the forest an inch at a time. Good, they would make love all night in front of the fire. It would be more romantic than any book or movie every created. She ran her fingers lower, wanting to feel the core of him.

He caught her hands and she cried out, irritation heavy in her voice. She stepped back so he couldn't distract her again with kisses. "Graeme, why won't you let me touch you?"

He stared at her for a long time, his head lowered, his expression guarded again. When he spoke, she didn't know what to make of it. "I'm afraid that will never happen. When a dragon ejaculates, it is the temperature and consistency of lava."

She frowned. "But you're a man. I won't be touching the dragon."

He took a deep breath and looked over her head, then back at her. "This is part of what I needed to tell you. When I say dragon, I am not saying d-r-a-g-o-n. I am a *dragen*, spelled d-r-a-g-e-n. I am not a dragon in my dragon form and a human in my human form, but rather a hybrid of both in both forms. When I ejaculate as a man, it is molten. It will kill you."

Heather gasped and stared at him, feeling very small. "I-I don't have to touch it."

He shook his head. "Never would I take that chance. I would die if I burnt you."

Heather's eyes widened. He didn't know! "Wait!" She ran to the fireplace and reached her hand in, as he shouted behind her. She pulled out a burning log and held it in her hands like an offering. "I can't be burnt, Graeme, I never have been burnt in my life."

He had been running for her, but he stopped when she turned, staring for a long time at the log in her hands. Finally, he took it from her and put it back in the fireplace, then returned to her, taking first one hand in his to inspect it, then the other. When he was done, her hands were as clean as the rest of her. She looked at his hands, trying to find the soot and ash, but his were clean, too.

He stared into her eyes but his expression hadn't changed. "I expected that to some degree, but it was still a shock. Forgive me for not believing it until I saw it fully. But I still won't take the chance. What if he made a mistake?"

Heather shook her head, her hair flying, feeling like

she was dreaming again for the first time in several hours. "Who?"

"The angel who made you for me. Your father."

The what now? Heather felt her knees go soft.

Graeme was there to catch her.

CHAPTER 26

Graeme took a deep breath. Where to begin? She was strong enough to hear it all, he knew that. He'd brought her out to his home because he had needed time to decide how to break it to her, but since she'd been there, he had been the one on an expedition of discovery. He hadn't known a female like her since his mother.

He would start with the obvious. "There's a lot about your world that you don't understand. That knowledge has been withheld from humans forever. Being who and what you are, though, I'm sure you have sensed something."

He stopped, then helped her over to the couch to sit, as she still looked a little shaky. She nodded gratefully and waited for him to continue, no sign of disbelief on her face.

He paced around the room a bit. "The creation stories of humans all dance around the reality, but none of them hit it quite right." He stopped to look straight at her. "You are most familiar with the religion of Christianity, is that correct?"

Heather nodded, but still didn't speak.

He bent into his story in earnest, trying to keep a balance between history and the present, fearing it was a *dragen* history he told, and she would need to hear it again from a *wolfen* in order to get all the pertinent bits and pieces. As he spoke, he saw the burning words she said she had written. *You are not the last dragon.* That would have to be addressed, dealt with. *Confirmed. Dragen* were not good beings, as a rule. They tended toward evil, toward killing for fun. If there was another *dragen* somewhere, hiding out, as he had hid out for centuries, he would have to be the judge, jury, and possibly executioner, if it came to that.

She interrupted him by holding up her hand, some life coming into her expression. "Wait, how old are you?"

"I am nine hundred and thirty-six years old."

Her face fell and her mouth dropped open. "These other beings fighting the demon, *shiften* you called them, are they all that old? Have I met any of them?"

"They are not. *Shiften* live much shorter lives than *dragen.* Aye, you have met a few. All of the police officers in Serenity are *shiften.*"

She stood and began to circle the room, a wider, more aggressive circle than he had made. "So that's why you didn't get in trouble for assaulting them. That's why cops always stick together no matter what. That's why…" She turned to him, her face open, wondering. "Wait, why did you grab those two guys, er, *shiften*, by the throats? What in the hell was up with that?"

Graeme looked out the window, not surprised she would ask that question, but not wanting to answer it. It would make what he was trying to do so much harder if she knew he felt a biological imperative to claim her as his own. She might even decide, if she could just get him to take her once, and she lived through it, he would give in to everything that came along with that. Worse, she was probably right. He stood tall and headed for the door. It would not happen. He had more years disciplining his body and mind than she had been alive for.

"Follow me," he said. "I need to show you something."

She cut through the room and exited right behind him without question. Once outside, he transformed.

Climb on.

Heather did and Graeme hoped he had successfully distracted her from that damning question. He leaped into the air, unfurled his wings, and began the short trip he hadn't made for over six hundred years.

***

Heather's brain boiled as her dragon flew them over the forest in the waning twilight, the moon high in the sky at their backs. On some level, she'd known the second she'd first seen Graeme, lying in that hospital bed, that her life would never, ever be the same, but could she so easily accept all of this talk of demons and protectors of humans and angel fathers?

She wasn't rejecting any of it yet. Was it the only explanation that let any of this make sense? She'd given up the notion that she could be dreaming hours ago, and here she was, riding on the back of a dragon again.

Even with all the talk of the demon and the danger to humans and this epic, ages-old fight, still, all she could care about was her dragon and how he felt about her and if he ever would make love to her. *Molten semen.* Those had been his exact words. Talk about a hot date! Her mind spun over the fact, not able to let it go. Was she really willing to try to have sex with a man—not a man, a *dragon*—who could burn her from the inside out?

But did she believe that? It made perfect sense that, if she had been created for him, if they were meant to be together on some cosmic level that resonated so strongly inside her she almost *had* to believe it, then she could handle the lava jizz. She laughed to herself. Lava jizz. Immaculate ejaculate. Boiling hot man chowder with a side of hot sauce. Man Chili. Spicy salty surprise. She giggled hard and had to curl her fingers around the base of his wings to keep from sliding to the left.

She felt his attention turn toward her as he asked a big question in her mind. *What's so funny?*

His sense of humor was much more refined than what she'd been thinking, but she still couldn't' stop herself. *So, your nut butter comes toasted, then?*

He didn't say anything for a moment, and she buried her face in his back, heat flushing up her cheeks. He thought she was childish. Of course, he did, he was more than nine hundred years older than her!

But then he laughed, a sweet chuckle that hurt her heart it was so sexy and so him.

He angled down slightly and she knew they were almost to the end of their journey. She took a quick look around, not wanting to miss one second of the flying because she'd been ruminating. She would think on it more, but if she had to answer yes or no right that second, she knew her answer would be yes, she was willing to bet her life that she could handle it.

She wouldn't be there, on the back of the dragon, head over heels in love with him, if she couldn't handle sex with him.

Heather's fingers loosened as she stared at the back of her dragon's head, her body going lax. In love with…?

Their angle dipped hard and she slid to the left, then screamed and tried to find a handhold. Graeme shifted and dropped straight down a few feet, getting under her easily, giving her time to hold on again.

He didn't ask why she had almost fallen and she didn't tell. She wished fiercely it didn't have to be so complicated. That they could have a normal courtship and a normal coming together. But it was not to be. What she got instead was something far more interesting and more satisfying, she was sure, if she could ever get him to put aside his fears and go for it.

Graeme flew toward a small clearing, then dropped lightly into it. Heather looked around from his back, not wanting to climb off just yet. She liked how powerful she felt from the higher vantage point, like nothing could ever harm her. Maybe that had something to do with the two-ton scaly beast between her legs.

Her dragon stood stock still and stared into the center of the clearing, his mood somber. Heather slid down and looked where he was looking, but there was nothing there. Or was there? Her eyes narrowed as she realized this clearing looked suspiciously like the one they had just left.

She focused her thoughts into a stream and imagined Graeme's little cottage right where they both were looking. She felt something happening, a shimmering of the air, a converging of energies.

It appeared. A cottage like Graeme's in some ways, but so different it startled her. She jumped backwards and ran into her dragon.

She turned to him, wondering if he was going to transform or not. "Did you make it appear?"

No, leannan, that was all you.

She nodded and studied it. The cottage itself looked proud, if a building could look that way, even in its state of disrepair. The beams for the roof shot straight up into the sky, scooping in a way that wasn't practical and she knew was all for show. No sort of roof covered it though, it had been destroyed by the weather years and years ago. The windows and doors of the place had likewise worn away a long time before, but the beams and walls of the cottage itself held. It was bigger than Graeme's, and something about it set Heather's teeth on edge. Her eyes ran over the corners of the building until she realized what it was that bothered her. Gleaming white bones lined the eaves of the house. She gasped and walked to her left to see the walls she couldn't see from her vantage point and, as she approached the back of the house, she found more bones, a pile of them. Heather shuddered, knowing what she would find before she did. Human skulls visible in the pile here and there, the empty eye sockets and toothy stares unnerving her. She ran back to her dragon and pushed close to him.

"What are we doing here?" she asked.

He didn't answer, only stared, and she tried to catch his feelings, which she thought she could, at least a bit. Sadness. Bitterness. Loneliness. Regret.

He peered into the trees, then back. *What does this place feel like to you?*

She chose her words carefully, as they seemed to mean something important to her dragon. "Bad. Like there's been a lot of suffering here."

Aye, it's in the ground and air here, even after all these years. This was the home of my oldest brother, Keir. He killed our mother and brother on this very spot we are standing on.

Heather shuddered. Her dragon's voice in her head held a note of melancholy that made her heart ache.

In her pocket, her phone began to ring. She reached in and silenced it, glad for the pull back into the present, but not wanting to talk to anyone. She looked around, surprised she even got a signal at the top of the mountain.

My brother Keir was ten years older than I was. He and Kendric were doublets, but Keir was the one everyone noticed. The one I idolized.

"Do you mean twins?"

Aye, twins. They looked the same, but in personality they were as different as night and day. Kendric was not very smart. He was a bit of a follower and relied on Keir to do his thinking for him. Keir was strong, commanding, a natural leader. He could get anyone to do anything, and if they didn't do what he wanted, he massacred them. Under Keir's tutelage, I unleashed my share of carnage upon the people of this land and other lands we traveled to in search of gold, fine food, and women.

His voice dropped on the last word and Heather felt her heart seize up. What was he telling her? Would her barely-acknowledged love for him survive this story?

Kendric and I traveled with Keir on his missions. I sometimes helped with the conquests, only because he wanted me to, not because he needed my help. As an adult, I learned that dragonslayers were mostly a myth. No knight could fight us in dragon form. We were too powerful. The only beings that even tried to stop our destruction and save the humans from us was the shiften. *It's been so long since most of them have seen a* dragen *that they may not even remember we used to be mortal enemies. Most* dragen *only joined in the fight against Khain if it gained them something personally.*

Inside her head, Heather heard the pain in her dragon's voice. She maneuvered herself so she faced him directly and lifted a hand to his cool cheek, her heart resolute. No matter what he told her, she knew him now. He was no brute, no killer. He was the kindest, most thoughtful man she'd ever met, and the fact that he was much more than just a man didn't change that one bit.

His red and yellow dragon eyes stared at her, the colors shifting liquidly until she saw purple, then more shifting until she saw fire again. She felt a new connection with him, making her want to open up to him. She would take on his pain if she could. Some of it, all of it, it didn't matter.

I was never a bloodthirsty dragon. I had never had it in me, even in our make-believe fights at home. Keir would always go for the throat, and so would Kendric, encouraged by Keir. I would go for a leg, or an arm, until teased and pushed to my limit by my brothers, and only then would I 'behave like a dragen', *in their eyes. It may have been my age, because I was much younger than them, or it may have been a temperament I was born with. I did not, however, begrudge my family and the others of my kind of what did seem to be natural dragon tendencies. They killed and maimed humans with no more thought than the humans themselves seemed to give to taking out those of their kind. It was a bloody, savage time, Heather, not good for women, or children, or anyone, really.*

He broke their eye contact and looked up at the sky, then back at his brother's cottage, then pulled in a deep breath and went on.

Our mother was the last female dragen, *so we all knew our time was running short. Even at our highest population, there were only three hundred or so of us, and dragen bairn were not easy to conceive, birth, or raise. Over the* millennia, *that number dwindled extensively, which might have been one reason why* dragen *felt so entitled to take what we wanted. My brothers and I never had mates. Never even had chances for mates. There were occasionally rumors of females, supposedly witches, who could withstand mating with a* dragen, *and this was one reason we traveled, bursting into a village from the sky and taking their best gold and food, killing the men and raping the women, witches or not.*

Heather gasped, making Graeme stop. He stared directly into her eyes.

You see, Heather, dragen *and humans were not meant to be together.*

She took a step backwards, shaking her head. No, she wouldn't believe it. She couldn't. The man—*dragen* she knew would never have done that. And suddenly she knew. She could hear it in the tone of his story. *He* hadn't.

"Did you ever rape anyone?"

He didn't answer for a long time and she wondered if he was going to lie. But why?

He unfurled his wings suddenly, stretching them out, lifting his neck to the sky, and then curling back in on himself. *No. I did not. But I stood by while my brothers did so to all the maidens in the village that caught their eye.*

She walked closer to him, reaching her hand up to touch his neck. "Is that why you're so scared to be with me? Have you seen many women die that way?"

He snorted hard and shook his scaly head into the sky, then calmed. *I used to hypnotize them so they wouldn't feel the pain of their death.*

Heather bit her lip, wondering at the life he had led. So

much experience and knowledge there. So much wisdom and goodness, and he didn't even know it, wouldn't acknowledge it.

"You killed Keir, didn't you?"

He transformed then, into a man. Into Graeme, his eyes intense, burning with some emotion she couldn't quite place. He grabbed her hand. "How do you know that?"

She stared at him. "You couldn't take it anymore. Even if people were killing each other, that didn't give your brother a right to do what he was doing to beings who couldn't possibly defend themselves from him. He wasn't searching for a female who could mate with him. He was destroying people for fun. That wasn't you. That was never you, even if you participated for a while out of loyalty, or just misguided youth. Eventually you couldn't take it anymore, so you killed him."

He took a deep breath, pulling the air into his lungs like he was drowning, then squeezed her hand so hard her bones rubbed together, but she didn't give an inch and kept her face carefully neutral and her energy accepting.

He opened his mouth to say something, then shut it again, then opened it, then ripped his hand out of hers and began walking in a straight line, away from the cottage. She followed, having to run to do so.

He stopped so suddenly she almost ran into his back, then turned, his expression bitter.

"I killed people, Heather. Humans. Your kind. *Shiften*, too, probably, I have no way of knowing. I did it for no good reason, none at all. No amount of wishing it wasn't true will make up for that."

This time, *she* took *his* hand, gently. She pulled it into her chest. "And how many years have you been trying to atone for that?"

He dropped his head, his hand limp in hers.

"It's not possible. I can't ever make up for it."

CHAPTER 27

*H*eather's eyes narrowed and her heart dropped. If he really believed that, most of what she'd seen of him so far was a smoke-screen, an external personality that very effectively hid the depression within. "What have you been doing since you killed your brother?"

His head hung at his chest. "I killed some other *dragen*, too. Others who were raping and killing like Keir. All of them, I thought."

Heather nodded. "Uh huh, and then what? How long ago did you kill the last *dragen* besides yourself?"

"Six hundred and fifty-two years ago." His answer came easily, like he wanted her to know this, at least.

"Ok, so you killed the last *dragen*. Then what did you do?"

His shoulders sagged, making him look smaller, less

alive. Like he had looked when she first saw him. Something dangerous seemed to coalesce around him, like electricity crackling in a lightning storm.

She pulled his hand closer and stepped into his space. If he was going to do something to himself, he would have to get through her. She reached up and took his chin in her free hand, encouraging him to look at her. "Graeme, tell me. Tell me what you did after."

His voice was dull. Dead. "I tried to kill myself."

It couldn't get much worse than that. "How?"

"I tried to drown myself in a loch. I tied a great anchor to my body and dumped myself over the side of a boat."

Heather's heart sped up as she tried to imagine the depths of her dragon's pain, but she couldn't do it. "That didn't work?" she asked gently.

His head hung lower still, but he seemed willing to talk, if not exactly eager. "*Dragen* are hard to kill. I thought drowning would do it, or at least put out my fire, which would weaken me, but apparently only taking the head clean off will do it. That's how I killed Keir and the other *dragen*."

Heather's breath shook, but she pushed on. Graeme needed to tell this and she needed to hear it. What happened between them when it was all out, she had no idea. Her phone rang again in her pocket and she pushed the button hard to silence it before she touched Graeme again. "How long did you spend under the water?"

"A hundred and two years, the first time. It's pleasant under the water. Almost like a hibernation. Everything slows down. I don't think. That's almost as good as death."

"The first time?"

"Aye. I've gone back in every time I've come out, so far.

I seem to have a built-in alarm clock that wakes me around every fifty years or so."

"So you've missed the last six hundred and fifty-two years? Don't… Can't… Isn't there anything that you want to live for these days? Can't you see the world has changed? Nobody is like they used to be. Life is not how it used to be, all hard scrabble and constant vigilance. There's comfort now. There's joy and laughter and love. Maybe you could find a good life today?"

He raised his head and stared at her and she saw that he wanted to believe, he really wanted to, but he wouldn't quite let himself. "As much as the world has changed, it's also still the same."

Heather shook her head emphatically. "That's not true! You give a person a loving upbringing and provide them with comfort and their basic needs, and they end up a good and kind being who chooses to help others."

He laughed once, a sharp, sad sound. "People, maybe. *Dragen*, no. I am still a *dragen*, leannan, no matter what you want to believe. There is no place in this world for my kind. Better to let the humans evolve as they will. They don't need *dragen*."

She bounced on the balls of her feet, trying to command his attention, unable to keep still. "Then why did you go to Serenity? Why am I here? Why did the cops there seem so willing to deal with you, to call you one of their own? The ones you weren't trying to kill even seemed to like you."

He put his hand on her shoulder and stared directly into her face. "I went to Serenity for one reason only, leannan, and you are not going to want to hear this, but you need to believe it. I went because I heard Khain, the demon, had resurfaced, and if there is one being on this planet left who can kill a *dragen*, it's Khain. I went hoping to finally finish the job. You, my sweet one, are a distraction, nothing more. Eventually, I will find my way back into the loch, or back to Khain's home." He pressed his lips against his teeth, all the blood pushing out of them and making them look white, like what he was about to say was hard for him, but he said it anyway, looking her directly in the eye while he said it. "You can take a *shiften* mate. There are thousands of strong, handsome *shiften* males out there who would sell their canines to have you notice them. You don't need me."

He stood straight and transformed, heaving a great roar as a dragon that sounded like an explosion, then leapt into the air and unfurled his wings. He waited until he was a thousand feet away before the burning began.

Heather watched him, her heart incinerated. Destroyed. She sank to the ground and stared at the dirt as tears fought to fall from her eyes, but she would not let them come.

"I don't want them," she whispered to no one. "I want you."

***

Heather didn't know how long she knelt there in the dirt as her dragon burned the forest. Her dragon? Really? He'd done everything possible to tell her he would never belong to her. Even told her to look for someone else. Her heart still seared from his final statements.

She tried to think of what to do. How to get home. Would he take her there? Why had he brought her all the way to Scotland if he had never planned on being with her?

As she knelt, crumpled on the forest leaves and needles, the hairs on the back of her neck stood up. She whipped her head around, looking behind her. She saw nothing at first, but as her eyes adjusted, a large, dark shape appeared in the forest. She stared hard at it. Was it her imagination? It was bigger than a horse but she couldn't make out any limbs or a head. She got slowly to her feet, staring, tracing the shape again and again with her eyes.

She took a step backwards, towards where Graeme had gone. The evil of the place sank into her bones, threatening to overwhelm her with sensation, with thoughts that didn't belong to her. Images of a mighty, scaly being killing a knight flitted through her mind. Remnants of some movie she watched? Or history she was absorbing through the air?

Heather took another step backwards and another, when a small snorting sound, almost derisive, came from the woods. The dark shape she'd been watching shook slightly. Her eyes widened. Oh, God, this was not good. As she watched, the shape moved again, stepping halfway into the clearing. She got a partial look at a golden shimmer down a bronze flank and big eyes over a hooked nose before she turned and ran.

GRAEME! She screamed in her mind as loud as she could, even as she tucked her elbows and her head, her feet pounding as fast as she could push them.

He was there immediately, swooping down to her, landing directly in front of her so hard the mountain shook. *What is it? What is wrong?*

"There, there," she screamed, running into the protection of his scaly chest and pointing behind her. She looked, but nothing was there. The weight of a stone dropped in her middle. Had she imagined it? "I—I thought I saw something there."

Graeme spewed fire where she was pointing, a massive stream that lit up the cottage, the clearing, the woods, everything. She saw nothing. Certainly, no shape. She hated looking like a fool more than anything, but that's where this was heading.

What was it? What did it look like?

"I don't know. It was big. Like, like a horse or a monster bear, maybe."

There are no bears in these woods.

"Oh."

Her face heated, but she knew she hadn't imagined it. She could still feel it watching her, whatever it was. Her phone rang in her pocket again and she pulled it out and swiped it, glad for once at the interruption. "Hello?"

"Is this Heather Herrin?" A male voice, official-sounding. "Yes."

"Are you in the company of Graeme Kynock?"

She shifted her eyes from the forest to Graeme, wondering who could possibly know that. Then she realized. The police. Oh, crud, what if they had called her mother to get her phone number? Even as she thought it, her heart hardened. Who cared what her mother thought. She was never going to speak to her mother again.

"Yes, he's here," she said and held out the phone to the dragon.

He transformed and didn't look at her, but took the phone delicately from her fingers, holding it to his head like he'd never done it before.

"Aye."

He listened and Heather stood close to him, not quite daring to touch him, but knowing she was safe in the circle of his protection, no matter what had been in the woods. She could hear the male voice on the phone speaking to him, but couldn't tell what he was saying. She let her mind wander, the part of her that never, ever said die, wondering if there was still some way she could get Graeme to change his mind, to realize that she could change everything for him.

"Aye," he said again. "It will take me twenty minutes to get there. Is it safe to bring the woman with me?"

Heather's mouth dried up. *The woman?* He wouldn't even say her name? And how were they going to get to Serenity in twenty minutes? Their flight here had taken longer than that just to get to the Atlantic Ocean.

He handed the phone back to her without saying goodbye. She looked at it, hearing the man on the other end still talking. Oh, well. She pressed the red end-call button and stared at Graeme, even though he would not look at her.

"Our time here is done. The *shiften* have an emergency they need my help with. I will return you to your home, but you'll need a *shiften* guard, so I'll ask you to go with me to them until they can arrange that."

Heather barely heard his words. All she could focus on was his tone and his coldness. He'd taken himself a thousand miles away from her in his heart. She lifted her eyes to the heavens, to the starry skies above her and said a prayer for help, for knowledge, for guidance. This couldn't be it. This couldn't be the way they ended.

The ping. The circular ping that she'd heard before from below his cottage. It started up again, insistently this time. She didn't know if it was an answer to her prayer, but she grabbed onto it with both hands.

"Graeme, there is something… that thing at your place. I never found it down in your treasure room. I think it wants me to find it."

He finally looked at her then, but his eyes were empty.

"Aye, you can have it, I will never use it. But it will not get what it wants."

"What it wants?"

By way of answer, he transformed and faced away from her, towards the moon, the way they would be going. She climbed on his back, feeling the weight of all his beliefs, enough to crush them both.

The trip back took only a few minutes, and she did not watch the moon or the stars because she could not stand to see their beauty.

When he landed, she climbed down and focused on the door to the rear of his cabin. It appeared, closed somehow. She walked toward it slowly, not wanting to make the trip down into the treasure room herself and convinced he would not go with her. But he stepped past her as a man and heaved on the door pull, then found the lantern and lit it, preceding her down at a quick pace.

They reached the bottom and she went about her business quickly, searching by feel. Near the back of the large room, next to the pile of mixed gold, silver, and gems, there was a stand that had one hook at the top of a tall spire. On the spire was the circlet of gold that had been calling to her. She lifted it gently. It was not what she expected and she wasn't sure what it was. The circlet was unbroken, unmarred, unscratched, like it couldn't really be gold. It was bigger than a crown, slightly larger around than a dinner plate, a fancy one. She put her hand through the open middle of the circlet, not sure what she was expecting, but gratified to hear a sweet, melodious tune erupt from it when she did so. Or was it only in her head?

"It's time," Graeme called from the other side of the room.

She tucked the gold circlet into her coat, surprised when

it seemed like it would fit in her pocket that she knew was not that big. Magic? She pushed it in the pocket it could not possibly fit in, then wound her way through the stacks and piles of wealth like some nations didn't own and met him at the bottom of the stairs.

In only a few moments, they were at the top again, with not a word passed between them.

She let her eyes wander over the forest and the cottage, wondering if she would ever see Graeme's home again.

CHAPTER 28

$\mathcal{T}$revor looked around the old, unused barn they had commandeered to use as a command post from the only farmer on the edge of Blue River Bluff. Trevor had given him and his family some cash and told them they had to clear out. Spend the night at a hotel or a friend's place. The official story had been a natural gas leak, but one look in the farmer's eyes as he saw the SWAT vehicles and scads of armed officers roll into his driveway had told Trevor the old man had not believed a word of it. Who knew what he thought was really going on, alien landing maybe.

He wished Graeme would hurry up. Unless the *bearen* thought of a better plan, nothing could happen until he arrived. Trevor's eyes rolled over his crew, who were jumping out of their skins. Some forward progress had to happen soon or there would be issues.

Harlan and Beckett were near the door, Harlan cleaning

blood off his hands and Beckett pacing and touching his chest and shoulder compulsively. Mac was with Wade at the map table, eyes alternating from the terrain map of the property directly to their north, to the cameras they had set up along the edge of the red zone. Trent and Troy were outside, functioning as guards, but ready to go at a moment's notice. They were both as amped up as the rest of them. A few *felen* played dice in the hay loft and the lone *bearen* that had been part of Ella's guard when this call had come in was in the corner behind the front door. He'd been functioning as a liaison between Trevor and the fire department but there hadn't been much for him to do yet. He'd taken one look at the spouts of fire streaming into the air on the edge of the property and declared any machinery that was going to fight that would have to be brought in from Chicago. That was plan B, if Graeme couldn't go through it. They had dozens more officers on the perimeter of the northern property, all waiting to hear the word *Go*.

He ran over everything they knew about the situation again in his mind, looking for holes, for something they had missed that would help them. The *foxen* had been rallying for weeks. Somehow, they had seen the video of Boeson long before one of them had decided to send a copy of it to the police. The *foxen* were divided firmly into two camps; those who thought the video was an affront to their basic *shiften* nature and who would never dream of following Khain, and those who stood behind it 100% and thought it was a war cry. Canyon and Timber, the KSRT's computer network experts and social media gurus, said there was a smaller, third camp who paid absolutely no attention to *shiften* business and lived entirely in the human world. Some of them didn't even know they were *foxen*.

A few days before, a vocal minority had started demanding one true mates, and that's when the plans for this debacle had apparently started cooking, although Mac insisted the two ringleaders were just using it as an excuse and had to have been planning something big for a while. Trevor agreed with him. There had been too much preparation into what they were facing for it to have been a spur of the moment thing.

Two *foxen*, both known criminals, had gathered the vocal minority, whipped them up into a frenzy, and convinced them to make a public statement at a local community college. They'd all loaded onto a bus and headed out there, but once the *foxen* had rallied support at the college, including a group of what seemed to be twenty human females, the two ringleaders had pulled out guns and ordered everybody back onto the bus and driven them out to the property Trevor was now staring at. Then the real demands had come in. Not one true mates, but ransom money from the families. They were threatening to start shooting women at random at noon tomorrow if every penny of the money didn't show up.

Trevor shook his head. Just the fact that they had given them over a day to gather the money meant they were completely confident in their ability to defend their position. They were in an underground bunker that had automatic guns on a tower above it, and three of the four sides were protected by the spouts of fire fueled by an underground natural gas reservoir they had somehow cut off from the gas company. So the gas company couldn't shut anything off. The pipes and the fire system must have taken them months to build. Trevor stared at the screens that showed the fires, their burning reminding him of Khain's home in the *Pravus*.

He rubbed his temples and wished again for Graeme to

hurry, then looked around. He spotted Ella in the corner of the barn, sitting in a folding chair, sipping coffee and looking at her phone. He approached her and sat down next to her, nuzzling into her shoulder. "I wish you would nap, El. The young need you strong."

She gave him a look. "Could you nap if you were me?"

He shrugged. "There's nothing going on right now."

"For a few moments."

As if accentuating her words, Mac swore from the map table and pounded on it. Trevor kissed Ella on the cheek and strode over.

Mac swore again. "I never thought any *foxen* would have the balls to pull something like this off, even these two!"

"It's a brave new world," Wade mused, looking at one of the screens. "That video and its message got them pretty riled up."

Trevor held up a hand to Mac and addressed him quietly. "Have you ever arrested these two *foxen*, personally?"

"Hell, yeah, I used to get them all the time for stupid shit like human-baiting or vandalism. You know, small-time stuff. Nothing like this."

Trevor knew what human-baiting was, a sick sport certain nasty *foxen* enjoyed that almost never went further than humiliation and assault. The *wolven* went after human-baiting like hate crimes, as aggressively as possible.

"Do you know anything about them that can help us? Anything personal? Any weaknesses?"

Mac thought for a few moments, pacing as he did so, then came back to Trevor. "Nothing I haven't already told you."

Trevor nodded. "Ok."

Mac looked at the screens again. "Too bad Harlan's one true mate isn't here. She could get past that fire."

Wade's head whipped up. "What?"

Harlan strode their way, his energy hostile. "What the fuck, Mac. She's not my one true mate."

Wade held up a hand, his eyes jumping from male to male. "Who? What are we talking about here?"

Mac scoffed, ignoring Harlan completely. "Harlan's one true mate. She's a ghost or some shit. We saw her a few days ago at Trevor's place. She appeared out of thin air, said his name, then disappeared again."

Wade addressed Harlan, who was shaking his head, his eyes shooting daggers at Mac. "Harlan, if she's not a one true mate, who is she?"

"I have no idea."

"How does she know your name?"

"She's appeared like that before. Always wearing that same outfit, like a hospital gown, and I can always see the same white hallway behind her. We talked a couple of times. I told her my name."

Wade turned his head to look at him almost sideways. "Appeared when before?"

"When I was eight or nine, again at thirteen, and then once last year, right before Christmas."

Mac shook his head. "See, she's gotta be a ghost, Wade. She was no older than twenty-five, for sure. Old Man River here is pushing ninety, at least. How could she have shown up when he was a kid?"

Harlan growled and Trevor turned away before anyone could see he was laughing. Fucking Mac. At close to fifty, Harlan was their oldest member, but ninety was insulting, and of course Mac knew that.

Wade held up his hand and raised his voice. "Everybody listen up! New rule! Tell every single *shiften* you know.

From now on, anybody in Serenity even gets a whiff of a female who could be a one true mate, I want to hear about it. Immediately. Got that?"

"Yes, Chief," Trevor said, hearing the *bearen* and the *felen* mumble in the affirmative behind him. Beckett said yes, still pacing, his energy topped off. Harlan nodded. Ella was silent.

"Ya vul, mein capitan!" Mac shouted and stood at attention. Wade shook his head and Trevor waited to see if Mac was gonna get it. Mac was in rare form tonight, on edge like the rest of them, but Mac being Mac, it was worse. He was gonna get something before the sun came up.

Wade went back to the screens, looked at his watch, then stared out the windows. They were all getting antsy, waiting for Graeme to show up so they could move on the situation. The longer they waited, the greater chance everything had of going to shit, and if he didn't get there before sunup, they might have lost their chance until the next day.

Trevor wandered over to the windows that lined the front of the building and stared out into the night. He could see the faint glow from the wall of fire the *foxen* had created, blocking their ability to sneak up to the property, forcing them to only enter from the front. Beckett had already been shot trying to go in under the cover of darkness. Trevor didn't know enough about *foxen* to know how their night vision was, but it didn't matter, did it? Not when night vision goggles existed. Mac and Harlan had acted quickly, pulling Beckett back behind cover, then Harlan had gone in with his fingers, pulling the slug out of Beckett's shoulder even as he screamed. Beckett had shifted, so he was as good as new, but his recent behavior said he wasn't going to forget being shot and the blunt bullet extraction afterwards for a long time.

Someone came up behind him and Trevor whirled around. It was only Mac, a grin on his face.

He lifted his chin to point at the *bearen* on the far side of the barn. "Hey, am I crazy or is that *bearen* carrying a gun under his shirt?"

Trevor looked hard and sure enough, he could see the outline of the gun and something else. "He's got handcuffs in his back pocket, too."

Mac frowned. "What the hell is that about?"

Trevor knew he was making a mistake, but he asked anyway. He was just as antsy as the rest of them and he wouldn't mind watching the show. "Think you can ask him without making an ass out of yourself?"

Mac snorted. "I doubt it," he said, and Trevor almost laughed.

Too late. Mac had already stalked across the room and had the *bearen* turned around in frisk position before Trevor could even say 'I told you so'.

Mac pulled the *bearen's* shirt up, slid the gun out of its holster, racked the slide forward, and dropped the magazine before the *bearen* even had time to say a word. "What the fuck is this?" he snarled into the *bearen's* face as he spun him back around and held the gun up.

The *bearen* didn't answer right away, and when he did speak, the tone in his voice didn't match what Trevor would have expected from him. His face didn't, either. Cool and calm is how Trevor would describe him. Like Mac didn't scare him one bit.

"That's Presley. She's my firearm."

Mac snorted. All the chatter in the large open room had stopped. "Your gun's name is Presley? And she's a girl?"

The *bearen* showed his teeth but didn't respond. Trevor

began walking that way. He didn't need this going sour, and, technically, he didn't even know if the *bearen* were allowed to carry a weapon on duty. If he had a concealed carry permit, and the fire department allowed him to carry on duty, he wasn't doing anything wrong.

Wade spoke up from across the room. "Hey, *bearen*, you got an on-duty carry permit?"

The *bearen* nodded. "Name's Bruin. And, yeah. My boss says I shoulda been a *wolfen*. Presley don't never leave my side."

"Mac, leave off him," Wade said, turning back to the screen. Trevor was close enough to see Mac's eyes narrow and hear him when he leaned in close. "What are the hand-cuffs for, huh?"

The *bearen* leaned against the wall behind him and crossed his arms. His tone stayed conversational and open, like he didn't know the words he said could get him killed. "I figure if you pups can't get the job done, somebody's gotta be the one to haul Khain in."

Trevor froze, his eyes on Mac. Calling an adult male *wolven* a pup was not a smart idea. Mac's eyes widened, then narrowed as Beckett started laughing from across the room and headed their way.

"You think you can handcuff Khain? You're a special kind of stupid, ain't you? You ever even seen Khain?" Beckett asked.

Mac laughed, too, and Trevor relaxed slightly.

Bruin faced Beckett. "No, have you?"

Beckett quit laughing and didn't respond. Mac got up in Bruin's face again. "I have. He was fifty fucking feet tall. You got handcuffs that big?"

Bruin scratched his head, and still his tone didn't change

to match Mac's hostility. "No, I guess I don't. What did he look like? Did you shoot him? Are you the wolf who went into the *Pravus*?"

Mac shook his head and looked at Trevor with a *do you got a load of this guy?* look. Trevor shrugged. *Bearen* were open and friendly, and notoriously hard to piss off, and clever if given time to figure stuff out. This guy was nothing more than a quintessential *bearen*.

Mac turned back to Bruin. "Wait a second. Your name is Bruin? Doesn't that mean Bear?"

Bruin nodded. "Yeah."

"Your parents named you Bear."

Bruin smiled and nodded harder. "Yeah, cool, right? But if you don't like it, you can call me Scorpion. That's what my friends call me."

Mac handed Bruin's gun back to him then wandered away, a look on his face like he couldn't believe what had just happened. Trevor grinned and stared back out into the night.

Any minute now.

***

Mac paced around and around the map table. That fucking bear. He got under Mac's skin like a tattoo of a tick. Thinking he could handcuff Khain. Walking around with his stupid name and his stupid gun's name and his stupider nickname. Fuck! If Graeme didn't get there soon, Mac was going to go out of his mind! *Wolven* were not meant to wait for hours and hours in a building while there were criminals a football field away holding a bus load of humans hostage.

Mac found the Rubbermaid container of food one of the

dispatchers had dropped by after it was clear they'd be there for a while. He dug through it. Spam. No. Beef Jerky. No. Chips. Fuck no. Candy. No. Wait. He turned the bag of candy back around. Gummi Bears. Ah, hell yeah.

He walked casually around the map table, eyeing Wade and Trevor, who had their heads together discussing strategy. Perfect. He strolled back over to the *bearen*, who watched him come, a welcoming smile on his face. Fucker.

He dropped a gummi bear in his mouth and chewed, then held one up between his thumb and fingers so the *bearen* could see it. He waggled his eyebrows. "Want one?"

As the *bearen* watched, he tossed the gummi bear into his mouth, then grabbed a huge handful and threw them all in there, chewing ferociously with his lips open while little gummi body parts fell out and landed on the floor.

The smile finally slipped off the *bearen*'s face. Jackpot!

"What is wrong with you?"

Mac smiled around the gummi carnage. "What?"

The *bearen* laughed. "You're one sick cheese-eater."

Mac swallowed his mass of gummi bears so he didn't choke on it. "Cheese—what?"

The goofy bastard held up his hands. "Hey, sorry, I don't know anything about wolves. Just that you're all rather bloodthirsty. Don't you like cheese?"

Mac frowned. This guy was a trip. Across the room Beckett snorted and yelled something.

"Look, Mac's got a boyfriend!"

Mac flipped him the bird, grinning. "Fuck off, cheese-eater!"

He snorted and looked around to make a joke, but the only one within joke distance was the *bearen*. Oh, well. "Monterey jackass," he muttered.

The *bearen* laughed hard and loud before he cracked his own joke. "Ah, give him a break. He's a Gouda boy."

Mac snorted, startled, then laughed and held up his hand for a high-five. Maybe Bruin wasn't so bad after all.

Now if only that inhuman torch would show up so they could get this show on the road, that'd be great.

CHAPTER 29

Graeme stood at the top of the steps as if he also were wondering about their future. He shook it off, tucked the lantern onto the top step, then closed the door. The door and the cottage disappeared. Heather felt tears threaten.

"We have to get back quickly, so I'm going to take you through another world. The transition is hard and dangerous, through a non-world that is nothing but fire, but it will only last a minute. Come, let me protect you."

Heather replayed everything he had said. Other worlds. Super awesome. More shit that made her feel like she was Alice down the rabbit hole. She narrowed her eyes. "You still don't believe I can't be burnt, do you?"

He didn't look at her. "There are many types of fire you can't possibly have encountered in your world."

Ok, then, message received. She stepped close to him. He

transformed and wrapped her into his chest with his wings tight around her. He sidestepped, and then there was a feeling of intense heat, darkness, and pressure, like it was a thousand tons of water around her instead of dragon wings. Like he said, it only lasted for a moment, and when he freed her from his wings, they were back in their world.

"That's it? We're in Serenity?"

He lifted his chin to the scene at her back and she turned around. Of course that wasn't it. The salty smell of the ocean hit her full in the face as she turned, even though they were still on the edge of what looked to her to be a Scottish forest, not that she knew one forest from another. Was it the Atlantic? Her eyes followed the sandy beach, then out onto the horizon. But no, she could see land across on some distant shore.

Climb on.

Heather did, her throat constricting at the gulf she felt between them. What if this was it? What if, once they reached Serenity, she never saw him again? She slid right down the other side, off him, holding a hand to his shoulder.

Graeme, can you at least tell me that you won't disappear? I'm scared. I don't want to lose you.

He tipped his head and spoke gently inside her mind. *Bonnie, you never had me.*

The tears started then and there was nothing she could do to hold them back. How could he deny what they'd had? What they shared? Who they were to each other?

He pawed the ground and she felt heat coalesce around them. His words in her head were harsher this time. *I never should have brought you here. I never should have kissed you or taken you in the manner I did. I'm sorry for that. I will regret that for the rest of my life.*

I'm not, she said through gritted mental teeth. *Even if you do disappear, know that I will never be sorry you brought me here. The last twenty-four hours of my life have been the most special I've ever lived. Thank you. I thank you for telling me in this manner. But please, Graeme, can we talk—*

The time for talking is done! Heather, don't make this harder than it has to be. You won't accept that I could kill you. You won't accept that I don't deserve you. But accept this. I will never bring a dragen *bairn into the world. This line dies with me. Now, get on!*

Heather bristled at the command even as she shrunk at the tone and the message. In his voice, she heard the call of a thousand kings, all equally convinced that they were right. He probably hadn't had much time to study history at the bottom of that loch and see just how often they were wrong.

She walked in front of him, locking their gazes, her expression just as proud as his. She could confess to him at that moment that she was unable to have children, and maybe stop all of this once and for all, but she would not. That would be like tricking him into her bed and she only wanted him there if he chose it. Because she wanted children someday, and if some miracle brought a baby to her, *dragen* or not, she would raise it willingly. After the last day and a half, she had to believe there was something more to her than a body that didn't do what it was supposed to and a lost love. There'd been too much magic floating around for her to think otherwise.

"You are wrong, Graeme. You can't see that because you've had too many years to think about it. But I promise you that you are making a mistake and thinking will never bring you what you want. Only action will. I don't know exactly why you say you won't bring a *dragen* into the world, whether it's because of how lonely you've been, or if you are afraid it would be like your brothers, but I'm standing before you, Heather, your fated mate who you are refusing out of nothing but sheer stubbornness, telling you that you aren't in control here. None of us are. You have to trust in the life that is brought to you and *quit hating who you are.*" She touched his nose. "I love who you are and I trust that you can love yourself again, too. You only have to let go."

Then, she returned to his side and climbed back on.

CHAPTER 30

Graeme took a moment before stepping out of the forest. He'd never been spoken to in that manner in his life. Never been challenged in such a manner. Life with that female would be… all he could come up with were words like amazing and wonderful, so he quit trying. Stubborn, he might be, but wrong he was not.

Was he?

He shook his head like a horse and set off to clear himself of the forest so he could take off. A family of beach wanderers a mile to their left took one look at him, screamed, and ran, mom and dad scooping up the littlest child and pulling on the hands of the older ones. Their archaic clothing of bonnets, full skirts, farmer's hats and pantaloons made Graeme think of his childhood.

Heather patted him on the neck. "Aren't you supposed to hide yourself, big guy?" He heard the hitch in her voice and knew her words and tone belied her true feelings. His fault. One more affront to add to his long list of grievances he could never make up for.

He could not pretend her pain did not eat at him like acid but he tried not to let her see it.

He spoke to Heather, the pull of his past still strong in his mind. *This is not my world. I dinnae care to follow its rules or conventions. I dinnae even know what they are. Mayhap they see dragons every day.*

"Wait. Are you saying there may be dragons living in other worlds? Then how can you say you are the last dragon?"

A being can only thrive in the world it is meant for. Anyone can visit for a short time, however naught but travelers can hop between worlds like visiting another city with the option of living there. I have never met a dragen *who was a traveler. It is not in our nature.*

She fell silent but Graeme could feel she was physically ready for his ascent, her body tight against his back. He leapt into the air, catching the wind, trying not to replay what she had said to him over and over in his mind.

They were across the short sea, the condensed version of the Atlantic Ocean, in only a few moments. This world was smaller than their own, so traveling took less time over its borders. In ten minutes, they would be back at the approximate location where Serenity was located, then they would sidestep back into their world. Easy.

When they arrived, he would do the one thing the *wolven* needed from him, then quietly disappear, leaving Heather safe with them.

Below them, a thriving open-air market bustled on this far shore. Heather was not looking down, but rather had her cheek pressed against his back as the fingers of her right hand ran circles over his scales.

He would miss her. Her smile. Her laugh. Learning more about who she was. Her incredible spirit. A thick yearning pushed its way into his throat, making him unable to swallow. He turned his thoughts away, to the water, to anything that would allow him to do what he had to do. What was best for all of them.

Heather shook slightly on his back and he knew she was crying. But he could not help her. She would get over him. He would never, ever get over her, but she had a full life ahead of her. She would choose a good male—

The thought made him snap at the air around him. Those thoughts were not safe either. He gnashed his teeth and stared at the sky. What could he think about? Nothing. But he'd never been good at that.

It was going to be a long century.

***

"Pull it together, girl," Heather whispered to herself. It wasn't over yet. Until he actually dropped her off somewhere and made like Houdini, it was not over. Even then, it was not over. She had some powers, she'd proved that already. Maybe she could follow him. Convince his big, dumb, stubborn ass some other way. There had to be something she could do that would open his eyes to the fact that he would suffer without her and that she would never take anyone else. That they were meant to be together and that only good things could come of their union.

She took a deep breath and sat up, looking around them for the first time. They were high up, but not so high she couldn't see the last vestiges of what probably passed for a big city in this world. Tiny huts a lot like Graeme's cottage were grouped in messy squares below them, stretching out between what looked like acres and acres of farm lands. She saw no roads, only foot paths and horse paths and a few double paths that probably allowed wagons. People dotted the landscape, all moving or working. Whenever any of them saw Graeme, they pointed and called out to their fellows, or just screamed and ran.

A forest slid beneath them and she watched the tree tops form strange patterns, until it ended at the edge of more vast farmlands.

A group of people on a path caught her eye and she watched them, thinking the energy of the small crowd looked strange. There were five uniformed men on horseback, their horses nervous, sidestepping and gigging. One man bent over his horse, his posture tense, talking to another man who stood on the path, his brown hat that reminded her of the Amish in his hands, his family behind him, a woman with three children hiding in her skirts, their faces covered.

What's going on down there? she asked Graeme.

He looked, but dismissed it quickly. *Not our business.*

Heather couldn't turn away like that. As she watched, the man who had been bent over his horse dismounted and punched the father in the stomach. He doubled over and his wife startled, pulling the children in closer to her.

Graeme, oh my God, that soldier just punched that man!

Graeme said nothing and Heather had to twist in her seat to continue watching. The punched man was on the ground and the soldier stood over him, then pulled a knife out of a sheath on his belt. The woman began to scream and plead and the children were barely visible, they were buried so far under her skirts.

Graeme, stop, turn around! We have to help them!

Nay, leannan, we do not.

Heather ran through everything she knew about Graeme. What could she say that would make him turn around? As she watched, one of the children stepped away from his mother. He was dressed in brown, with a hat just like his father's. He approached the soldier, his head high, his posture saying he would fight for his father. Was he nine? Ten?

She shifted her weight. *Turn around Graeme, I will help them, even if you won't. I swear to God, I'll jump if you don't turn around.*

You'll die, he responded, his voice dull.

So be it, she said, pulling her right leg over his back to meet her left and pushing off into the open sky. She would rather smash to a pulp on the forest floor than see that little boy get killed in front of his mother and father and not do whatever she could to help. As she plummeted through the air, her hair streaming out above her, the soldier sliced a gash up the little boy's cheek. Even from her height, she could see the blood well up immediately.

She screamed, hoping to get their attention. If the soldiers ran to find her body, maybe the family could get away.

But then her dragon was under her. *Hold on, leannan!* he cried as his angle sharpened and he screamed towards the ground. She curled her fingers around his wingmounts and held tight with her legs. Thank goodness he had come. She was not ready to be a meadow hamburger.

Before she had time for another thought, they landed on the ground next to the horses. The three closest horses, including the one the soldier had been on, reared up and ran. Heather could not tell if their riders went willingly or not.

She slid off Graeme and stepped forward on shaky feet, taking in the scene. The woman had fallen to the ground, her eyes wide on Graeme, and the two children left with her were blubbering in terror, trying to disappear against her body. They were younger than the other boy.

The man who had been punched scrambled to his feet, grabbed his boy who was bleeding from the face, and backed away from Graeme, unnoticed by the soldier, who was also staring at Graeme, mouth open, knife in his hand forgotten.

"What is going on here?" Heather cried, having no idea if they would understand her or not. She ran close to the soldier on the ground while Graeme snorted behind her and another horse whirled and ran. "Why did you hit this man?"

The soldier on the ground looked at her, his face astonished, then back at Graeme.

"Answer me!" she screamed. "Or I will have my dragon eat you."

Seriously? Graeme said in her head. *No thanks.*

Play along, she urged him. This wouldn't work without him.

The soldier licked his lips, then looked around. The last horse, with another soldier on its back, had backed away, both rider and horse looking ready to bolt any time. "H-He did not have his taxes. King Dilmer only gives one warning. That was his warning. I am only following orders."

"Ah," Heather said, her thoughts whirring. "King Dilmer. Ah. Right. You tell him that Graeme, the fierce and hungry dragon, is displeased with the way he runs his kingdom. You tell him that Graeme the fierce will visit him in his sleep if he does not change his ways. The people need compassion. The king is there to provide *for them*, not the other way around."

Graeme chuckled in her head. *Not happy with saving the family, are you? You have to save the entire world.*

Quit it! she snapped. *Do something.*

Like what?

I don't know. Chew on him.

Graeme laughed again, but stretched out his neck and opened his mouth, shooting fire just to the right of the soldier. The man screamed and turned around and ran, trying to catch the last horse and rider who were already fifty feet away, the hooves of the horse barely touching the ground, he was running so swiftly.

Heather turned her attention to the family. The man was throwing them terrified glances and trying to get his wife to stand and run. But the boy. The boy with the homemade clothes and the knife slice down his cheek. Heather's heart broke for him. His eyes were far away, looking at nothing. He didn't even try to stop the drops of blood that dripped openly onto his shirt.

She went to him, her hands open, telling Graeme to stay back in her mind. She spoke to the parents. "We aren't going to hurt you. You don't have to run. I just… can I talk to your boy?"

The father nodded slowly and watched as Heather approached him. She bent to look into the child's face. He was tall, but his soft features told her she'd been right in her assessment of his age. She tried to touch his hand. He startled and took a step backwards, his eyes haunted and rolling in his head but not finding her. "That was very brave of you, sweetheart. I know that was scary. Terrifying. But you're ok, alright. Your father is ok. Your family is ok. You can go home."

He lurched, then turned and threw up a pitiful thin stream of nothing in the weeds to his right. His mother made a sob that told Heather her heart was broken. "Caius, come away," she called, her voice shaking. He wiped his mouth and stood, but finally his eyes met with Heather's.

She smiled at him, reaching in her pockets, hoping to find a piece of candy for him, anything to make him feel better. All her fingers settled on were coins. She pulled them out. Two pennies, a nickel and a quarter. She held her hand open with the coins on her palm and smiled wider. "Here, these are money where I come from. I doubt they will help you, but you can have them if you want them."

He only stared. She glanced at the rest of the family and saw the other two children had finally emerged from under mom's skirts. Two girls with soft blonde hair and big eyes. Caius looked at the coins on her palm and made as if to reach for them. The cut on his cheek had finally stopped dripping blood.

She held perfectly still, noticing the little girls had come her way a few steps and the parents hadn't stopped them. Caius took the coins, holding them in both hands like a treasured live animal, then backed away.

Heather, Graeme called in her head. *You need to send them on their way before those soldiers come back. Send them through the grass, not on the path.*

Heather crouched in the grass, wishing she had something else to give them before she did so. She was going back to her own world, where things were different, better, softer. They would have to stay here. She wanted to see them smile, if only for a moment.

She checked her coat pockets. Gloves and her hat. She dropped them on the ground in front of her. "Here. These are for you and your sisters." Her hands flew to the inner pockets of her coat. On the left side, her fingers grazed the circlet she had taken from Graeme's treasure room. *No. You will need that.* She heeded the voice, though she did not know if it was her own or not. On the right side, something heavy dropped into her pocket as she was reaching her fingers that way. She thrust her hand after it and felt something cool and bumpy, with a chain attached.

She pulled it out by the chain and stared at it. The pendant. The pendant she remembered stealing from her mother's home, then putting into her safe at her house, how many days ago? She stared at it. The angel with the raised hands on one side, the dragon, her dragon, on the other. A fierce knowing shot through her. This would do it. If she could put this around Graeme's neck, he would realize what a mistake he had been making, see that they belonged together and he deserved to be happy. *It is not for him,* the voice whispered again. *You may see it again, but it is for the children now.*

Heather stared at it longer, then looked up as she heard someone gasp. Everyone was staring at it as it spun and twinkled in the sun on the end of the chain, the angel's yellow eyes and the dragon's purple ones catching the light.

She pressed her lips together, remembering the speech she had given Graeme about letting go. She held the pendant out to the boy. "Take it. It's yours. Take it and lead your family through the grass away from here. Go. Quickly."

CHAPTER 31

*H*eather watched the paths recede behind them and the family hurry through the grass until she couldn't see them anymore and Graeme began to descend slowly at a gentle angle.

Her brain was threatening to shut down. She didn't know how much more craziness she could take. Had she really just given away the pendant with the dragon on it?

They dropped lightly to the ground and Graeme lifted his head and turned in a circle, as if he was trying to find something.

"Are we lost?"

This spot is where the police station is in our world, but it seems empty. No one I know is left there to ask where I am to go. They told me the street names, but I dinnae ken Serenity, so where they correspond to in relation to the department is a mystery.

"What are they?"

Elm and Locust.

She slid to the ground. "Orient me."

He did, showing her the layout of the police station in front of them.

She pointed to her left. "About seven miles that way."

Graeme took a few steps in that direction, his head still up and moving strangely. At five steps, he dropped his head and tilted it to the left, looking like an overgrown, scaly dog. *Troy*, he said in her head.

"Troy?"

You'll meet him soon. A good male. Come to me.

Heather did, pretending that he meant more by those words than she knew he did. He wrapped strong leathery wings around her and stepped to the side.

Pressure. Heat. Nothingness.

Then they emerged on the other side, into a crisp Illinois night that made her smile, it felt so much like home. It confused her, though. Where they had just come from it had been daytime, with the sun overhead. No matter. She would never go to that world again.

Graeme transformed next to her, still with no shirt on. She averted her eyes from his strong, solid form. Looking would make her want to touch, and he'd already made his feelings about that clear. Their short non-fling was over, according to him.

She focused on the street next to them, instead. Elm passed directly in front of them and she saw the red and blue lights of a police blockade in both directions. Directly across from them was a side road and that's where Graeme headed.

In the ditch, a small white sign with writing on it stood, positioned so that cars driving by could read it.

Serenity is a town of LIES, it said, with a small, messy rendition of a wolf howling at a spray-painted moon in the left corner. She frowned at it.

Graeme ignored it, walking so fast she had to run to catch up, the emotional distance between them wider than ever. Ahead of them and to their left stood a driveway, with a farm house at the end of it and a large barn to one side. Graeme turned down the driveway, his boots crunching on the gravel. A black form, larger than any dog she'd ever seen, appeared from between two bushes.

Troy, she heard Graeme say in her mind. *Good to see you, old wolf.*

The wolf bared its teeth and Heather stopped walking, fear overtaking her.

But then she heard the wolf answer in her mind and she relaxed slightly. He sounded friendly enough, and happy to see Graeme.

Graeme, hell yeah, it is. They are waiting for you in the barn.

Graeme turned and motioned to her to come forward. *Heather, meet Troy, a good friend of mine and a Serenity police officer. Troy, this is Heather...* His words trailed off, like he wasn't sure what to say about her.

Heather stared. She didn't know how to greet a wolf.

The wolf smiled in her mind but didn't show her his teeth. She was quite glad about that. *Heather, so good to meet you.*

Thank you, she squeaked out, glad when Graeme took her hand and pulled her up the path and the black wolf stayed where it was.

Graeme pushed open the door to the barn and Heather looked inside nervously. There were several men in there, some she'd seen before, each bigger than the last, all with guns at their hips, some with assault rifles slung over their backs. Every head turned to them as they entered.

Her eyes flitted to each face in turn, wondering if these were all wolves. Graeme had said all the cops were *shiften*, but were they different kinds of animals?

They stepped inside and one of the males, with a hard face and glittering eyes, called out to them. She recognized his voice from the woods. "Damnit, Sparky, cover that shit up. I'm tired of looking at your dragon titties."

The men (men?) laughed and the tension was broken. Graeme pulled her inside and introduced her to each of them in turn. She tried to remember names. Mac. Trevor. Wade. Beckett. Harlan.

Mac introduced a lumberjack-looking guy at the back with a brownish-reddish beard and intense eyes. "This here's Bruin."

"Call me Scorpion," Bruin said and Mac snorted.

Heather waved politely, glad when the males in the room said hi, then seemed to go back about their business.

Graeme pointed to the exact other side of the room, his voice kind enough that she could almost believe they were together again. "That's Ella. I do believe she's your half-sister."

Half-sister! It was the woman she'd seen days earlier at the police station, the one she'd felt the connection with. Ella raised her hand and waved and Heather tried to smile and wave back.

Beckett chose that moment to walk across the room toward the map table, passing within a few feet of Heather. Graeme made a sound like a chainsaw starting up deep in his throat and grabbed Beckett by his shirt, tossing him across the room into a wall. Beckett hit the wall snarling and came down in a fighting stance. Heather screamed and backed up a step, having no idea what had come over Graeme. It was like back in the police department the last time.

Mac ran to get between the two as everyone in the room stopped what they were doing and stared. Mac squared off with Graeme. "Damnit, Pop Rocks, you didn't mate her yet, did you? You were gone for two damn days. Why else would you disappear from the continent, if not to do some secret *dragen* ritual that would calm you the fuck down? Did you forget how it works? You need a fucking lesson? You need me to show you where everything goes?"

Graeme roared and launched himself at Mac. Heather backed up into the corner, as far away as she could get from everyone, as all the males in the room piled on Graeme's back, trying to pull him away from Mac.

Ella ran around the melee and grabbed her by the hand, pulling her over to the spot where she'd been sitting, putting Heather in a chair. "Don't move, whatever you do," she told Heather, then ran back to the fray, careful not to get too close.

"Stop! Everyone stop and Graeme will stop, I know he will! Slowly, the males climbed off of Graeme, who stood in the center of the room, his chest heaving, his hands on Mac's shoulders.

Mac shoved Graeme off him. "What the fuck, Wade, we can't work with this lava lamp going off every two seconds. Get him out of here and bring in the heavy equipment from Chicago."

Ella addressed Graeme. "Look, Graeme, she's safe over here with me. Can you calm down if she stays over here and no one gets near her?

Graeme shook his head as if to clear it. "Aye," he finally said, looking at the ground. "Let's get this done and then I swear we'll never have this problem again."

Wade and Trevor held out hands to Graeme, guiding him by the elbows to a large table with a map spread over it. Heather watched him, her eyes narrowed. That had been about her. All about her. He really was fighting his every instinct not to—what had Mac said?—not to mate her.

Ella returned to her and smiled gently, then flopped in the chair next to her. "I'm so glad you're here. It's really hard being the only female around all this testosterone. That happens more often than you'd think, and Wade says it's only gonna get worse."

Heather allowed herself to be pulled into a hug by her sister. Someone who was in this with her. She smiled into Ella's shoulder, a sigh escaping her lips.

When Ella finally let her go, she stared at the other woman for a long time, trying to figure out which of her many questions she should ask first. Or should she tell Ella that Graeme had rejected her? No. Too hard. She looked around at the males, picked out the one she'd seen Ella with before, and pointed to him. "That's your, ah…"

"My mate, yes. Trevor." Ella smiled happily, watching Trevor's back, her expression adoring.

Heather looked at her feet. She wanted what Ella had more than anything. That simple assurance that someone— not just anyone, but Graeme—was hers no matter what. That feeling of love and contentment that Ella was steeped in.

Heather swung her feet and stared at the floor. "He's a… a what? Does he change into a wolf?"

Ella looked back at her, eyes wide. "Yes, a huge one. Black and silver and he has a mark on his shoulder that's white and in the shape of a boomerang." She grabbed Heather's hands. "You can't imagine how good it is to have someone to talk to about this. Have you seen Graeme as a…?" Her voice trailed off like she wasn't sure if she should be saying anything.

Heather smiled and nodded. "Yes. As a dragon. He let me ride on his back and flew me to Scotland."

Ella stared, her mouth a perfect O of astonishment. "Oh, wow, that must have been amazing! I would have been scared."

Heather shrugged, then nodded, feeling like an imposter all of a sudden. Ella thought they were happy. Probably on their way to mating. She changed the subject. Something drastic had to happen between her and Graeme before she could talk any more about him. "What's going on here, anyway?"

Ella shrugged. "Police officer stuff. Mostly it's been one big snooze and a whole lot of waiting. But then I'm not a cop, so I don't get to participate in that." She waved her hand at all the males bent over the table. "They are planning some sort of attack on somebody who took a bunch of people hostage. I'd be nervous about it, but Wade already said Trevor doesn't get to go on the raid when they do it, because someone has to stay with me, but I'm still a little nervous because his brothers will be going in. But mostly I've just been sitting here reading my book. I have a friend who writes stories about this kind of stuff." She waved her hand again at the males in the center of the room. "You know, men who can turn into animals and the women who love them." She laughed and Heather laughed, too, startled into it. She'd never heard of such a thing.

"Anyway, she's writing this really good one right now and publishing a chapter at a time on her website about a woman who finds a stray bobcat kitten in the forest caught in a trap. She frees the kitten and takes it home to nurse it back to health and then all the bobcats come looking for her. I just finished the last chapter she wrote, where a certain male bob-cat sneaks into her bedroom and steals the kitten away from her, but falls in love with her when he sees her sleeping. His love for her makes him able to turn into a human. He takes the kitten to its mother and then goes back into the house and that's where it ended. I'm hooked. I hope she writes the next chapter soon."

Chills ran up and down Heather's spine and she shivered, thinking of Dahlia and the bobkitten. She opened her mouth to ask Ella her friend's name, but Ella stood. "Stay here, ok, I really gotta pee." She looked over at the group of males around the table, then back to Heather. "Seriously, stay here."

Heather nodded. She took off her jacket and tucked it under the chair, then turned her attention to Graeme's back. The older guy, Wade, was explaining something to him. "We can't shut the gas down off-site, but our eyes in the sky say there is a manhole cover set in the ground twenty-five feet inside the first ring of fire that *probably* leads to whatever valves these two have fashioned. They have to have a way to turn it on and off. That's what we need you to do. Get in there and shut it down."

Graeme nodded thoughtfully. "I can get in there. Is there anyone who shouldn't see me? Because I can sneak in there in human form or fly in as a dragon."

"We don't know what kind of surveillance they have, but if you stay on the ground, we don't think you'll get caught by any bullets. They are holed up in a separate area more than five hundred feet farther north. According to infrared, there are no warm bodies below the manhole cover guarding whatever is down there. They are counting on this fire to keep out everything smaller than a helicopter. They must not have heard we have a *dragen* working with us yet."

Trevor cut in. "We have to move soon. Dawn is in fifteen minutes. Visibility is poorest then, and they won't expect us to try any sort of attack till tomorrow. If we're lucky, we'll catch them sleeping."

Heather's eye was caught by the twelve foot walls of fire dancing on the screen.

They looked drastic enough.

***

Ella washed up, glad the old barn had plumbing by some miracle, her mind on her new-found half-sister. Heather seemed normal enough, and sweet. Nothing like Shay. Guilt shot through her as she imagined Shay, still unconscious in the hospital bed, a baby, Ella's niece or nephew, growing inside of her limp form. Ella dreamed about it every night, thought about it constantly, and still could not bring herself to tell Trevor.

Because she didn't know who the father was.

Ella stared at her hands, suddenly more glad than ever that Heather had surfaced. She would ask Heather what she would do. Maybe not now, but tomorrow, or the next day. Heather wasn't going anywhere.

She hurried back out into the open room to where she had left Heather, but the chair was empty. She looked around. Trevor and all the males were still gathered around the map, deep in discussion. She walked around the perimeter of the room, but knew there was nowhere Heather could be hiding. She would not have gone up in the loft with the *felen*, and the only other place in the old barn that was hidden was the bathroom. Which meant Heather had gotten past the males somehow and gone outside.

Ella's eye was caught by movement on one of the video screens. A female form, running straight for the fire. A strangled cry escaped her throat. "Heather!"

Graeme was the first one out of the pack, looking hard at Ella. He followed her gaze and saw Heather leap into the wall of flame. Her clothes and boots blazed instantly, falling off her, but her hair and skin seemed to hold the fire, caress it lovingly. On her face was a wide smile. Her lips parted and Ella imagined her laughing, even though she couldn't hear it.

Mac spoke first, as all the males stared, dumbstruck at the woman disappearing willingly into the fire. "Damn, Sparky, she really is the only female you could have sex with, isn't she?"

Graeme grabbed him by the back of the shirt and heaved him across the room as he had done to Beckett earlier, then a screeching roar erupted out of him that broke every window in the place. He transformed as he ran to the front of the building, then flew out a window, after his female.

Trevor came up behind Mac and helped him to his feet. "Nice one, Mac, you really have a death wish."

Wade shouted into the radio for everyone to get in position, ready to move on his mark.

Mac brushed himself off. "Totally worth it if it gets him to come to his senses and mate her as soon as possible. We can't afford to play kiddie games around here." He pulled his gun out of his holster and headed for the door. "Damn, why I gotta be the only adult around here, getting shit done?"

CHAPTER 32

Graeme flew as fast as he could into the dawn, swearing on his life that, if she survived, he would do anything she asked. She was right. He couldn't live without her. He wanted to trust. He wanted to live, truly live, for the first time in his life. But he could not do that without her. If she died because he'd rejected her, he would take off his own head. The realizations sank into his bones, thrust there by fear and terror that he'd just ruined his life for the second time.

But no, he would not die today. There, he saw her light and lithe form bent over something in the grass, no longer on fire. He landed, shaking all over, but still with the presence of mind to look around, ensuring they were alone. The night was quiet on this side of the fire, only the sound of the gas hissing out of the ground and the clean, quiet flame it created marring the silence.

"Good," she said. "Help me open this."

He changed into his human form, and the shakes hit him hard when he did. He clamped down on his emotions. They were in enemy territory and she wasn't safe yet. He wanted to throw her over his shoulder and march out of there, but, if she made a commotion, it could draw attention to them. He had no doubt she would tear into him if he tried it.

He bent to see what she needed help with. The manhole cover. He dipped down and fit his fingers into a socket hole and lifted it easily, tossing it to the side, peering into the darkness below, while trying to hold her back from doing the same thing.

"We need a light," she said, dropping her legs down the hole and descending the rusty ladder in bare feet. Bare everything. Graeme swore. Didn't he say she would be the death of him? That had been a thousand years ago, right?

He transformed again and flew to the bottom quicker than she could reach it, then blazed fire up and down the corridor. Empty. Quiet. Dank. But definitely the right spot. Huge pipes ran vertically into the ground, then off towards the fire, with large wheel attachments at the front of them. Heather was already on the first one, grunting to spin it to the left. Graeme transformed and picked the next one. They leap-frogged like that, without a word, until all the gas pipes were shut down.

***

Heather stood at the bottom of the ladder, shivering and trying to get her pounding heart under control. She wished she could ask her dragon to come warm her. She wished he was her dragon again. She peered into his face, wondering if he'd seen her go through the fire.

She heard something above them and wondered if the fire had been put out after all. She scrambled up the ladder as quickly as she could, but Graeme was there, right behind her, holding on to her shoulders, not letting her stick her head out. Instead of arguing with him, she squeezed sideways and pushed hard with her legs, popping up just enough that she could see. Two black wolves were racing at full speed toward them. Yes! They'd done it. The wolves passed them, teeth bared in silent snarls, making Heather shudder. Behind them came Mac and Beckett and Harlan. Mac's chest was bare. Graeme popped up behind her, scolding her in her mind.

Mac threw something at them. It was blue and made of cloth and it opened up slightly as it flew through the air. His shirt. "For your female, Sparky," he called softly, then he was gone.

Graeme leaned into her. "Come back down with me. Put this on."

"Ok. You gotta go first." He gave her some room to move and she took it, following him back down. He handed her the shirt and she pulled it over her head, as more heavy feet ran above them. The shirt hung off her shoulders and came down to her mid thigh. Perfect.

Graeme smiled, looking at the still dark sky through the circular hole. "That Mac, he's a good male. Strong. Fearless. He should have been a *dragen*." His smile grew wistful. "All of them should have."

Heather considered. "Maybe you should have been a wolf."

He looked at her, surprised. "Maybe." The word was soft.

She gestured up the steps. "Go after them. They might need you. I won't move till you get back. I swear."

Graeme shook his head. "That will never happen. I must get you back to the barn first. I won't leave you alone."

Heather knew better than to argue. They climbed up and out, hurrying back the way they had come. Just as they reached the barn and pushed the door open, the crack of three gunshots rolled over the grassy field.

"Damn," Wade swore as he snatched up his radio and stared out the windows at all they could see; which was nothing.

Graeme took Heather to Ella, who hugged her, but Heather could only watch Graeme as he turned to go out the door. Before he made it, a report came over the radio. "All clear. All civilians safe. One *foxen* casualty, eleven *foxen* in custody. All officers unharmed. Tower disabled. Send us some medics."

Wade and Trevor whooped and high-fived and Ella hugged her tighter. "Oh, thank God," Ella said in a cracked voice.

Trevor turned to talk to Bruin in the back of the room, but he was already on his radio. He tucked it back in his pocket. "Medics on their way."

Heather watched out the window as the first light of the sun began to show in the sky. She was still alive, but was she whole? She didn't know yet. Her eyes tracked Graeme as he turned and came back across the room.

He went to Wade. "Am I needed here? Because I have something important to tend to."

Wade shook his head, looking tired, but triumphant. "You're not needed, no. Go do your thing."

Graeme's eyes met hers and Heather's heart leapt, then sank. He couldn't be leaving. That hadn't sounded like a good-bye.

He stared at her across the room, speaking, but not to her. "I need a clear running stream somewhere that I won't be interrupted all day, and especially not at sunset. Any ideas where I could go?"

What? A stream? Sunset?

Trevor spoke up. "There's a stream on my property. Behind the house about four acres back, in the forest. I don't know what else you need, but just, ah, for your general information, there's a cabin back there, too, that no one is using. It needs a little work but it's livable. Just in case someone needed something like that."

Graeme stared at Heather still and she began to heat up from the inside out. A smile spread over his face. "A cabin. Imagine that."

Trevor glanced at Ella and Ella's head bobbed up and down emphatically as she nodded at her mate.

"We've, ah, also got a guest room, if anyone wanted a place to stay while, well, while things were getting fixed up. Safety in numbers, that kind of thing."

Graeme nodded but didn't break eye contact with Heather. "Your kindness knows no bounds, my friend. I'll discuss your offer with my bond mate."

Heather's limbs felt too heavy all of a sudden, and her chest too tight, like she couldn't breathe. She stared, then blinked, then stared again, as Graeme crossed to her and held out his hand.

She tried to lift her hand and, when she couldn't, he bent and took it, then pulled her to her feet. "If she'll still have me," he whispered to no one but her.

She tried to talk, but her vocal cords had taken flight with the rest of her. She had no control over her body.

Graeme pulled her into his arms and nuzzled her cheek

with his nose and mouth. "I hope you'll give me another chance. I know I was a stupid fool, and I cry your pardon a thousand times, leannan. I'm ready to let go. I'm ready to listen to your wisdom and take you as my own, if you'll agree."

Even Heather's eyes were revolting. They filled with the tears she hated so much. She couldn't see, so she let them drift closed. The talking in the room and on the radio receded, as did her knowledge of the existence of anyone else on the planet. All that was left for her was Graeme, tall and strong against her, pressing soft lips to hers.

Her *dragen*.

CHAPTER 33

Heather rocked against Graeme, next to the stream in the forest behind Trevor and Ella's house, him sitting cross-legged, her on top of him, her legs hooked behind his back, both of them naked. The forest was quiet, only the tinkling of the stream and a gentle wind through mostly bare tree limbs, reminding her they were outside.

He kissed her softly, first on her upper lip, then on her lower, his tongue moving gently in and out of her mouth. It was art, the way he'd been kissing her for hours, like there was nothing else in the world to do. Like he'd been put on the earth solely to worship her mouth. Like he drew food, warmth, and water from her lips, but only if he plied them just right.

His attention made her feel whole, complete, not crazy, and not a freak, for the first time in her life. She was different, but she belonged somewhere.

She moved against him, feeling his hard cock between their bodies. Her fingers itched to touch it, but so far he hadn't let her. Drops of pre-cum leaked out of the tip occasionally, heating her belly as it touched her, but it certainly did not feel molten.

"Graeme," she whispered into his mouth. "I get that you don't want to have sex until sunset, for whatever reason, but can I touch you? Please?" Her fingers inched downwards.

He caught her hands again and spoke into her neck between kisses. "I have not explained it properly to you, leannan, because your body distracts me. Your lips and what you allow me to do to them capture my full attention, making me forget what you don't know. We are here to bond. That is what the binding ring is for and that is what will happen at sunset."

Her eyes flew open and she stared over his shoulder at her jacket hanging on a tree limb. "The binding ring is the circlet of gold, isn't it."

"The very same." He returned to kissing her.

She smiled into his mouth. "You were going to bond with me all along, or you wouldn't have let me bring it."

She felt him smile back. "Perhaps you are right, my sweet one. You do seem to have much power over me. I fought a good fight, but I should have known, back in that hospital bed, that there was no use denying we were meant for each other." He kissed her again, then whispered into her ear. "Ta ma hurry, chi annit."

She jumped. "Oh, that's what you said when you first saw me! Say it again, spell it for me, tell me what it means."

"It is Gaelic." He spelled it for her, then pronounced each word slowly. "Tá mo chroí istigh ionat. It means, my heart is within you, or, more simply, I love you."

Tingles spread through her body. She bit her lip, trying

not to let one tear spill. Oh, God, she would love him forever. Do anything for him. Had she known it way back then, too?

She smiled as he kissed his way around her earlobe. "I don't mind that you fought. I like my *dragen* feisty."

He threw his head back and laughed, returning to kissing her before his laughter had stopped completely.

"What does the binding stone do?" she asked.

He looked up into the sky, as if sensing the time. She figured sunset must be getting close. "I'll show you," he said.

He deposited her gently onto Mac's shirt, which was spread on the ground, then retrieved the circlet of gold from her jacket. She watched him until the golden ring appeared, and then she couldn't take her eyes off it. Its pull was strong. She could see it was the same size as she remembered it, slightly bigger than a dinner plate. He sat down, pulled her back onto his lap, then held her left arm out to her side, entwining his right fingers with her left ones, then sliding the golden ring up and over their hands till it sat just above their elbows. The ring tightened slightly, just enough so that it wouldn't fall off.

She stared at it, feeling her stomach flutter. "Now? We do this already?"

He took her chin in his other hand, turning her eyes to his. "Isn't that what you wanted, leannan? There is no in between for *dragen*. We bond or we separate. We do not date. This particular binding ring will not tether us if we have already had sex. That comes after."

She stared into his eyes, her nervousness falling away at his words. There was no question. "This is what I want."

He smiled and she saw the rest of her life in his expression.

He frowned slightly, and stared at the bonding ring. "It is time. I will start. Don't be scared, leannan."

She licked her lips and waited, for what she had no idea. Graeme stared at the golden ring until one half of it, the half covering her arm, burst into flames, then melded around her skin. It felt warm and good. A promise that could not be broken.

He looked back to her. "Your turn. You must do my half."

Uh oh. "I—I don't know if I can."

"You can. Or you would not be here."

She snickered. When did he suddenly become so sure about that? But she didn't have the slightest idea how to begin. "Wait," she whispered. "The binding ring won't work if we have sex first? Does it only work on virgins?"

"Aye, this particular one does."

"You are a virgin, too?"

"I have never been touched in this manner before. Only by you."

She sighed and let her eyes drift closed. "Relax me."

He kissed her, running his tongue over her lips again, nibbling slightly, her entire body thrumming with the need he created inside her. She almost forgot about the binding stone, until he smiled against her mouth again. "There. It is done."

She looked, and his side of the ring was in flames, then it melted around his upper arm just as hers had. She expected the connection between them to be broken, but it wasn't. The ring was still bound in a figure-eight, holding them tightly together.

"Does it ever come off?"

"Never. Not unless I die. Then it falls off when you are ready for it to go."

She closed her eyes against the idea. "I guess *dragen* can't cheat on their mates very easily if they can't take their rings off."

He chuckled. "If a *dragen* cheats, the binding ring tightens until it cuts off the limb, then it falls off and the binding is dissolved."

Her eyes flew open and she sat up straight. "Wow."

He nodded. "Loyalty is everything to *dragen*."

"I guess," she breathed. "Is that why what happened with your brothers and the other *dragen* bothers you so much?" He stiffened slightly. "And is that why you have such a hard time committing fully to the wolves? I know they want you to work with them full time. I can see it in that Chief's eyes."

He didn't speak for several moments. "You see much, leannan. The *wolven* are not *dragen*, and, as such, their loyalties are different, but I am finding their way may be better." His eyelids half-lowered. "But that is a conversation better left for another day."

She sighed and let her eyes drift closed and her arm droop as he kissed her again. She could still feel his erection between them and damn if it didn't feel bigger, longer. When would she get to touch it?

"There is but one more thing we have to do before the ceremony is complete."

"Yes, do it. I can't wait another moment."

"You don't have to," he whispered, then wrapped his free arm around her hips, lifting her easily and pulling her farther forward. His cock slid underneath her and she gasped and opened her eyes at the feeling, the solid friction of skin she had not yet been allowed to touch sending a warm line of sensation across her middle. It nudged her swollen lips as Graeme settled her completely against him.

He plied her breasts with his lips. "Tell me when you are ready, leannan." She heard no trace of fear in his voice. He trusted. He knew.

She wiggled slightly, positioning him better, the touches of their skin delicious. "I'm ready, Graeme."

He let her weight go, one millimeter at a time. Her head fell forward onto his shoulder as she gasped at the sensual intrusion. The slow, tortuous friction was wonderful, but it hurt, too. A bit of pinching and grabbing that faded into an ache she could quickly ignore as other sensations built.

Even more slowly, he continued to drop her onto him, until finally, he was fully seated inside her, the feeling one of rightness and fullness that she would never forget. A tear dropped out of her eye onto his shoulder and she smiled into his neck.

A lovely metallic ringing sound bounced off the trees around them, and they both looked to the binding ring. It had separated. Heather stared at the gold ring around her arm, then flexed her elbow. It seemed to meld perfectly with the muscles there.

Graeme began to move underneath her and she turned her attention back to her bond mate, her *dragen*. Her life.

"Leannan," he whispered, wiping more tears from her face and stopping the undulations of his hips. "Does it hurt?"

She shook her head and smiled, leaning on him until he let himself fall backwards to the forest floor. "It feels so good."

"Aye." He smiled back. "That it does. I never could have imagined how good sex feels with a female. It is not quite the same with one's hand."

She threw back her head and laughed at that, thinking that was a good thing for the continuation of the species. Darn. That thought tried to darken her mood, but she would not let it. This was her bonding. The connection with her bond mate that all other connections would build from. Sad thoughts had no place at a bonding.

"Are we bonded now?" she whispered. "Was that everything?"

He pushed her hair back from her face as she picked up his rhythm, met it with her own, then dropped down to kiss him as he continued to thrust into her, spanning her hips with his hands.

"There is but one more thing," he whispered, his teeth gritted with pleasure, his eyes closed. "I've heard it is to be said during the washing, which comes later, but I feel we should say it now. I'll say it, then you repeat it to me."

She nodded against him.

"I, Graeme of the line of *dragen*, choose Heather to be my bonded mate, and I will hold no other before her until the day I die."

Graeme's rhythm stayed steady below her, the sliding and friction as lovely as his words. She took a breath and repeated them into his chest. "I, Heather…" she stumbled over the words, not sure what to say, then picked them up again. "I, Heather Herrin, choose Graeme to be my bonded mate, and I will hold no other before him until the day I die."

Power shot through her, lifting her chest, but pushing her down onto her dragon. She cried out as wings burst from her back. Dragon wings? They folded around her and Graeme until they were wrapped in a cocoon of her love and flesh, and then they rocketed into the air. Graeme smiled at her as if he expected it, and before she knew what to think, they were back on the ground and she was normal again.

"What was that?" she panted.

"Your true nature showing its face, I believe."

Heather went with it. It wasn't any crazier than anything else that had been happening. She smiled at Graeme as a lovely sensation began to build in her, so different than any she'd felt before. Her breath came harsher and faster and she let it take her, lift her, move her as one with Graeme. He growled under her, thrusting harder and faster, lifting and lowering her hips with his hands to meet his advances with more energy, more power.

Every slide inside her was ecstasy, pushing her closer and closer to that edge, that delicious edge she reached for, knowing they had all night to do it again and again, to explore, play, get to know each other more deeply and fully than either of them had ever known anyone.

The push of sensation finally broke and she cried out into the forest, a strong cry that echoed back to them both. He didn't stop, slamming into her with a single-mindedness that elongated her pleasure, made it go on and on, until he groaned, low and deep in his throat, and she felt the spilling of his cum deep inside her. It spread a hot warmth around her middle and her orgasm, instead of winding down, intensified until she thought she would die of the pleasure.

He held onto her hips, pulling them hard onto him, as his cock continued to pump and jerk inside her. When he finally relaxed and dropped his hands to the forest floor, her crests and eddies of pleasure began to ebb away enough that she could fall onto his chest, all her muscles relaxed, even her mind quiet.

It was done. They were bonded.

CHAPTER 34

They lay that way until their breathing returned to normal. She sat up on his chest, surprised her muscles obeyed her commands. They felt like used-up rubber bands that would need rehab to learn to work again.

"Molten, huh? Did you make that up just to scare me?"

He laughed. "I would not do that. I assure you that you are special. No one else could have survived that."

She leaned forward, pulling him out of her, then sat next to him. "It felt warm. I'll give you that. But I liked it."

He sat up and kissed her on the nose. "Good. Because I'll be wanting to do that again when we've finished."

"Finished?"

"We must bathe our bodies and the rings in the stream. Then the ceremony is over and we can leave the forest if we like. Go to your place. You can feed me hot dogs and introduce me to your reptiles in between sessions of love and deciding what to do next."

She stopped, halfway in the process of standing. "You know I have lizards?"

"I apologize, leannan, but I saw them. The night I walked you to your home. I stayed outside and checked on you through the window, then followed you the next morning."

Her forehead creased. "But why?"

He frowned. "Have I not made it clear that you would be very valuable to the demon, Khain? Until the *wolven* have vanquished him, you will never be without a guard again."

She stood straight up, remembering something Ella had said, about somebody having to stay and guard her. Her chest tightened slightly. "Oh." She would think about it later. Deal with it later. For now, she would keep her thoughts in the forest, with her bond mate.

He stepped into the stream and held out a hand to steady her as she stepped in also. He bent and cupped his hands to gather freezing-cold water, and began to wash his legs, his cock, his hips, then up his chest and finally his arm. When the water hit his ring, it resonated again, sending out that sweet, melodious note they'd heard before. The sound filled her with happiness and hope. Being a one true mate wasn't all bad, or all good. Just like anything else in life, it just was. She would face it all head-on.

She followed his lead, shivering slightly. "That's cold!" she cried as she tried to wash her legs.

"Let me help," he said, and a blast of heat radiated out of him, warming her right away. She smiled at him and continued her washing. When the water touched her own ring, the sound came again. She stared at it, then flexed her elbow to see what would happen. The note's echo changed slightly, resonating at a higher frequency, making her smile.

"Oh," she said, deciding to face one thing right there and then. It would make Graeme happy. "You don't have to worry about me getting pregnant. I can't have kids, anyway. I didn't tell you before because I didn't want you to think I was making it up. I wouldn't have been able to stand that."

He blinked a few times and stared hard at her, water dripping from his hands, the sound soothing. "Who told you that?"

"My ob-gyn." She bit off the rest of it. She wouldn't tell him about the C-word. All of that seemed so unreal that she couldn't bring herself to say it.

He shook his head. "I would never believe what a human doctor said about a female intended to mate with a *dragen*. I'm sure you look different inside than what he is used to. Wyrmlings come out on fire. Heck, for all I know they start that in the womb."

Heather's hands fell to her side and her mouth dropped open. Graeme bent and finished her washing for her, then pulled her out of the stream and began to dress her gently, reverently.

She hit his hands away, shock still numbing her from the inside out. "Wyrmlings… that's a *dragen* baby?"

He dipped his head, looking nervous now. "Aye."

"And they come out of the woman's body on fire."

"Aye. So I've heard. I've never seen it."

Her voice turned frantic and there wasn't anything she could do about it. "And you think my gyno is wrong. That I can have babies, I mean wyrms. Wyrmlings!"

Graeme stepped toward her and pulled her into him. "Heather, I'm sorry I've made ye scared. This is part of why I fought us being together for so long. *Dragen* life is not what you are used to. But it can be a good life. I see it when I look in your eyes. I never, ever thought I'd have a bairn to call my own. But when I'm with you, I want one. I feel something here." He made a fist and pounded on the center of his chest twice. "And here." He pointed with two fingers to his throat. "Something stronger than any fight or conviction that points my thoughts towards family and wee ones with all the need in the world."

His touch soothed her and his words! How did he know the exact right thing to say to make everything ok? The C-word sprung to her lips and as it did, she knew she'd been lying to herself. It scared her badly. And she needed Graeme to soothe it. She spit it out in a rush. "My doctor said if I didn't have surgery to take out my uterus I'd almost certainly get cancer in a few years."

He smiled and she almost freaked. How could that make him smile?

But then he shook his head. "No, leannan, no. You have no cancer and will not." He took a deep breath through his nose. "I would smell it on you if such a thing were brewing inside of you, waiting like a snake in the bushes to strike. You smell of robust health, of happiness, of fire, and good tea. There is no sickness within you."

A dam broke in Heather's mind. One that had been holding back those worries since she'd first stepped out of the doctor's office. The worries flooded out, then streamed away. Gone. "Oh, thank God," she cried, falling into her *dragen's* arms, letting him kiss every bit of it away, until they fell to the forest floor and made love again, while night fell around them and the world went about its business somewhere far away, so far away, it couldn't touch them.

CHAPTER 35

*E*lla woke up in a rush, her eyes flying open, her dreams interrupted. Something was happening, or about to happen. Something big. She climbed off the mattress Trevor had called God knows who to bring in for her, then strung sheets across chairs and tacked them to walls until she had a tiny nest in the corner to sleep in. She'd been so glad when her head had finally hit the pillow. He was right. She needed sleep. Being pregnant taxed her enough that she could sleep even through all the noise.

She made her way out of the little tent he'd constructed for her and looked around at the old barn. They'd turned it into a processing station, bringing all the evidence and even the hostages there for a short while for cataloguing and processing. Officers were everywhere, talking to each other and poring over boxes and items.

Trevor saw her and ran over. "I'm out of here soon, I

swear. My part is just about done and then I can turn everything over to Mac."

She waved her hand and stared at the sky out the broken windows. "It's ok. What time is it?"

He looked where her eyes were glued. "Almost six. The sun will set soon."

She walked forward, waiting. Any minute now…

Trevor followed her till she stopped. "Ella, are you ok?"

She didn't answer. It was coming. Whatever it was.

A blinding light filled the sky, erasing everything, making her shut her eyes and cry out. Trevor grabbed her and held her, while all other people in the room vocalized surprise, alarm, and then wonder. Ella blinked her eyes and opened them slowly. The initial blinding light had faded, but a steady band of red and yellow illumination was shooting straight up from what looked like the woods in the direction of her house. It reminded her of a volcano, one big enough to reach the heavens.

Her back tingled and she arched it, as a power shot through her chest, making her remember her claiming. She grabbed for Trevor's hand and moaned lightly. He was there, his eyes searching hers.

"I feel it, too." He looked over her shoulder, then ran his hand along her smooth back. He growled deep in his throat. "I have to get you out of here. Get you somewhere private. I never should have made you stay so long."

"You were doing your job," she said, turning to stare at the light in the sky, which was beginning to fade. "But take me home, now, I need you to take me… home."

"Yes," he murmured, knowing exactly what she wanted.

On the other side of the map table, Mac spoke up, pulling Ella back to where they were. "He did it, Sparky did it! Good for him. I knew he had it in him."

A few males laughed, while most continued to stare out the windows. Trevor pulled her over by Wade and whispered something in his ear. Wade looked at them both, then he nodded. "We got this. Get your mate home."

Trevor didn't wait to hear any more. He pulled Ella across the room and out the door, and, by the time they'd hit the driveway, he'd picked her up and was running with her.

EPILOGUE

*E*lla lay in her mating bed, staring at the beautiful ceiling Trevor had fashioned out of lovely birch logs before she'd ever met him, her breath slowing, her body melting into the mattress.

He'd taken her with the fervor of their claiming and she felt a strange connection with her half-sister in the afterglow of it. Like maybe Heather was thinking of her, too, or talking about the life they would all share, now that another one true mate had been found. What it all meant. What they meant to each other.

She let her mind wander, feeling her mate's warm body beside her. He'd fallen asleep on his stomach almost immediately after their love-making, but she didn't begrudge him that. He'd worked all night and not slept like she had.

What would it be like? Not only would they have their own lives, but the lives of the males would be connected in a stronger way than they'd ever been before. Trevor had invited Heather and Graeme to move onto the property. To stay in their guest room.

The reality of the massive family and community that she would soon be a part of hit her hard, making her swallow convulsively and run her fingers through her hair, trying to soothe her thoughts. She could see it. Couples that she loved like family, because they *were* her family, lined up in front of her. Babies everywhere. Like a constant family reunion. One steeped in danger no one would name until they had to.

The genius of it flooded into her. They would fight for each other. Die for each other. Because they would love each other. The group that would be created by the mating of half-sisters with wolf after wolf would have to be able to fight the demon. To win. Even if nothing else could. They would have the power of love. That had to win over evil. Had to!

Trevor snorted next to her, then held his head straight up, his open eyes staring at the wall. She rubbed his back. "Shhh. Go back to sleep."

He turned his head towards her and the strange look on his face unnerved her. His eyes were wide open. "I can't believe I never gave it to you."

"What?"

He sat up, looking towards his closet. "The pendant. I bought it for you back before I even knew who you really were. I bought it from that crazy old lady. And I forgot all about it. Everything's been so busy. I have to give it to you."

Ella pulled herself into a sitting position. "Trevor, what are you talking about?" but some part of her tingled like she knew. Her breath caught and a strange fear filled her.

Trevor stood and stalked to his closet, naked, running his fingers through his hair and making it stand on end. He disappeared and she heard him pulling clothes off hangers and swearing.

A few minutes later he emerged, a chain dangling from his fingers, and at the end of it, the wolf and the angel. She gasped and held her hands to her throat. "Trevor, how did you know that was mine?"

"I don't know. It just called to me. When I stared at it I saw your face in my mind."

"No, Trevor, I mean I sold that the morning before I met you, to Mrs. White."

A frown line appeared between his eyes. "You didn't want it?"

She blew out a shaky breath. "It's not that I didn't want it. It scared me. It's powerful. I didn't know then what I know now."

He walked toward her, holding the chain open like he wanted to put it over her neck. She stared, her mind warring. Should she let him? She bit her lip, almost told him to take it away, hide it, put it somewhere she'd never run across it, but then she bent her neck to accept it.

The cold metal of the pendant grazed her face as he lowered the chain around her head, then positioned it, and stepped away to look at her.

Memories, emotions, smells, and impressions of what had to be the future came to her in a sizzling rush that she could not interpret. The room in front of her faded. Horrified alarm appeared on Trevor's face and he reached out for her, but then she wasn't there anymore.

She looked around. She was sitting in a grassy field that smelled different than Illinois. She scrambled to her feet and glanced up. The sun was high in the sky, no people were around, and a rutted path ran next to her. On the path, the dirt was scuffed and pitted as if there had been a struggle there.

She took a step backwards. "Trevor?" she said under her breath, stress chemicals dumping into her bloodstream. Where in the world was she?

Hoof beats sounded behind her, and she whirled around. A lone horse with a rider was coming up fast, the form on the top of the horse bent over it, the horse's nostrils flaring and its eyes rolling.

The horse slowed at a command from its rider and the person sat up straight. Ella could see it was a male wearing a strange soldier's uniform and armor. His eyes widened and his mouth fell open.

Ella looked down and realized she was naked. Oh, God. This was a dream, it had to be! A flash of gold caught her eye. The pendant! She ripped it up over her head and held it by the chain.

The instant she did that, the world flickered and disappeared and she was back in her own bed, Trevor screaming frantically for her in the hallway outside their room.

"I'm here," she called weakly, still holding the pendant out.

He ran in, his eyes wild, his face flushed and terrified. Relief flooded it when he saw her. "You disappeared."

"Take this," she said, thrusting the pendant at him. "I never want to see it again."